PRISONERS

OF

TWILIGHT

DON ROBERTSON

PRISONERS OF TWILIGHT

★ ★ ★

CROWN PUBLISHERS, INC.
NEW YORK

Published by Crown Publishers, Inc., 225 Park Avenue South, New York, New York 10003

CROWN is a trademark of Crown Publishers, Inc.

Manufactured in the United States of America

Library of Congress Cataloging-in-Publication Data

Robertson, Don
  Prisoners of twilight / Don Robertson.
     p.   cm.
   1. United States—History—Civil War, 1861–1865—Fiction.
I. Title.
PS3568.0248C66   1989
813'.54—dc19   88-20326

ISBN 0-517-57134-X

Book design: Shari de Miskey

10   9   8   7   6   5   4   3   2   1

First Edition

For my friend, Clyde C. Taylor

My bowels boiled, and rested not: the days of affliction prevented
    me.

I went mourning without the sun: I stood up, and I cried in
    the congregation.

I am a brother to dragons, and a companion to owls.

My skin is black upon me, and my bones are burned with heat.

My harp also is turned to mourning, and my organ into the voice
    of them that weep.

Job 30:27–31

PRISONERS
OF
TWILIGHT

TIDWELL

Saturday, April 1, 1865.

They needed firewood, and so they smashed the tables and the chairs in an abandoned cotton warehouse. They carried the lumber and a haunch of mule up the hill to Hollywood Cemetery, and they made a fine snappy fire just behind the fussy tomb of President James Monroe. But no one—not even Sgt Patterson, who they figured was the smartest of them—knew who President James Monroe had been. The feller surely had been planted in a fine tomb, though. All curlycued and filigreed it was, with little arched stainedglass windows, and the skeletons in attendance were impressed as hell. And McGraw said: "It surely do make a feller proud, don't it?"

"Be quiet air," said Sgt Patterson.

"Try to show a little respect," said Ratliff to McGraw. Ratliff had found a large castiron skillet, and he was slopping and greasing it with fat he'd sliced from the mule and then had fried up nice and bubbly. That goddamn hot mulefat would be as good as lard any old day, and maybe twicet on Sundays. And Ratliff grinned up at McGraw and said: "No offense, but maybe oncet in your fuckin trash life you can try to be decent, you hear me?"

McGraw's left hand was wrapped in a gray and maybe green rag that oncet probably had been some fancy fambly's fancy tablenapkin. His teeth were loose and black, but he was smiling.

1

And he said: "Don't mind me. I'm just makin conversation—at's all. I'm bad at way. All the time too much of the old blah an blah, you know? I mean, I expect sometimes it makes me almost believe I'm alive, you know?"

A man named Tidwell was sitting against a treetrunk. He'd personally butchered the mule. He did that sort of work for the commissaries, and he was a first cousin of McGraw's, and blood was supposed to be thicker an water, correct? So he had made the suggestion to McGraw that maybe a supper of old mule was in order, and he hadn't had to make the suggestion twicet, no indeedy *sir*. He and McGraw and the others hadn't been able to carry off much more than the shank, but it would be enough, at least for tonight and probably even for tomorrow, if the Yankees didn't come storming in and put them all to rout. Tidwell more or less was a silent feller, and he cleared his throat a great deal (which was about all the sound that came from him), and he liked to remember his boyhood and what he saw as its innocence. He'd been reared on a farm up near Fredericksburg, and he'd watched his dad slaughter all sorts of animals, and his dad had told him not to take any joy in it. His dad had said: *Do her quick, Jasper. Ain't nothin good bout pain. So slit the throat in one move, you hear me? An step back from the blood real quick, so you don't drown in it, all right? After all, a beast of the field is a creature of God, and don't you forget it. You don't want to be takin a bath in its blood, now do you?* And Tidwell . . . his full name was Jasper Donald Tidwell, and he was thirtysix years of age in that spring of 1865 . . . had taken his dad's words to heart, and the killing of animals had become a loving and careful thing, as far as he was concerned—and sometimes, when he knew no one was looking—he would embrace some poor doomed horse or cow or pig and breathe its heavy hairy odors and tell the sad scared creature it was in sweet loving hands, and he guaranteed it wouldn't feel hardly a goddamn thing. Oh, he didn't *always* hug an animal before dispatching it. He *couldn't*—not if any of his friends were around. Christ, what would they have *said?* But this didn't mean he was without feelings. Sometimes it seemed to him that his whole entire life had been dedicated to the slaughter of animals, but he didn't have to *like* what he did, did he? No indeed. No *sir*. His wife had accused him of taking what she'd called unseemly pride in that sort of work, and sometimes old Rosemary had sat at the kitchen table and had wept and had told him she'd never again eat fatback or even a chickenleg, on account of the cruelty involved. Tidwell had tried to argue Rosemary out of that foolish notion, and he even had tried to laugh her out of it, but his arguments and his laughter hadn't done much good, and she'd usually ended the discussion by telling him *he* was the one who was the *real* beast, and *at* was the plain truth of *at*, you bloodthirsty assassin you. Ah, that Rosemary. She'd attended some sort of normal school up in the District of Columbia, and her father once had been a state senator, so she believed herself to be some real cookies, and words such as *bloodthirsty* and *assassin* came to her easy as the pale watery stink of babymess on a hot day. And surely she and Jasper Tidwell knew a thing or two about babymess, now didn't they? She'd given him four sons in seven years, and then she'd given him four daughters in four years, and all eight of those children had survived, and Lord God, you didn't have to tell him how lucky he was. Hell's bells, the couple who lived on the next farm—Bert and Lizzie Poling by name—had produced six dead babies before poor Lizzie had given way to some sort of demented melancholy and had thrown herself into the Poling cistern, drowning herself and causing the cistern's water to go sour and poisonous. So all right, Jasper Tidwell knew he wasn't exactly unlucky, and he rejoiced in the eight children he and Rosemary had caused to enter the world, and he supposed there was a lot to be said for the work a man had to put in when he and his woman did their bounden duty to help the race avoid commiting suicide, but by God there wasn't an awful lot of *peace* involved when a man had eight children running and whooping and colliding and in general rolling and tumbling underfoot. Which meant that this here war was a sort of relief as far as Tidwell was concerned, and the high scary whir of minnyballs and the screams of the scorched and the torn and the mutilated and the explosions of various cannonballs and the like, the shouts and the whoops of a man's companions as they charged the bluebellies and showed those sleek smug miserable cowards who was boss . . . well, the whole shebang maybe was *almost* as loud as the screams and whoops of Tidwell's four sons and four daughters, and sometimes he just about smiled when he brought it all to mind. But he didn't smile a whole lot, and neither did anyone else. It wasn't exactly no little old Easterbonneted *church social* when a man marched off and fought a war, and it was a whole goddamn less than that to suffer and starve and then *lose* the goddamn war, and finally . . . *finally* . . . nobody wanted to be abandoned and more or less left to flop in the road like a speared fish. Which was what was happening along about now. All the fine patriotic THE CONFEDERACY FOR-EVER!!! words had gone to earth like nothing more than god-damn . . . *seepage*. Everything was shit, and nothing but shit, forever shit, world without end, kindly pass the plate. Oh, but suregod Tidwell wished he could think different on all this. Blinking, he glanced around at the fellers who were lounging with him here on this hill in Hollywood Cemetery. None of them except old Ratliff the cook were doing much of anything. Tidwell shivered. He figured they all thought the way he did. He figured there was no other way really to think, what with the things that had happened in the just about four years of this here war. The weather was too damp, and everywhere were mud and a killing gray chill, and he was aware of rags and torn bones and dead breath. He frowned. He blinked at headstones that said SMOOT and McNAIR and SACRED TO THE MEMORY OF. He blinked at the syrupy mud that had curled itself against the headstones, and he blinked at all the ragged dead winter sticks and wet torn leaves that had dug themselves into the corrupted earth. He wished he didn't have to think the way he did, especially seeing as how everybody thought that way, and that surely made his thinking common as sour milk, and he God damn didn't want to be like everybody. But what was a feller supposed to God damn *do?* Tidwell embraced himself. He ached to be a boy again. He ached to squat in the clean oldtimey uncorrupted dirt of his mama's vegetable garden and breathe fresh onions, say, or simply breathe the moist and splendid dirt itself and gather the dirt in his fists and squint thoughtfully at worms and ants as they poked and wiggled and danced. Nobody had aggravated him when he'd squatted in the dirt that way. And there'd been no currupted earth in those days, and the breathing of that oldtimey earth had created a hunched and clenched joy within him, and nobody had said anything harsh to him when he'd grimaced and damn near had wept because the odors of that fine abiding dirt had gone thick as new molasses and somehow had invaded his mouth and his tongue and his spit. Hell, he was a farmboy and then some. Before the war, he'd owned sixty acres, two horses and a mule, and he'd planted corn, cotton, beans, potatoes, and the earth had been all clotted and grand, and his Rosemary had been the best cook between Fredericksburg and Our Nation's Capital, and you could just bet your bottom dollar on *that*, by Jesus. She was a creature of pies and stews and creamy puddings, and she kept telling him by golly one day she'd actually fatten him up. And Tidwell, who usually wasn't the sort to laugh and carry on, allowed himself a chuckle or two when Rosemary spoke that way. And every so often, in fact (just as long as no one was looking), he would tweak a cheek of her plump hind end, and he always enjoyed the way she shrieked and bleated and blushed. He hadn't seen her since early June of '63, when the Army had given him a brief leave, and he'd hurried home in an RF&P daycoach that was full of wounded soldiers and flashy tophatted politicians and natty little drummers and a number of glittery whores, and the glittery whores wore shiny stuff on their cheeks, and they also wore heavy perfume, the sort that engorged the nostrils and caused the eyes to water, and Tidwell was in a fair and proper state when he walked home from the depot, trudging seven sweet miles out past the old Fredericksburg battlefield from December of '62, glancing at all the craters and all the splintered trees from that terrible fight, then smiling as the road climbed into the calmly rolling country-side south of the Rappahannock. And his children saw him walk-ing up the road. And they came running. All of them came running—even Barbara, the baby of the litter. And several chick-ens came running. And old Oliver the dog came running, and Oliver's old black mouth was foaming a little. Then came Rose-mary, hands happily fisted, tits flapping, her torso swaying from side to side and her short legs churning. And later he drew the bedcovers up to his chin and grinned like some great gray bony old bird and hugged himself and shuddered a little and said to her: *I've missed you, Miz Tidwell.*

I expect you have, said Rosemary, and she rolled toward him and hugged him. She kissed his neck. She giggled. *It's all I need . . .* she said.

What? said Jasper Tidwell.

One more.

One more what?

Old number nine, said Rosemary.

Jesus have mercy, said Jasper Tidwell.

His wife laughed.

And now Tidwell was remembering all this with a clarity that was just about enough to scorch his eyeballs and his brain. Rosemary never exactly had been what a feller would call skinny, even after the war had come along. She always had been smilingly proud of the fact that she had places a man could take hold of. Knobs and handles of warm flesh. Ah. Oh. Sonofabitch. Even now, tired and whipped as he was, Tidwell couldn't think back on his times with her without damn near—

"Hey, Jasper boy," said McGraw.

Tidwell flinched a little.

McGraw still was smiling. "Come back to the livin," he said. "I expect you're thinkin bout old Rosemary, ain't you? Well, I ain't never seen her but maybe three, four times, but she surely looks like she's a load, an at's a fact, ain't it?"

". . . never you mind," said Tidwell.

"Leave him be," said Sgt Patterson to McGraw.

McGraw's smile went away. He rubbed the hand that was wrapped in the rag. The hand was all gray and swollen. It had been mashed when a wounded and shrieking runaway horse had stepped on it during a skirmish in the Petersburg trenches. No one knew where the horse had come from, but it had trailed a rope of its guts, and it had been all foamy and red, and its knees had kept giving way. Sgt Patterson finally had shot the goddamn thing, but not before it had mashed McGraw's hand. And in the meantime they'd all been grappling with the Yanks who'd tried to take the trench, and the horse had bellied down on three of them, and Sgt Patterson had got to kicking the dead horse, and McGraw (by his account, understand, since Tidwell hadn't been there) finally had got to laughing. Now, though, he wasn't laughing.

6

Now, though, he was rubbing his stinking hand. He hadn't seen a doctor about it for something like a week. No one knew where to find a doctor, and so McGraw hadn't bothered with it. Tidwell never much had liked McGraw, who'd been a barber in Fredericksburg before the war and who'd given maybe the worst haircuts in town. He always had nicked and sometimes downright *slashed* his customers, and the wonder was that they hadn't dragged him to the nearest lamppost and strung him up like the foul whining cur he surely was. His mother was a sister of Tidwell's mother, and everyone in the family knew poor Emily McGraw had married beneath herself. Why, those McGraws weren't much more than river trash, drunkards most of them, inhalers of snuff, with snaggled grins and an urgent liplicking way of talking that was all oily and even vaguely menacing, as though they were advising some frightened victim to let them quietly pick his pocket, lest they loudly bash him on the head, hwa hwa, take your pick, sir. Now, though, there was nothing of the hwa hwa in the suppurating Clyde McGraw. He sat with his spine resting against the haunch of mule, and he was sweating (it was a cold day for April, and he had no reason to sweat), and peculiar little humming sounds seemed to come from somewhere behind his nose, or maybe his goddamn eyes. He had helped Ratliff slice the fat from the haunch of mule, and now he sat with a bloody knife in his lap, and it was matted with shreds of raw mulemeat, and he kept rubbing its blade with a finger, as though he were trying to wipe away all the blood and mess. He looked around. He looked up. No sun was to be seen. Nothing much of any worth was to be seen. Nothing much more than the ornate tomb of this here President Monroe. Noisily he inhaled, and his lips flapped, and then he nodded toward Tidwell and said to the others: "This here cousin of mine, he's got him a soft job with the commissaries, an he don't never go hungry, an ain't he just the grandest thing on two feet though?"

"Shit," said Tidwell. "If you think I'm goin to answer back to a crazy man, you got you another think acomin."

"I gettin to you?" said McGraw to Tidwell. "Why, Lord have mercy on my poor stupid ratty old *soul* . . ." And McGraw's grin reappeared. His gums were bleeding, and he spat a pale red stream. His gums hadn't been bleeding yesterday, and maybe he didn't have all that long to live. Maybe it all had to do with the, uh, the gangrene.

Sgt Patterson walked to McGraw and stood over him and said: "Go see a doctor. Go on. Get out of here."

". . . what?" said McGraw.

Sgt Patterson kicked McGraw in the chest, then bent over and pulled him to his feet. McGraw swayed, and his eyes were leaking. His mouth was working like the mouth of a sick fish. Sgt Patterson said to him: "Take a walk. Go to headquarters. They'll give you bandages or somethin. An maybe old General Lee'll come along an *kiss* at air hand of yours. Like maybe your mama kissed it when you was a little boy and slammed a door on it or somethin like at."

Now Ratliff was slicing meat from the shank of mule. He grinned at Sgt Patterson and said: "Hey, Rufus, at's tellin the sonofabitch."

Said McGraw: "Hey you, who's a sonofabitch?"

Said Ratliff: "You talkin to me?"

Said McGraw: "I ain't talkin to the angel Gabriel."

Said Ratliff: "No. I wouldn't suppose you would be."

Said McGraw: "Put at fuckin knife down an fight me like a man, you dumb old pisser you."

Said Ratliff, sighing, laughing a little: ". . . shit now, Andy, you ought to have better sense an to get into somethin you can't nohow finish . . ."

A boy named Pendarvis (he was slight and pale, and he'd said he was nineteen but he didn't nowhere appear to be more than fourteen—or maybe fifteen, if a person stretched the old imagination) was lying on the grass. He was barefoot, and the veins in his feet stuck out. He sat up and smiled at everyone. His daddy was a Baptist preacher over to Staunton, and he almost always smiled at everyone. He said: "Hey now, you fellers, we ought to save our fightin for the Yankees, don't you expect I got a point?"

Sgt Patterson still was facing McGraw. "I think," he said to McGraw, "our friend here's got a point."

"Fuck you," said McGraw, "an fuck your friend."

"Shit," said Sgt Patterson. He looked around. He shrugged.

He appeared to be trying to smile. He also was barefoot. In point of fact, almost all of them were barefoot. Some of them had feet that had been streaked green by the wet grass of this here Hollywood Cemetery. Sgt Patterson blinked at all of them. He couldn't have been much more than twenty years of age or so, but he was bent forward like somebody's exhausted granddad. Everybody figured he'd fought in one fight too many, but then who of this here wornout bunch of foolish skeletons hadn't? Oh, almost all of them liked Sgt Patterson well enough, and he surely went where the rest of them went and put himself to the test probably more often than the rest of them did, but the time was long gone when that sort of thing earned him much respect. Too many people were dead for respect to amount to much. There was too much of a stink, and words were worthless . . . unless a man had the good sense to make fun of them. And now, since Sgt Patterson appeared to be trying to smile, maybe he wanted to make fun of something or tuther. But all he did was look around, blink at the sky and the naked springtime trees and the tomb of President Monroe, moisten his lips, study the earth and the flattened stringy grass, then take several large breaths and allow himself a pale tight grimace and place his hands on his hips and say to McGraw: "You know how tired I am?"

Said McGraw: "I don't give a welldigger's fart how—"

Sgt Patterson gave McGraw a despairing little push, not really much of a push at all, but it was enough to knock McGraw down. McGraw landed on his bad hand, and he shrieked. He writhed. His legs flopped, and his bare heels pounded the earth. Sgt Patterson carefully kicked him in the balls, and McGraw's hands made clawing movements, but they simply were clawing at air.

". . . no," said Pendarvis.

". . . hey," said Petrie, a skinny little fellow who wore spectacles and had a blotchy purple birthmark on his neck. He rubbed the birthmark and shook his head.

". . . shit," said Ratliff, glancing up from his fire. He was laying out mulemeat in the skillet, and the meat and the fat were making a jolly bubbling sound, at once busy and loud.

Two fellers came up the hill. Their names were Coy and

Miller. Coy had lost his right arm in The Wilderness, and Miller walked with a limp on account of the villainy of some Yank who'd swiped at his legs with a bayonet. Miller had shot the Yank between the eyes, killing the Yank deader than a rock in the desert, but the Yank's bayonet had seriously gashed both of Miller's shins, and Miller had walked with a limp ever since. That particular fight had taken place at a place called Hatcher's Run back in October, and fourteen of the thirtytwo men remaining in the company were put out of action through death or wounds, and three others ran off. Now, on this first day of April in 1865, just thirteen men of the original company remained, and all the officers were dead, which meant Sgt Patterson was the goddamn company commander. But the thing was, Coy and Miller were included in the survivors, and neither of them was worth a damn. They should have gone home, but they didn't like their wives all that much, so they'd elected to stay and probably starve to death. Which maybe—probably—was saying a whole lot. Sgt Patterson had sent them off in search of maybe a bottle of whisky, and he'd told them he really didn't give much of a shit if they had to kill for it . . . especially if it belonged to a civilian, preferably a War Department clerk or a member of the Confederate House of Representatives. Coy and Miller, though, hadn't come up with dog shit, and this was apparent from the weary crouchy way they walked—or, in Miller's case, limped.

Pendarvis and Petrie stood up and took a few steps toward Coy and Miller, but Coy and Miller were shrugging and looking away, and so Pendarvis . . . pious Pendarvis, Pvt Alvin G., the preacher's son . . . said: "Shit."

And Petrie rubbed his birthmark and said: "I be damn an go to hell."

And Sgt Patterson fell on McGraw and began clubbing him with the sides of his arms and said: "The world ain't nothin but fuckers."

And Tidwell ran to Sgt Patterson and began kicking him. "You stop your beatin on my cousin," said Tidwell.

"Stand clear of this here food, boys," said Ratliff, pushing mulemeat around the noisy skillet.

And then everybody (except the busy Ratliff, of course) went at it. And many were the grunts and terrific expulsions of breath thereof. Everybody tumbled and kicked, and Tidwell and Pendarvis collided with tombstones as they grappled, and they damn near knocked themselves out. It wasn't but maybe five minutes at the most before someone began to laugh, and of course it was Sgt Patterson. Then Pendarvis laughed. So did Coy, while at the same time rubbing his left shoulder. Miller kept hollering at the other fellers to be careful when it came to whacking him across the shins. Everyone rolled and clutched and made high mad happy sounds. Ratliff fussed with the mulemeat, and he whistled something thin and tuneless, and from time to time his tongue tapped the roof of his mouth, and he said he suregod didn't know what the fuckin world was comin to. (McGraw never did look for a doctor.)

PATTERSON

Saturday, April 1, 1865.

There was mist that night, but at least there was no goddamn downright rain, and so the fellers were able to get some sleep in the same cotton warehouse where they'd broken up the tables and the chairs for firewood. There were no windows in this warehouse, but then there just weren't many windows remaining in all of this part of Richmond. Maybe windows were worth their weight in gold, what with all the destruction from the war, but those days who *really* gave a damn about windows? After the war, there would be time enough for windows. Sgt Patterson, who was a virgin, lay a considerable distance from the others, and he kept reaching inside his britches and playing with himself. Sometimes he almost wished the other fellers knew he was a virgin. That way, he wouldn't have to hide himself away from them like a thief in the night so he could pull and whip his poor old weary wizzle. He could pull and whip the silly thing in full sight of Man and God, and those who objected could go jam their heads up their hind ends. Ah, such a grand state of affairs *that* would be!

Scratchings. A sound of loose bricks.

Sgt Patterson opened his eyes.

". . . heynow," said a whispery voice, and it was the voice of goddamn Pendarvis, the preacher's son.

Sgt Patterson exhaled. He linked his hands and cracked his knuckles. "Yessir?" he said, and his voice was just as whispery. He shook his head. He didn't know why the hell he and this Pendarvis were whispering. Outside was a sound of explosions, bells in the night. The talk was that the Army of Northern Virginia's engineers were blowing up the railroad yards, round-house facilities and the like. Any day now General Lee would be giving the orders for his wornout troops to abandon Richmond and probably try to make their way west. At least this was what everyone believed, although Sgt Patterson for one didn't figure they could hold out more than a couple of weeks, and then . . . well, and then somebody would have to be doing some surrendering . . .

"How's she lookin?" said Pendarvis.

". . . how's what lookin?" said Sgt Patterson.

Pendarvis hunkered down next to Sgt Patterson and said: "Outside air. Things blowin up an all. Air been flashes ever since nightfall. I mean, it's all real bad, ain't it?"

"I expect so," said Sgt Patterson.

"I talkin like I'm fresh fish?"

". . . a little."

"Well," said Pendarvis, "I *am* fresh fish, by God."

"Surely," said Sgt Patterson, yawning. He made a soft groaning sound as he yawned, and he hoped this Pendarvis would take the hint and go away. He was tired beyond tired, but at the same time he knew he wouldn't really be able to sleep until he fooled with himself, found the necessary relief, then relaxed his muscles and his bones and dozed off. Fooling with himself provided a fine way for a feller to relax his muscles and his bones. Right now Sgt Patterson lay in a loose exhausted sprawl on a pile of torn burlap bags. One thing about this old cotton warehouse . . . it had plenty of burlap bags, and they surely did provide relief from the place's cold stone floors.

Said Pendarvis: "My daddy told us he was proud of us as proud could be. When we jined up, I mean. Me an my brother Lutey, I mean. At was only seven months ago, an me an old Lutey rode here in the steam cars. Lutey . . . I feel bad bout him. I mean, I believe he could of lived longer, you know?"

"I expect I do," said Sgt Patterson.

"He just wasn't cut out for none of this," said Pendarvis.

Sgt Patterson lay back and closed his eyes and said: "Right." He pressed a cheek against one of the burlap bags. He breathed through his mouth.

"You member him good?" said Pendarvis.

"At I do," said Sgt Patterson.

"You think bout him much?"

"I don't think bout him a tall," said Sgt Patterson, opening his eyes and staring at the shadowed rafters of this here old cotton warehouse.

". . . oh?" said Pendarvis. "How come?"

Sgt Patterson blinked. He made loose fists. He said nothing.

"You got no answer for me?" said Pendarvis.

"You expect me to?"

". . . maybe," said Pendarvis.

Sgt Patterson looked directly at the squatting Pendarvis. He rubbed a booger from his right eye. He wiped the booger on the front of his shirt. It was an old black shirt, but at least it wasn't torn. He'd taken it off the body of a dead Yankee sergeant after the battle at The Crater. Both the dead Yankee sergeant's legs had been blown off at the crotch, but the black shirt hadn't been damaged, nor had it been bloodied. Sgt Patterson had stripped it from the feller, and it had carried the feller's odor for a week or two, but repeated washings with hard grainy homemade soap gradually had done away with the odor, and now that black shirt had a new odor—the odor of Sgt Patterson, Rufus B., and no one else. But now was no time to be remembering the history of his goddamn shirt and its goddamn odor. This here Pendarvis had asked Sgt Patterson a question, and he supposed it deserved some sort of courteous answer. So he shook his head and shrugged a little and said to Pendarvis: "I'm real sorry, an I know it'd be a good thing if I was to think bout all the ones at's dead an gone home to Jesus, but I don't even know for sure they've gone home to Jesus or Anyone else. Your brother, I member him just fine, but I don't *think on him*. I mean, I got other things on my mind. I try to think of what's Here an what's Now. I try to keep us one step ahead of The Dark Place. I want us to pull ourselves through

14

this here war. I mean, I know we look like shit, and I know we *feel* like shit, but maybe we'll amount to a little somethin when it's all over an done with an we go home an . . . an the noise dies down. But I can't . . . well, I can't just lay here an *think* on your dead brother an all the other dead ones, on account of shit, boy, my mind keeps bein pounded by all the other stuff I keep memberin . . . like the fight at The Wilderness last year, when every ten feet we kept stumblin over the skeletons of em who'd been killed in '63 at Chancellorsville, an what kind of war is it when two battles is fit on the same ground? I mean, ain't air enough *other* ground so at sort of thing don't have to happen? Oh, God damn you, Pendarvis, don't get me started on all this, all right? I just want . . . well, I just want to be left *be*, you hear me? Please do at for your old Sergeant Patterson, all right? I mean, looky here at me. Looky here good. I'm real *tired*, Pendarvis. I mean, ain't the light good enough so you can *see* how tired I am?" And Sgt Patterson reached up and seized one of Pendarvis's wrists. Pendarvis lost his balance and slipped out of his crouch and abruptly sat down. Sgt Patterson squeezed the wrist. Now Sgt Patterson's voice was hissy and wet. "Shit, old friend, you don't want to know what I know," he said. "It ain't none of it pretty, an you don't *learn* nothin from it, an anyways, listen here, you already know all I know. You been here long enough an en some. It ain't like, hey, I'm carryin round the secrets of the ages. I mean, at's one thing bout this here war—it ain't no secret, you know? No sir. Ha. Listen to me. I'm real funny."

Pendarvis reached behind himself and leaned forward and rubbed his tailbone. "I ain't laughin," he said. "Swear to God I ain't."

"So maybe you can go away an let me sleep."

"You aggravated with me?" said Pendarvis, his voice thin and whiny. He kept rubbing his goddamn tailbone, and now he was grunting.

"Shit," said Sgt Patterson. "I ain't aggravated with *nobody*. I'm just *tired*, at's all. I mean, is at so hard to understand?"

". . . no," said Pendarvis, and now his voice was pursed and hollow, maybe even sullen.

"So you expect you can go away an let me sleep?"

15

"I don't know," said Pendarvis, and he tried to clear his throat.

"How's at?" said Sgt Patterson.

"Air's been too much noise," said Pendarvis. He reached toward Sgt Patterson and touched one of Sgt Patterson's shoulders.

Sgt Patterson said nothing. He simply glanced down at Pendarvis's hand.

"You member how you was with me when Lutey was chopped down?" said Pendarvis.

"I expect I member how we both was . . ."

Pendarvis squeezed Sgt Patterson's shoulder, and then he touched Sgt Patterson's cheek. Easily. Softly. With the side of a finger.

Sgt Patterson exhaled.

"I'm younger an you, but I know," said Pendarvis.

". . . know what?" said Sgt Patterson.

"What this here is like."

"What?"

"Me and Lutey, well . . ."

"Oh, sweet Jesus," said Sgt Patterson.

"We couldn't hep it none," said Pendarvis. "But oncet it's begun, well, a man's got to be stronger an we was to back off from it . . ."

Sgt Patterson pushed Pendarvis's hand away. "Leave me be . . ." he said, and he covered his face with his arms and squeezed his eyes tightly shut.

"I loved my Lutey," said Pendarvis.

Sgt Patterson quietly wept into his arms. Sgt Patterson, who was a virgin except where death was concerned. He supposed what he really needed was to crush his skull with his fuckin stupid useless arms.

Grunting, Pendarvis stood up. (Sgt Patterson heard a crack of Pendarvis's joints, the dry slap of Pendarvis's bare feet. He saw nothing, but he heard all that was necessary to hear.) Then Pendarvis said: "I won't bother you none. I expect I know what you must be feelin." More sounds, and they were slow and reluctant, but they meant Pendarvis was walking away, back to wherever he'd been sleeping.

Sgt Patterson exhaled. His arms relaxed a bit. Then he was able to rub his eyes. Pendarvis was pretty, and there was no other word for him. He was blond. Even his eyebrows and the hairs on his arms were blond. He and Sgt Patterson and the rest of them had gone swimming often enough so that Sgt Patterson knew that Pendarvis even had blond hairs surrounding his prick. Why, Pendarvis was so pretty he reminded Sgt Patterson more than a little of a girl named Elizabeth Strawn, whom Sgt Patterson had loved since maybe the beginning of time. His hometown was Suffolk, a Tidewater community down near Norfolk, and before the war he'd worked as a clerk in his father's drygoods store, and Elizabeth and her parents had lived across the street from him and his family. She'd been almost as blond as Pendarvis was, and she'd been a lively one, and at the age of eighteen she'd eloped with a feller named Ben Ferrell, a cavalry lieutenant then serving in the command of no less a person than J. E. B. Stuart. And back in '62, during the Shenandoah Valley campaign, this Ben Ferrell had personally captured a genuine Yankee colonel, a deed that had made that flashy grinning braggy showoff sonofabitch maybe the biggest hero in all of Suffolk. And so of course he'd made off with Elizabeth, and the last Sgt Patterson had heard, Elizabeth had given birth to a baby boy whom she and Ben Ferrell had named James Ewell Brown Stuart Ferrell, after the martyred Gen Jeb Stuart. The thing was, Suffolk had been in Yankee hands the better part of two years, and Sgt Patterson didn't know *what* was happening; he didn't even know whether his parents were alive. And now he was hoping the war would end soon, so he could go home and find out what was what. No one had much doubt that the Confederacy had been defeated, and the only remaining question was when the politicians and the generals would accept the goddamn truth of the situation. God, Sgt Patterson and the others were hungry—and for more than haunch of mule. For one thing, they were hungry to be shut of blood and death. For another, they were hungry to be done with detonations and shrieks and the claptrap tinhorn sound of distant bugles, the shouts of officers trying to be brave, the groans and the obscene imprecations of the dying. Sgt Patterson wanted to be able to spend one day without hearing anyone mention shit or piss or puke. He wanted to be waited on, to empty himself, to reach for the warmth of a tit, a belly, sweet hands, an abiding mouth. He wanted to acquaint himself with kisses and hugs and moist pussy. He needed to fuck something and kill nothing. He would be twentyone years of age on the First of May, and his virginity made him feel as though he'd stuffed his pockets with stones and rammed a cluster of iron rods up his asshole. He rubbed his eyes. He tried to remember his Elizabeth, and she was smiling at him, and she was telling him oh yes, all *right,* he was kind of sweet and maybe even a little goodlookin, but who on earth was *he* when compared with the heroic likes of a Ben Ferrell, heynow, tell me at, dear Rufus? And these words of course made his face go all knotted and grim, and he knocked her down, and he kicked her, and it didn't matter a damn to him that she was a wife and a mother, and he kept hollering to her that he was a man and had killed people and was too goddamn weary to put up with her snippy talk of her heroic husband, and he asked her who the hell did she think she *was?* And he told her there were other fish in the sea. And Pendarvis smiled. And Sgt Patterson seized Pendarvis by the back of the neck and held up Pendarvis's head and told Elizabeth hey, girl, talk bout *pretty* . . . what do you think of *this* when it comes to pretty? And Sgt Patterson waved Pendarvis's head from side to side to side to goddamn *side,* and Pendarvis smiled and smiled and goddamn *smiled* bright enough to snuff the sun, and Pendarvis's lips went all plump and kissy, and there were bells in the night, but no one paid much mind to the bells in the night. There were rustlings and timid slapping sounds, and Sgt Patterson grew, and he touched himself, and he moaned. and Elizabeth kissed him and licked his ears, only she wasn't Elizabeth, and maybe she was even prettier. And she didn't have no husband, and she didn't have no baby, and there wasn't no hero for miles around, and she told him she wanted to hep him, seeing as how wasn't that the best way a person could show true love? Didn't the Lord bless lovers? Now that Lutey was dead (she said, voice hissy and quick), who else was there in her life, and yes, you can touch me, o kiss my ears; you're goin to be surprised how beautiful it all is, an I'll be comfortable for you; just you wait an see, my darlin love. And the voice had fragrant breath, just as girlish and happy as a warm afternoon in some bright secret wicked little fussed and chintzy female dancing academy, full of damply carnal ambitions and deceits, and Sgt Patterson wanted to seize his love and dance him around the room and listen to the wild rustlings of his love's skirts and petticoats and breathe his satins and his laces and his delicate unguents and powders. The music scratched and tootled, and Sgt Patterson moistened his lips and displayed his teeth. He had unbuttoned the front of his britches, and Pendarvis's hands were stroking his prick, and Pendarvis said I'll love you just as much as I loved my Lutey, an don't think you're dreamin all this, on account of you ain't, an I won't never tell no one. I don't want to lose you, o my Rufus. I love your darlin starvin bones, an I love your tallywhacker, you know at? Well, it's true. It's all true, an you're so tired, ain't you, o my beloved? Which is just fine, seein as how it's best when a feller is tired, o take my word for it. And Sgt Patterson nodded in response to all this. He told himself none of it really was happening, which meant he could do whatever he liked. Gently he tugged down Pendarvis's britches and stroked Pendarvis's tallywhacker, which was small and warm and tough. He sucked Pendarvis's ears, and he spoke to Pendarvis of love, and none of this was happening, and he licked the fuzz that lay across the back of Pendarvis's neck, and he smiled, and none of this was happening, and none of this was happening. Pendarvis squealed and gasped, and Sgt Patterson said o, o, o, Elizabeth mine, you surely should be seein this here thing at's happenin. An *ain't* happenin. Whatever. Sgt Patterson's lips felt hot and cracked, and he supposed he was going through quite a lot, especially seeing as how none of this was happening. Now Pendarvis was facing away from him, and he was embracing Pendarvis, and his fingers were gentle with Pendarvis's balls as well as Pendarvis's tallywhacker, and Pendarvis whispered something having do with a certain place where the sun didn't shine, you follow me, my darlin sweetheart? O, Rufus my perfect one, you're so brave an strong an all, an you surenough have lasted through all of it; give me some of your strength; spread me; work me over real good; suck my flesh; make me forget my Lutey. Kiss my shoulders, o yes. I am your one an only Pendarvis. O yes. Squeeze me. Ah. O. I love you. It surely feels good, don't it? I mean, it's better an not havin nobody, right? You fixin to fill me up, you beauty you? Oh, good for you. I tell you, you're my love an en some. And Pendarvis's sweet whisperings persisted while Sgt Patterson adjusted himself, pushing his tallywhacker against Pendarvis's bunghole, o such a precious bunghole, and spreading Pendarvis's cheeks (as Pendarvis giggled and mewled) and sucking Pendarvis's ears and squeezing Pendarvis's nipples while at the same time thrusting, retreating, thrusting again, and Pendarvis's bunghole was pink and large and warmly easy, and Pendarvis reminded him that dear dead Lutey had been there before, and so it wasn't as though that particular highway never had known a traveler, and Sgt Patterson fucked Pendarvis; he clogged Pendarvis's dark passage with seed and more seed, and Pendarvis called him adorable, and Sgt Patterson wept a little. Later he and Pendarvis lay quietly and kissed one another, and their mouths were wet, and then Pendarvis slid down and sucked Sgt Patterson's prick, and Sgt Patterson came in Pendarvis's mouth and seized Pendarvis by the ears and twisted those ears and spoke brokenly of joy and true love, and Pendarvis looked up and smiled and said: Want to fuck me again? Whereupon they both snickered and wept. Sgt Patterson allowed as how this was a whole lot better than pulling his pudding, and Pendarvis made a number of nickering sounds. Which were deeper than his particular snickering sounds—deeper and more knowledgeable. Which meant more corrupt. Which was all right and didn't matter a damn, seeing as how none of this really was happening. Sgt Patterson and his beautiful Pendarvis lay with their bellies touching and their legs entangled. They kissed, and their tongues touched, and they trembled. Sgt Patterson kept stroking Pendarvis's hair and he supposed he no longer was a virgin, and he told himself he never had imagined giving up his virginity this way. But he just bet it was a good a way as any, and maybe better than most. The thing was, a man just never could tell. Sgt Patterson wanted to lie on his back and howl, but this would have meant waking up the other fellers and they would have found out something they didn't really need to know. He and Pendarvis linked their fingers and held hands and swore their love would outlast the sun and the mountains. Sgt Patterson fell asleep while sucking the comely Pendarvis's dear thin fingers. He heard more bells, and he heard detonations. He reached out to hug Pendarvis, but somehow Pendarvis wasn't there, and so Sgt Patterson hugged himself. And smiled. And said to himself: Pendarvis called me Rufus. O, he surely loves me, all right. No doubt bout it. An so it don't matter where he is right now. I expect he'll be back, an he'll tell me he loves me, an we'll hug an kiss an do all the rest of it, an we'll be just so—

"Heynow," sand Pendarvis, whispering.

Sgt Patterson saw nothing. He was sweating, though. That much he knew.

"You all right?" said Pendarvis.

Sgt Patterson opened his eyes.

Pendarvis was squatting next to him. "You was moanin in your sleep . . ."

". . . what?"

"Was you havin a bad dream or somethin?"

Tears came in great blots from Sgt Patterson's eyes, but he managed to make no sounds. He reached up and touched one of Pendarvis's hands. He squeezed it with both of his own hands and then said: "I was . . . well, I was somewheres else, you know?"

"I think so," said Pendarvis. "I hope it was nice . . ."

"It was like the nicest thing at's ever happened to me."

"Next time maybe it won't be no dream."

"You know at for sure, don't you?" said Sgt Patterson.

". . . yessir," said Pendarvis. He touched Sgt Patterson's hands. He teetered. He sighed. "A dream don't get nothin done . . ."

"Tomorrow night?" said Sgt Patterson.

"I surely do hope so," said Pendarvis.

"We'll find somewheres quiet," said Sgt Patterson.

"Good," said Pendarvis, and he bent over Sgt Patterson and gently kissed him on the forehead.

Grunting, Sgt Patterson freed his hands from Pendarvis's and poked with curved fingers at the sweat and the tears on his own face. The bells and the explosions were a sight louder. He wanted to kiss Pendarvis, but, well . . . maybe tomorrow. Or maybe whenever . . .

PATTERSON

Sunday, April 2, 1865.

By daybreak the world more or less was beginning to fall down. The time had come for everyone to skedaddle. Nothing much remained of the Army of Northern Virginia, and Sgt Patterson for one didn't quite know what to do. Also, his britches were messed and sticky, and he kept having to scratch his tallywhacker and his balls and the hairs down there. He'd had better mornings, and that was for sure. He caught Pendarvis smiling at him several times, but he managed to look away. He kept clearing his throat, and he wished to God he had a spare pair of britches. He and his fifteen men had been detailed to guard duty at the RF&P yards, and that really was funny. The RF&P yards had been blown all to hell, and the only thing they'd seen moving for the past week and a half had been a stray Leghorn chicken, which they'd immediately caught and had boiled and had eaten. Or at least three of them—Coy and McGraw and a big rough bearded feller named Llewellyn—had partaken of that stray Leghorn chicken. Several of the others had grumbled, and the opinion had been offered that decency demanded that all stray Leghorn chickens should be shared and shared alike, but Coy and McGraw and the substantial Llewellyn had laughed at *that* one, seeing as how the goddamn little Leghorn had been skinny as a pile of sticks. Coy and McGraw and Llewellyn hadn't wasted much time with plucking and boiling the bird, and they'd shouted angrily at the pot as they'd waited for the water to boil. Why, the truth was they'd just about gulped it down raw, and strands of its meat had glistened pinkly at the corners of their mouths, and the sight hadn't exactly been the sort to help a man keep down his breakfast of mush, say, or grits, or a slice of fatback, or whatever other handful of scraps he'd managed to appropriate for himself. But Coy and McGraw and Llewellyn really hadn't much concerned themselves with that sort of thing, and they'd crunched down that chicken without hardly looking up. That morning the company consisted of Sgt Patterson, commanding, plus McGraw, Ratliff, Coy, Pendarvis, Miller, Petrie, Goodfellow, Llewellyn, Tidwell and fellers named Vincent, Appling, Pope, Nelson, Barber and Boom. In point of fact, Tidwell and Appling and Boom weren't in truth members of the company at all. They'd attached themselves to the company because their own units had been broken up. Tidwell, the commissary man, no longer had any animals to slaughter, and so . . . once he'd been reunited with his cousin, McGraw . . . he'd slaughtered that final mule and had walked away with the haunch, and he wouldn't be returning to the halfdozen or so pasty and dirty loafers who remained in his commissary outfit. So in one sense he was a deserter, but he surely wasn't a deserter in his own eyes, and he'd told Sgt Patterson he'd be happy to tote a rifle just as soon as he found one. Appling, who hailed from Alabama, was an artilleryman whose battery had been destroyed when its position had been overrun at Petersburg. As for Boom (stocky and bowlegged, with dark and heavy eyebrows and strange pointed cheekbones), well, he'd simply appeared three days ago down there in the RF&P yards, and he'd told Sgt Patterson he was a cavalryman whose troop had been wiped out in a skirmish northwest of Richmond. He was wearing a black top hat and a grimy white shirt and a pair of scuffed boots, and he looked more like a politician or a feed merchant than any goddamn cavalryman Sgt Patterson ever had seen, but what the hell, at this stage of the situation, if a man wanted to announce that he was the Pope of Rome or the Emperor of the Heathen Chinee, did anyone really care? And did it matter that the man carried the preposterous name of Boom? By

rights, he should have been in ordnance, correct? Or at the very
least the artillery. But this here Pvt Boom (an older man, maybe
forty, maybe even fortyfive) said very little about himself, and he
said nothing at all about his name, and he kept *to* himself, but at
least he'd brought along a rifle, and he hadn't complained when
he'd taken his trick guarding the nonexistent trains at the nonexistent RF&P yards, and Sgt Patterson figured there really wasn't
much more he could ask of the feller. And of course Boom had
been included when it had come to sharing the shank of mule,
once the curious and abundantly crazy freeforall at the Hollywood
Cemetery had run its course, but he'd offered no opinions on the
freeforall—or anything else. And as far as Sgt Patterson was
concerned, it was good to serve with a man whose opinions
weren't exactly a matter of public knowledge. (Boom's eyes were
especially puzzling. They were a soft and almost mushy brown,
and maybe they even were girlish, and they didn't have much to
do with his stocky body and his strange cheekbones. Ah, the poor
feller probably was trying to hide something—but then who wasn't?)

A tall dusty lieutenant riding an exhausted snuffling old
spotted mare told Sgt Patterson and his men to get out of there.
Sgt Patterson didn't know this lieutenant's name, but what difference did *that* make? It was about eight o'clock in the morning
when the lieutenant came riding across the abandoned RF&P
tracks, the sad loosegaited mare's hooves clattering and stumbling,
and the lieutenant spoke in a breathless and melancholy voice,
telling Patterson and the others it was every man for himself,
boys; Petersburg's a goner, an at means Richmond's a goner, an
the best thing we can do is head west; air's supposed to be a whole
lot of trains full of food an ammunition waitin for us at a place
called Appomattox Station, an I don't know bout yall, but at's
where *I'm* headin, long as this here old Betsy of a horse of mine
don't drop dead on me. I mean, *I* ain't givin up. Not just yet, by
God. The lieutenant briefly waved his hat at Sgt Patterson and
the others, then went clumping and clattering away. For a few
moments everyone just stood there. Sgt Patterson coughed. He
glanced at Pendarvis, then glanced away. He spoke as quietly as
he knew how. He allowed as how he couldn't blame anyone who
wanted to run off, and he said he wouldn't lift a hand against any

man who sort of faded away, you hear what I'm sayin? He reminded the others that the war wasn't over until the people in charge said it was over—but at the same time he said he'd just about given up having much faith in the people in charge. Except old R. E. Lee, of course, an maybe, well, ah, maybe old R. E. Lee had a last trick or two up his nervy old sleeve, you know? Now I ain't askin you to be no heroes, an I don't blame nobody who wants to go on home right now, but I know *I* got maybe a drop or two more of fight in me, an if at makes me crazy, well, so be it. I ain't noways perfect, an at's a fact. (Sgt Patterson was smiling at all of them, and he felt as though he was trying to sell them some sort of particularly poisonous and obscene patent medicine made maybe from the balls of camels and the assholes of sheep.) The men all fell in line behind him—even Coy and Miller, the crips—and he led them away from that place, and their feet made hollow listless sounds, and no one said anything. Not even McGraw spoke, and Sgt Patterson wondered whether maybe McGraw was dead and didn't know it. Then Sgt Patterson grimaced. His sticky crotch tugged at his hairs down there. He wanted to look back at his beautiful Pendarvis, but of course that was out of the question. He rubbed his mouth. Only eight of these men—nine, counting himself—had rifles, and barely two hundred rounds of ammunition were available. Pendarvis, Coy, Petrie, Tidwell, Ratliff, Nelson, and Goodfellow were unarmed, and Sgt Patterson surely hoped they would find abandoned rifles along the way. It was difficult enough staying alive while carrying a rifle; it probably was impossible staying alive while carrying nothing but hope and prayers and boiling puke. So they trudged, and they heard churchbells, and McGraw finally was the first to speak, asking whether it was possible that all the whisky in the whole goddamn Confederacy had been swilled down by the politicians and the government clerks and the goddamn stinkin fuckin whores. Ratliff and some of the others laughed, and Ratliff suggested that maybe all of Richmond's holy pissy hypocritical Temperance ladies had banded together and had poured all the whisky into the James River. And McGraw said he didn't believe Ratliff's suggestion was all that amusin, you fucker you. The sound of the men's footsteps was a sort of cum gum cum gum, except in the

case of Miller, who wasn't able to maintain the cadence, what
with his damaged shins. He in fact did little more than hunker
and lurch along, and he winced and gasped with every step. They
marched out of the ruined RF&P yards and headed west through
the streets of Richmond. People were running in every which
direction, and they were shouting. Their mouths were cavernous.
Their clothing was torn. Never in his life had Sgt Patterson seen
so many poor claptrappy wornout holey top hats and dresses and
britches and shoes. Some of these people shook their fists at Sgt
Patterson and his men and accused them of being cowards. Sgt
Patterson almost smiled. He wondered whether maybe his men
were the planet's first cowardly skeletons. A copy of yesterday's
edition of the *Richmond Sentinel* came skipping and flapping across
the street toward Sgt Patterson, and he picked it up, and his eyes
skimmed its front page, and then he read:

> We are very hopeful of the campaign which is open-
> ing, and trust that we are to reap a large advantage
> from the operations evidently near at hand.

Again Sgt Patterson read those words, and then he made
certain of the date, and it indeed was yesterday's date, by Jesus
Christ, and he shook his head and wadded the paper and threw it
away. Godalmighty, he said to himself, if bullshit was chocolate
cake, we'd all be fatter an the moon. Pope, who was walking along
next to him, asked him what he'd just read that was so terrible,
and Sgt Patterson told Pope shit, you wouldn't want to know,
take my word for it. Pope chuckled. He was tall, and he had a
fine tenor singing voice, and he didn't particularly mind when the
other fellers called him the Pope of Rome and the Fuckin Holy
Father. At one time he'd carried a banjo with him wherever the
Army of Northern Virginia went, but he'd lost it one morning
back in October when someone apparently had stepped on it and
had crushed it while the company was repulsing one of the
Yankee attacks on the Petersburg trenches. Pope missed his banjo
a damnsight more intensely than he resented being called the Pope
of Rome or the Fuckin Holy Father, and he often would speak of
the goddamn injustice and cruelty of a war at deprived a man of

26

his banjo. Sometimes he was asked whether the noise and the pain and the dirt and the killing and the maiming and all the bugs and hunger and sickness and trenchrats bothered him anywhere near as much as the loss of his banjo, and he always shrugged and grinned a little and said: Listen, you fellers, it ain't at I ain't got no *feelins*, an I mourn the dead just as much as any of you do, an all this goddamn death an pain makes me bawl like a boy baby who's got his little balls caught between the blades of a pair of scissors. I mean, I take it hard when one or tuther of us is goddamn, ah, *erased* by some fuckin Yankee sniper's bullet or some Yankee footsoldier's bayonet or whatever, but ain't it all right for me to, um, to mourn my banjo as well without taking nothin away from my respect for the dead? And Pope always smiled hopefully as he said those words, and they always ended in a querulous upward curve, as though he were some sort of urgent nervous lawyer pleading a righteous (but maybe just a wee bit shaky) case that he wasn't really sure even a jury of certified saints would accept.

Sgt Patterson liked Pope. There were times Pope almost made Sgt Patterson laugh, and this was important. Sgt Patterson surely wished he could laugh along about now. God damn but what this whole business was becoming too complicated for him. This morning he'd almost convinced himself he didn't know what to do, and then he'd gone and made a little speech that he wanted all the fellers to head west with him to that place Appomattox Station, where food and ammunition awaited, and it would enable the skeletons to continue their skeletal war. At the same time, he figured he honest to the Lord was, ah, in love with a . . . with a . . . well, with a *boy*. No. No. That was craziness. He was too tired. He didn't know what he was thinking, much less what he was feeling. He was lonely, and he'd messed his britches because of a terrible *dream*, an air wasn't much more to it an at. So he blinked. He pinched the bridge of his nose. A buggy clattered past. It was driven by a man who wore a blue checked suit, and two women were riding with him, and the horse was a tottery bay gelding with sides that more or less had collapsed. The women were young, and they wore dresses that appeared to be made of satin, and Sgt Patterson supposed they were whores. Being a virgin, Sgt Patterson didn't know a single thing about whores, but he *supposed* they were whores. And these whores (or whatever they were) actually were plump. Well, he supposed whores didn't hardly ever starve. He supposed some things just went on forever. The street was lined by trees that scratched at the sky. Fine spindly houses, cunningly filigreed and gingerbreaded just about half to death and then some, were set back from the street, and men and women and children ran in and out of the houses. They were yelling, but Sgt Patterson couldn't make out their words. They surenough appeared to be ascared of the approaching Yankees, though. Evidently they believed the approaching Yankees would tear each of em apart like the carcass of a chicken and gobble em down quick as lightnin an maybe a humminbird's fart, ha ha. He heard a crash, and a chair came sailing through a window. A man jumped out the window, and another man followed him, and the second man was brandishing a pistol. Neither man was particularly young. The second man fired two rounds in the general direction of the first man, and Sgt Patterson and his skeletons wearily dropped to the earth, where they lay and twitched and softly moaned. The second man's second shot struck the first man's left elbow, and it blossomed redly, and the first man seized it, and his legs gave way, and the second man stood over him and said to him the time is at hand, Pettis you sonofabitch. And the second man began kicking the first man, and the first man screamed. Sgt Patterson, who didn't for the goddamn life of him know what he was doing, stood up and began walking toward the wounded Pettis and the man with the pistol. He carried his rifle loosely. He didn't figure he'd be using it. No matter what happened, to hell with the goddamn thing. The second man blinked toward him, and now Sgt Patterson was able to see that this feller was crying. The one named Pettis, though, simply lay on the ground and made no sounds whatever. The second man tried to smile at Sgt Patterson. He nodded down at his pistol and said something to the effect that he'd never fired a pistol before, and wasn't it truly remarkable how warm a pistol could get after it had been fired? Sgt Patterson nodded, and then he shrugged a little and told the second man heynow, feller, whatever's the matter, you don't want to do no more shooting. (It abruptly occurred to Sgt Patterson that he may have been going through all this in order to show his Pendarvis how brave he was. Surely there was no other reason. After all, what did *he* care about these two men and their dispute or feud or whatever it was?) The second man was trying to smile at Sgt Patterson. Then he dropped the pistol. Behind Sgt Patterson, out in the street, one of his skeletons applauded, and another got to whistling, and a third let go a quiet and bemused rebel yell. (The quiet and bemused rebel yell came from old Pope, unless Sgt Patterson missed his guess.) The second man poked at his eyes with his knuckles. He told Sgt Patterson his name was G. W. Mossman, and he said he didn't live in this particular house, but rather this piece of . . . this piece of *carrion* named Albert W. Pettis owned this establishment you see here before you, son, an I came over here this mornin on account of the game is up (an I don't have to be tellin *you* at little fact, do I?), an so air's a reckonin due, seein as how this man an my sister Maisie have been creatin a scandal for the past two years with air carryin on . . . I mean, ever since his poor wife Abigail died of the fever back in the spring of '63, why, this man has absolutely *debauched* my sister, don't you know, an her a woman who's buried two husbands an won't ever see forty again, an no amount of reasonin with em, boy, no appeal to decency, no attempt to make a polite effort to call on air what you say *better instincts* . . . none of at sort of thing has made the slightest difference, an I mean I've talked to em an I've *talked* to em, an it's been like my tongue was fixin to come flyin from my mouth, what with all my damn words an words, an my pilin of words on top of words on top of *words*, but I ask you—what else could I do, especially when you stop to consider that he's an assistant secretary of state while I'm only a damn member of Congress from away to hell and gone out in Chittenden County, and I ain't never been married, an my sister Maisie means everthin in the world to me, an only this mornin she said to me: George, why don't you peddle your fish somewhere else and leave us *be?* Well, I ask you, after all I've done for Maisie, an after all at my pride's had to put up with ever since she an this Pettis here got to behavin like pigs in a mudpile an takin a room at the Spotswood Hotel sometimes three and four times a week for purposes at I, bein a gentleman, don't believe I need to describe . . . ah, well, you'd think the *least* she could do was treat me with a little respect. But not *her*. An not this Pettis here. Oh, God! God! *Maisie!* And then, maybe on a quick and hotly urgent impulse that couldn't be denied or laughed away or reasoned away, G. W. Mossman scooped up the pistol, raised it to his mouth and blew away the back of his skull. His corpse did not fall. Rather, it seated itself on the grass. The pistol dropped into its lap. A crimson chunk of G. W. Mossman's skull lay maybe ten feet behind the corpse. Sgt Patterson released an involuntary fart, soprano and absurd. Down on the grass, not far from the corpse, the man named Pettis squeezed his elbow and bleated. Sgt Patterson glanced at Pendarvis, and Pendarvis's arms were curled around his head. Sgt Patterson exhaled. He didn't for the life of him understand why this death was much different from all the other deaths he'd seen, and so he didn't suppose it was. He nearly shrugged, but then he figured a shrug probably wouldn't have been proper. He and the other fellers stood around for a few minutes, and then—without saying anything—Pettis managed to stand up and stagger back inside the house, pushing and flailing his way back through the broken window and leaving behind little clots and knots of blood from his wounded elbow. There was an insignificant stink of gunpowder, but then it went away. Sgt Patterson motioned to the men to follow him. Now the newcomer, Pvt Boom, was walking along next to him, and Sgt Patterson said something to Boom about a man never knowing what to expect next when it came to this goddamn war. Boom said nothing. He adjusted his top hat and tucked in his filthy white shirt. He grimaced, and he inhaled, and his breath had a shaky sound to it, but he said nothing. Behind them, G. W. Mossman's corpse still sat on the grass, and from a distance it could have been an outline of a man seated on a picnic blanket while waiting for some nice woman to serve him a platter of sausage and beans. A feller in a tattered uniform with corporal's stripes ran past and hollered something having to do with a breakout by the Union prisoners at Belle Isle out in the James. The feller said all available troops were supposed to seek out those escaped Yankees. Sgt Patterson nodded. He glanced back at his fellers and told them never mind; it was too late for at sort of thing. All the fellers nodded. All of them. More carriages clattered past.

The skeletons marched past the Armory and they marched past the Capitol Building, and the cum gum cum gum of them was drowned out by the carriages, by horses, by shouts, by a sound of tears, by the harried and bewildered sounds of children bouncing up and down and from side to side in the buggies and all the high clattery wagons that went careening past. Sgt Patterson kept pinching the bridge of his nose. He didn't know what to think of first. He kept reminding himself that he was in love with Pendarvis, but then he asked himself: How come, if I'm in love with him, I got to keep remindin myself of at little fact?

The streets were muddy, most of them, and the mud was sticky, layered with a sharp surface scum, and that sort of mud was no comfort to bare feet, but then neither was this goddamn war, and would there really be food and supplies at that place Appomattox Station? Why didn't Sgt Patterson simply turn to these fellers and shrug and tell them to skedaddle, an good luck to yall, an don't forget me in your prayers? Ah, a good question, and he only wished he could answer it. He and the others watched a wagon full of Confederate battle flags go hurtling past, and the driver was fiercely laying the whip to the horse (a foamy old black mare), and Sgt Patterson for one wondered where in the name of God that wagon was taking those flags, and he asked himself why the flags hadn't been left behind. Did someone believe the occupying Yankees would spit on them and wipe up their shit with them and then by God *burn* them? He shook his head. He and his fellers marched past a cigarstore that was being looted by men wearing sleeve garters and men wearing frock coats. An elderly man sat weeping on the curb in front of the store, and Sgt Patterson supposed the old feller was the cigarstore's owner. He decided the best thing he could do was not give the old feller a second look, and so he didn't. They saw men looting a furniture store, a drygoods store and a saloon. Sgt Patterson frowned at the drygoods store. He thought briefly of his daddy's drygoods store where he'd worked a million years earlier. Again he shook his head. Fuck it.

Sgt Patterson and the rest of them all flopped down for the night in a railroad culvert maybe ten miles west of the city. Pendarvis came to Sgt Patterson, but Sgt Patterson told him he was tired. Pendarvis nodded. He smiled. He touched one of Sgt Patterson's hands and said yes, yes, he surely understood. A little while later, Pendarvis and Nelson went off to see if they could rustle up any food. They both were killed.

TIDWELL

Monday, April 3, 1865.

Tidwell and the feller named Boom sat up most of the night and watched the sky and various thin vague reflections of distant fires. The reflections came from the east, and clearly Richmond was burning, and Tidwell and Boom could only speculate why. "Maybe em Yanks got off Belle Isle," said Tidwell. "Em Yank prisoners, I mean."

"But I've been told air a sorry lot," said Boom.

"I don't expect they get enough to eat," said Tidwell.

"Well, who does?" said Boom.

"You got a point," said Tidwell.

Boom and Tidwell had built a fire, and now they were sitting crosslegged in front of it. Most of the other fellers had been too tired, though, to bother with a fire, and so they lay hugging their knees and now and then twitching like sick dogs. Boom reached into a pocket of his britches and came up with a tin of snuff. He took a pinch and inhaled it, then sneezed. He held out the tin to Tidwell, but Tidwell's head went from side to side, and he told Boom he'd never really been able to come to terms with snuff. Boom shrugged. "Jack's son has the gout," he said.

". . . pardon?" said Tidwell.

"Oh. Sorry. At's what we used to say when I was a little feller."

"Jack's son has the gout?"

"Yessir," said Boom. "My brothers an myself, we had a tutor named Mister Tudor, and he taught us a little French, an one of the phrases we learned was *Chacun à son goût*, which loosely means each one accordin to his choice but which loosely *sounds* like Jack's son has the gout. Or at least Sam an Carter an myself thought so. An we always sort of covered our mouths when we said *Chacun à son goût*, an Mister Tudor, Mister Tudor the tutor, ha ha, told us we were frivolous an silly, an you know, I can't help but agree with him . . ."

"Yall had a *tutor?*"

"Right. We were real fancy, we were."

"I expect so . . ." said Tidwell. He sighed. He rubbed a palm against his stubbled chin. "I expect yall ate good too, didn't you?"

"Oh yessir. Yessir. Indeed we did. Why, we even had afternoon tea. Mister Tudor the tutor was English, you see, an he taught Sam an Carter an myself to *expect* to have our tea every afternoon at four o'clock, seven days a week, come what may. Tea an little cakes an cookies, you see, an he made us sit still while we were drinkin our tea an eatin our little cakes an cookies, an he told us our afternoon tea was as good a way as any to calm us down an keep us from goin *altogether* wild. An he said it was important at we be kept from goin altogether wild, on account of boys such as Sam an Carter an myself would grow up to be such . . . well, such *leaders* . . . an it was important at we be at least a little civilized . . ."

"Was the little cakes an cookies good?"

"Oh, yes *sir*," said Boom. "We had this nigger woman who cooked for us, an her name was Clytemnestra, an she used so much butter an sugar in those cookies an cakes at it was a miracle all the butter an sugar didn't get stuffed into us beyond redemption an, well, an sort of come out of our noses, you know?"

"Can't say as I do," said Tidwell, "but I would like to, an especially long bout now . . ."

"I used to miss it," said Boom, "but at's all gone now."

"Oh?" said Tidwell. "How come?"

"I'm too tired for all the fuss."

"I expect I don't know what you mean," said Tidwell.

Boom shrugged. "Well," he said, "who wants to eat little cookies an cakes when instead he can go skedaddlin acrost the countryside while Yankees keep shootin at him with rifles an cannon an tryin to slice him all to hell with bayonets an swords? An don't forget the starvation. I never in my life thought I'd eat my horse, especially seein as how I'm cavalry an I come from a fambly of cavalry, an my daddy early on in my life—and early on in the lives of Sam an Carter—told us we'd roast forever in the Final Conflagration of Perdition Almighty if we treated a horse with anythin less an courtesy an the utmost respect, but three weeks ago myself an my . . . ah, I mean, myself an, ah, well, some of the fellers I was servin with . . . well, for the better part of four years my Old Catawba was my friend and companion nonpareil, if you know what I mean. Nonpareil. Yes *sir*. An at mornin three weeks ago I woke up an had myself a cup of hot sassafras tea, an it sort of reminded me, you know, of the little teaparties myself an Sam an Carter used to have with old Mister Tudor the tutor, but air wasn't anythin more to my breakfast an at cup of hot sassafras tea, an I looked around an I saw Old Catawba sort of standin in a slump, an his sides was stove in, an his eyes was all gummy, with sort of a yellowish cast, and I stood up an said to myself: Ah, fuck it. I still had a pistol at day, an so I pulled it from my belt an walked to Old Catawba, an he looked at me like maybe he was honest to God *welcomin* me, an he blinked, an he neighed ever such a little bit, so I shot the poor sucker dead. I pressed my pistol's muzzle smack between his eyes an pulled the trigger, and I'd forgotten air would be a lot of blood, so I more or less was drenched, but at day by God we ate pretty good. Not *real* good, you understand, on account of air wasn't all at much meat on Old Catawba's loyal old bones—but it was good enough, and we'd whipped Old Man Starvation for one more day. An all the fellers came to me an told me I'd done the right thing, but I kept wonderin what my daddy would have said. Only he's been dead for ten years, so why was I worryin myself about him? Strange the stupid things we bother ourselves with. Stupid oldtimey fears. God, when's it all goin to end?"

"You askin *me?*" said Tidwell.

"At I am," said Boom.

"I'm real sorry," said Tidwell, "but you're askin the wrong feller. I don't know when nothin's goin to end, and I ain't even all at sure none of this ever *will* end. Hey, but maybe you can tell me somethin . . ."

"Oh?" said Boom.

"You an me, we're havin us a nice little talk, ain't we?"

". . . yes," said Boom, after thinking about it for a moment or so.

"So how come?" said Tidwell.

". . . how come what?" said Boom.

"I mean, pardon me for bringin up the subject, but you ain't had but maybe ten words to say to any of us, so how come now air's all this talk comin from you? Your horse an all. Your teaparties an your brothers an I don't know what else."

"Oh," said Boom. "I see what you mean . . ." His voice trailed away. He was wearing his top hat while he and Tidwell sat by their fire. Thoughtfully he patted his top hat, as though he were trying to keep it from blowing away. He coughed. He rubbed his mouth, especially at the corners, where a string of spittle may have gathered. He rubbed his forehead. He picked at a fingernail. He looked up, and his eyes were imprecise. He shrugged, and of course Tidwell didn't have the slightest god-damn idea why. Then, after another cough, Boom said: "I believe I've sprung a leak. It's like maybe sawdust's comin out of me. Like maybe now I got to speak, on account of *somebody's* got to speak—an maybe talk his way through to the truth of all this. The truth's important. It helps cause the sun to come out an the birds to sing an the clocks not to fall down in a heap, you know?" A pause. Boom rubbed his imprecise eyes. He shook his head. "I'm full of shit," he said, "an it's a mile wide an I couldn't tell you how deep. The thing is, I ate my horse, all right—but under different circumstances an I've described. More, ah, desperate. Hey. Don't look at me at way. I'm not the village lunatic, my friend. I'm only a feller who's lost . . . ah, never mind . . ."

"Lost what?" said Tidwell.

". . . never *mind*," said Boom, and abruptly he stood up. He walked away from Tidwell without saying anything more. He scrambled up a side of the railroad culvert and vanished into the shadows up there.

Tidwell shrugged. He grimaced into the fire. It was too hot, and so he scrunched back from it. Twigs scratched and rustled, and the earth was too goddamn damp. He had no idea what anyone was supposed to do. He wanted to go home to his good old plump wife Rosemary and his four sons and his four daughters and even old Oliver the dog. That was what he *wanted* to do, but was it what he was *supposed* to do? He didn't believe so. The choices in this war always were harder than that. Either you ran or you flopped in the mud. Either you killed people or they killed you. You dug up everything. You erected claptrap barricades made of logs and stumps and fenceposts and broken wagons and caissons. You rooted up trees. You demolished houses and barns. You slaughtered farm animals and sometimes you made off with shoes you tugged off the feet of corpses. You scampered away with shoes and shirts and whatever else you could find, and who gave a rat's shit where they came from? You drank hot raw moonshine and passed out on some buggy and humid whorehouse pile of sheets and rags with a woman whose pussy had an odor of lard and onions. Whoo, some life, and Tidwell wouldn't have hesitated to trade it for two broken sticks and a handful of cow flop. Now he lay back and blinked toward the pink and ominous sky. The terrible light seemed to be coming from Capitol Square and maybe even the commissary depot, and Tidwell supposed there was a good chance the looters they'd seen today were having themselves a high good time. (He'd worked in the commissary depot, and he knew the place couldn't have been guarded by more than a dozen men, and he felt sorry for those dozen men if the looters had decided to take the building. The guard detail wouldn't have lasted five minutes against looters, and that was the absolute undistilled fact of *that*, by dear bloody Christ.) He wondered whether the Confederate generals had had the presence of mind to order that the bridges over the James be destroyed. Not that this would delay the Yanks a whole lot, but at least it would show the world that the fall of Petersburg didn't mean the fight was altogether out of the Army of Northern Virginia. By God,

Petersburg wasn't the world, and the Army of Northern Virginia lived on, by God, by God. And here Tidwell grimaced. He jammed shut his eyes. He watched explosions of afterimages; they scooted across his skull's interior like mad insistent lightning. He summoned images of Rosemary and the children, and he almost was ready to believe his mouth held a flavor of milk. Now he was sucking straw, and Rosemary was whispering earnestly of her breasts and her anxious nipples. He smiled, and he poked the straw through the openings between his teeth. She was his virgin bride, and she lay fearful and pale in the bridal suite of the Fredericksburg House, and it was 1851, and he heard a toot and whumpf of locomotives, and she kept trying to smile at him, and he told her everthin would be just fine, my lovely one, an don't you . . . ah, don't you worry bout a thing, o you're surenough my darlin you are, you are, an I wouldn't hurt you for the world an all the tea in China an all the gold in old Castille, don't you know. So he moved as gently as he knew how to move, and she welcomed him with kisses and secret fragrant fluids, and the necessary penetration was accomplished, and she hardly bled at all, and later that night she said to him: You think maybe I'm in the fambly way yet? And he grinned and said: I got no way of knowin, but it surely would be a nice thing, wouldn't it? And he gathered his Rosemary to him, and he made hissy comfortable sounds, and now he slept with his arms curled over his ears, and he awakened with a smile. For he was remembering that she'd given him eight healthy babies in just nine years, and he supposed the two of them were sort of a scandal, but there were scandals and then there were scandals and some scandals were more pleasant than other scandals, and their particular scandal had been pleasant beyond measure, and its contemplation surely did help a man pass through a day when he was plowing a field or planting beans or uprooting a stump or helping a mare through her time of foaling. Ah, such a time it had been, and God *damn* this war for interrupting it and knocking everything down in a dismal despondent heap. Still, Tidwell did manage to smile when he awakened. And he still was smiling when he boiled himself a pot of chicory coffee. His newly talkative friend, the mildly mysterious Boom, demon of the teaparties and Jack's son's gout, wearer of an enigmatic and perhaps even scarifying top hat, hadn't returned from wherever he'd gone, but Tidwell figured the poor feller sooner or later would come straggling back. After all, where else would the man go? Maybe this bunch of tattered murmurous skeletons didn't amount to a hill of beans, but it was better than no bunch at all, and at least it offered the sad starving companionship of the sad starving walking dead. Oh, haw haw. How real funny. Tidwell shook his head, and he sipped his coffee. Petrie came to him and hunkered down next to him and asked him for a cup of coffee. Tidwell nodded. Petrie had brought his own cup, and so he filled it. He told Tidwell of the disappearance of Pendarvis and Nelson, and then he said Sgt Patterson had taken McGraw and Appling in search of the missing men. Petrie said he suregod hoped Pendarvis and Nelson had come acrost a couple of little old girls . . . friendly girls, girls with big tiddies an not much religion, hee hee. Tidwell nodded. He said that surenough was a nice thought, and he said he supposed that was what they all lived for, wasn't it? Petrie snickered. He was dark and slight, and he wore spectacles that had bent wire frames. The spectacles hung crookedly from his nose, giving him a clownish aspect. In point of fact, the poor feller appeared to be damn near blind, and this was one of the reasons he went without a rifle. What the hell, no one wanted him to shoot off one—or maybe both—of his goddamn feet. At dawn Sgt Patterson and McGraw and Appling had set off in their search for Pendarvis and Nelson, and Ratliff had been left in charge. Most of the fellers respected Ratliff. He'd been in the army since '62, and he roasted a pretty mean haunch of mule, and he'd once been a sergeant himself . . . until he'd told some gleaming spitpolished little lieutenant to go fuck the dog when the feller had ordered the company to make a third attack in six hours against the Yankees' Petersburg trenches. The gleaming spitpolished little lieutenant had screamed at Ratliff that he (Ratliff) was being cowardly and insubordinate, and Ratliff had screamed back at the feller, telling him yessir, yessir, at's absolutely true, but it ain't the *whole* truth, seein as how I'm also bein *alive*. The next day Ratliff was given a summary courtmartial by a panel of exhausted jabbery distracted officers, and the presiding officer, a colonel named Abernethy, was drunk. The courtmartial lasted twenty minutes, and the gleaming spitpolished little lieutenant was the only complaining witness, and the tired officers all nodded and thanked him for his devotion to duty, and then they sighed and yawned and reduced Ratliff in grade to private. The day after that, and Ratliff barely had ripped off his stripes, the gleaming spitpolished little lieutenant was killed by a sniper's bullet, and no one was quite sure where the bullet had come from. The feller's name had been Abner O. LaFarge, and he had hailed from some jerkwater town in South Carolina, and his boots were stripped from him by his friend Ratliff, and his sword and pistol were appropriated by a feller named Robertshaw, who traded them two days later for five quarts of moonshine, who then drank himself into a state of staggery pukey lunacy, who finally for no real good reason scrambled from the trenches and launched a loud shrieking singlehanded attack on the Yankees, advancing perhaps fifty feet before he was chopped down by a burst of annoyed riflefire. Actually, the fact that he'd advanced as many as fifty feet was looked upon as a hell of an accomplishment, and there were those who said poor old Robertshaw had been so lucky it was just about as though he'd been touched by the Hand of God. Others, though, didn't think any of it was very funny. Ratliff, for example, was promptly promoted back to sergeant by the company commander, a frail young captain named Purcell who'd been a teacher at the Tidewater Latin Academy in Norfolk before the war—but Ratliff, ornery and toughly stubborn, refused the promotion, and he told Capt Purcell he meant no offense, but he just didn't no more want the bother of being a sergeant, seeing as how he wanted to spend most of his time trying to make sure no one shot his ass off. Capt Purcell nodded and said he understood, and about a month later Capt Purcell was killed leading a charge on a Yankee gun emplacement at the top of a low hill about a hundred yards from the Confederate position. He led sixtytwo men in that charge, and thirtysix came back. Ratliff remained in the rear rank, and by his own admission he'd remained back there, but no one thought the worse of him for that. The war had lasted too long for accusations of cowardice. That sort of talk was too damn trivial. It was feathers and eiderdown. It was blabber. It was bullshit. It did no justice to anyone.

So, as it usually did, noon came, and smoke was rising from Richmond in ropes and plumes, and wagons were rattling past on a road just beyond the lip of the railroad culvert, when that Alabama artilleryman, Appling by name, came sliding and scrambling down the side of the culvert and told Ratliff the bodies of Pendarvis and Nelson had been found lying on their backs, hands tied, with bullet holes in their chests and skulls. Appling was breathless, and his voice and lungs made squealing sounds, and he told Ratliff the fellers all was to go where the bodies was, so air could be a proper funeral service—and them was Sgt Patterson's orders. Ratliff snorted. He told Appling he hadn't attended a fuckin *proper funeral* since before the war. Appling shrugged. He told Ratliff he only was doing what he'd been told to do by Sgt Patterson. Appling still was gasping, and he placed his hands on his hips and confronted Ratliff. He told Ratliff he was new to this company—or bunch of straggling skeletons, or whatever it was. He said he was from Alabammy. He said he was proud to be from Alabammy, and he suregod couldn't wait to get on home. In the meantime, though, he said, he would do like he was goddamn *told*, even if it involved a *proper funeral*. He turned away from Ratliff and began climbing back up the side of the culvert. Ratliff spat. He motioned to the others, and they all followed Appling up the side of the culvert and back toward Richmond along the road that was carrying all the refugees—some in the rattling wagons, some on foot, a few on horseback—no doubt as far away from Richmond as they could get. They saw children, and they saw men in frock coats, and they saw chattering whores and solemn disheveled mounted officers. No one glanced at them, and not a soul waved, not even the children or the chattering whores. Tidwell wondered whether anyone in the world had a name anymore, or opinions, a place in time and space. All these fleeing people were gray and apparently eyeless and for the most part silent. For all he could figure, all of them could have been dead, and so why hadn't they been buried? Shit. Fuck. Always there were too many questions, and they made about as much sense as did smoke. Ah, the smoke. The sky was torpid from all the smoke, and ashes came down, and everyone brushed the ashes out of their eyes. With Appling hurrying along at the head of their lurching tattered procession, the skeletons marched maybe a mile back toward Richmond. It occurred to Tidwell that his new friend Boom was nowhere to be seen. Well, maybe the feller lived somewheres nearby and had decided that the war was over for him. Tidwell couldn't blame Boom for that. The war was over for all of them, only the war carried its own awful tormented momentum, and he and the others simply were going through the motions because what the hell, they'd been in the army so fuckin long they didn't know what else to do. The bodies of Pendarvis and Nelson were sitting at the base of a large fingering elm that leaned across the road from a general store that appeared to have been pretty well bashed and looted. A large torn cardboard sign was nailed to the tree directly above the bodies, and the sign carried the single word: LOOTERS. Sgt Patterson and McGraw were squatting next to the bodies. Sgt Patterson's face was damp, and he was hugging himself. He stood up, and so did McGraw. The bodies were faceless and crimson. Tidwell had known Pendarvis slightly, so he remembered what Pendarvis had looked like. Nelson, though . . . well, Nelson had been a gray and barrelchested little feller, maybe as old as forty, with a heavy chest and knotted legs, and early in the war he'd made a bit of money running footraces against fellers from other companies. But then, what with all the times of short rations, he'd lost weight and strength, and he'd no longer won the footraces, and in the past year or so he'd kept to himself. Or at least that was what the other men had told Tidwell, and it represented all he knew about old Nelson. But Nelson's history no longer really mattered, did it? Nelson was dead, and dead was dead, and enough said, don't you know. The men gathered a few feet from where Pendarvis and Nelson sat against the base of that elm tree, and Sgt Patterson nodded toward the smashed and obviously looted little store and told the men they knew as much as he did. He said he had no idea who'd executed Pendarvis and Nelson. He said he hoped whoever had done it would rot in Hell. He was shaking. Standing (slouching, rather) next to Sgt Patterson, McGraw was picking his nose. Tidwell, who was McGraw's cousin, for Christ's holy sake, would have to give the sonofabitch a talkingto. Sgt Patterson told the men it was absolutely necessary Pendarvis and Nelson received a decent burial. He said it was about time decent burials were restored to the, ah, the daily scheme of things. He said he only wished Pendarvis and Nelson could be carried down to the river so their blood could be washed away. But there wasn't the goddamn time, was air? The time was needed for skedaddlin, wasn't it? The graves were dug in a grove of wild cherry trees a few yards from the road. No shovels were available, so the men used the butts of their rifles to dig the graves. Sgt Patterson poured water from his canteen and more or less washed the blood from Pendarvis's face. This didn't do an awful lot of good, seeing as how Pendarvis's face had no flesh. Sgt Patterson grimaced and groaned. He walked to the demolished store and kicked a number of loose boards with his bare feet.

BOOM

Monday, April 3, 1865.

Boom spent the morning sitting on a hillside overlooking the place where Pendarvis and Nelson had been executed. He talked gently to himself, and he was aware that his words didn't make a whole lot of sense. He listened to morning birds, and he kept patting down his top hat, and from time to time he embraced himself in order to try to keep out the damp and the cold. Earlier, he'd literally tripped over the bodies of Pendarvis and Nelson in the bloody goddamn dark, and his right hand and arm had been soaked in Nelson's blood and tissue. He'd gone flailing and flopping up the side of the hill, and he'd shrieked and whooped. Then he'd lain back and had blinked in the direction of Richmond and the fires. And certain quiet lunatic words had come from him: "Mother, you never explained any of this. You an Mister Tudor the tutor kept us too busy sippin tea, which was all the rage back en, wasn't it? An you kept tellin me my poetry an my little paintins made me what you called special. Yes ma'am. Special. Surely. Special as mud is more like it, am I correct? I should have gone to VMI the way Sam or Carter did. I'd have died content, firm in my knowledge of the right an the wrong to all this. You know somethin, Mother? I can't even hear an *owl* without jumpin an dancin out of my skin. Jumpin an dancin. Like a nigger with his feet on fire. Ha. I wish I was like an engravin in the *Southern*

44

Illustrated News. Nice an neat an steadfast, you hear me? Hey, how come I got no tit to suck on? What happened to all my boys? Were they boiled down for air fat? Ha. *What* fat? Oh, an whatever happened to Jesus? He's supposed to be ever bit as gentle as you are, isn't at so? Mother, how come you keep your dress shut? I mean, I'm the only one remainin to you, so why don't you show me your tits? I want your tits, Mother. Maybe I could drape em round my neck like jewelry, do you think, ha ha? So many of my boys died, Mother. Too many. Always it was too many, even when it was only one. Mister Lee an I drank coffee in the shade of those willowtrees at twilight at time after we'd whipped em at Chancellorsville, an he told me he was happy bout how it turned out, but his old *face* wasn't very happy, an he went on to say at too many good men had died, an he even had kind words for the Yankees, an en he said a brave an remarkable thing. He said: *I wish I were simple an impoverished, a tobacco farmer maybe, or a section hand on the railroad, rather an what I am, which is nothing more an a . . . a famous claptrap hero whose picture is in too many magazines an whose pronouncements somehow have achieved the dimensions of holy writ.* An en, Mother darlin, he climbed up onto old Traveller, an at fine horse gently cantered away, an Mister Lee rode easy in the saddle, an it was like he was inspectin the cotton crop, or maybe ridin off to church. I do wish I could talk to him. Maybe he'd tell me what to do, or what I should have done. Maybe he'd say I was a coward. Maybe he'd say I was stupid. But at least by God I'd *know*, wouldn't I? I mean, I have a top hat and a white shirt to my name. I don't have my sword, an there is no plume in my top hat, an I am by any measurement a discredited ass who equates plumes with the deaths of fine boys, who doesn't understand the difference between gallantry an grace on the one hand an vainglory an butchery on the other. I am trapped by the wrong varieties of words, dear Mother. But then what are the *right* varieties of words? Are you capable of listin em for me, o Mama mine? Do you understand how deeply I—"

A scream, quavery but at the same time every bit as urgent as rainstorms and hailstones and quick blanketing thunder, came tearing up from the place where the bodies of Pendarvis and Nelson lay. Boom squinted into the darkness, and he was able to make out the shapes of three men who appeared to be blundering back and forth and waving their arms. Boom slid partway down the hill on his rump, and he hoped he wasn't making too much noise. He sat crosslegged, resting against a fallen log. It had damp bark. He plucked and tore at the wet bark and it gave off odors of brown. He squinted down at the three men, and he watched them drag the bodies to the elm tree and prop them up at its base. Then, as dawn came clustering in through the morning mists and various wisps and hints of the hard curling smoke from burning Richmond, he recognized the men . . . Sgt Patterson and two other fellows from the company, and he believed their names were McGrath and Appleton. Something like that, at any rate. He did not move, and he barely breathed, and he was able to hear their voices . . .

"The officer who ordered this, his asshole is where his head ought to be," said McGrath or whatever his name was.

"Be quiet . . ." said Sgt Patterson, and his voice was papery. He and the other two were lounging on the earth a few feet from the dead men.

"I'm just offerin an opinion," said McGrath. His voice was pouty. He nearly sounded as though he wanted to cry.

"God damn you, McGraw," said Sgt Patterson, "I don't need to hear your fuckin *opinions* . . ."

(Up on the hill, Boom nodded. All right. The fellow's name was McGraw and not McGrath. Now Boom knew, and he no doubt was enriched by the information, haw haw.)

They fell silent down there, and they appeared to lie back and drop off to sleep. It wasn't until long after dawn that Sgt Patterson awakened, sat up, rubbed his eyes, then stared whitely at the corpses. The whiteness was quite apparent against the grayness of his flesh. He could have been waving a goddamn battleflag with those terrible eggy eyes of his. He sat motionless. He didn't even stand up and go into the underbrush for a quick piss. He simply sat there and stared at the corpses, and he appeared to be concentrating on the man Boom for one believed to be the pretty Pendarvis. After maybe an hour of sitting there, Sgt Patterson stood up. He stretched. He balanced himself on the balls of his feet. He teetered from side to side, and then he tiptoed toward the tree. He squatted in front of the dead Pendarvis and stared at Pendarvis's ruined face. Then, carefully leaning forward, he kissed Pendarvis's chest, and he appeared to be kissing Pendarvis's wounds. Boom sighed and looked away. He shook his head, and he gnawed his lips, and he needed to say something more to his mother, but he didn't know what the words were. So he lay back and closed his eyes and left poor Sgt Patterson to whatever it was Sgt Patterson needed to do, and he, this tophatted and formerly silent Boom, decided to lecture his brain and its interior darkness, to harangue the elements, to scold history and to admonish God, and he said: "It's all too goddamn trivial, if anyone were to ask the likes of me. For one thing, we sleep too much, an at's like rehearsin for death, isn't it? A man of sixty sleeps fifteen or maybe twenty years of his life away, doesn't he? An he remembers nothin at happened before he attained the age of five, an onethird of five is one an twothirds, subtract the one an twothirds from five and you come up with three an onethird more years of waste, an you add at to twenty, say, and the total is twentythree an onethird, an if you throw in the time a man spends shittin in the privy an prayin to Almighty God in church an fightin in some goddamn war or other, then the total comes to more an a quarter of a century, which is a whole bunch, by Christ. A whole bunch. An for what? A whole lot of time, an a whole lot of trains hootin an smokin, pullin golden glowin steamcars through the night, an a whole lot of men an women bouncin in the sheets, yes *sir* . . . an I only wish I could figure the sense in any of it. An I mean, now see here, I didn't go rushin an careerin into this war all bright an cheery like a churchbell on Easter mornin. I had more sense an at, an I said to Lenore, I said: Don't you smile at me an wave your handkerchief at me like I was some sort of sweet knight settin off to joust an flail an jab in the name of the Honor of the Confederacy. I just can't put up with at sort of thing. An Lenore tried to smile, but I said to her: No. Don't you do at. You don't know what you're doin. You read too many books at tell lies, and I mean *real* lies. Hey, tell you what you ought to do, Lenore. Just sort of, um, *arrange* yourself where everythin's pretty, an your mama can serve you cakes an milk, an you can fill your mind with music an poetry an the heroic utterances of famous men. I mean, the best things for you are daffodils an banjomusic an the Sermon on the Mount. Be calm, Lenore. Be of good cheer. Vex not your sweet skull with disturbin thoughts. Always keep a plenteous supply of coolin sachet on hand. Practice your titterin an the battin of your eyelashes. Keep a cat. Have a nigger woman teach you how to roast chicken an pork an bone a fish an pour wine. Keep your heart pure an your loins dry an your bosom all pinkly aglow. Don't expose your tits to the wind, old girl. You might catch you a rash. I mean, you see us in the goddamn tintypes, Lenore, an we're frozen as though we're already dead but no one's told us to lie down, an our faces are drawn an glum, an our uniforms never are pressed as well as they should be, an our hair never is trimmed as well as it should be, an we look like we're propped up by ropes an boards, don't we? An at's really bout the size of it, Lenore. We're paralyzed, and we almost never know whether we're feelin much more an plain dog weariness, an why is at? Well, we can't help but wonder what's comin next, an whether we'll survive, or who among us will survive, an myself . . . well, speakin for myself, you understand, I stare into all air faces an I keep wonderin which one maybe could be a poet, which one a brave an incorruptible politician, which one an engineer, which one a writer of music havin to do with love an pretty girls an the perfume of honeysuckle. Oh, it all passes through my mind, an I . . . sometimes I want to shriek like maybe a pig with a sparkin fuse up its ass. Tell me why I feel what I feel, Lenore. You too, Mama. Join right in with *your* opinions. I honest to God can't wait to hear what you two fine ladies have to say. I mean, I wanted to scold the elements an admonish God just now, but I never did get around to all at, did I? Well, maybe tomorrow'll be another day. Maybe . . ." And Boom opened his eyes and blinked into the early grayness. He hoped he hadn't been talking too loudly. He didn't want to make himself known to Sgt Patterson and the others. Not just yet, at any rate. He figured he eventually would get around to confronting his particular disastrous history, once his tonsils and his courage had been brought forward in force. But then, instead of talking, he wept. Boom wept. Boom. Ah: wept. Yes. His boys did the best they could, but they were so hungry they kept fainting, and he told them there would be plenty of food in the next town, at the next railway depot, the next granary or fish cannery or slaughterhouse. And he was such a liar as to make Satan toss his stinking Satanic hat in the blistering Satanic air and issue the most vigorous congratulations. There never was a next town or a next railway depot—or at least not the sort Boom had promised his boys, and one by one their horses died and were skinned and roasted and eaten, and some of his boys wept, and he couldn't blame them. And now, murmurous and hunched, his head wobbling from side to side and his voice threaded with his own particular grief, he said: "We are damned an forever debauched, an we have been betrayed, an we have been pulled down, razed, sold for scrap. Our ideals are fraudulent, an our poetry is shit, an we have been lied to an flummoxed. Hear me, Mother. Listen closely, Mister Tudor, you tutor you. Our poetry is *shit*, I tell you, an air's nothing left to us beyond dust an weariness an crippled words. Nothin in the damn war is what we were told it would be, an I was one of the ones who did the tellin, on account of I was a—"

A sound of hollering interrupted Boom's monologue, and it was Patterson who was doing the hollering, and Patterson's words were directed at McGraw: *"You lazy sonofabitch you! Air's a farmhouse maybe half a mile back towards Richmond, an I expect the farmer air will give you the loan of a shovel or two! Just tell him two fuckin heroes of the Confederacy are dead! Don't say nothin, though, bout how they died! For oncet in your life, show a little good sense!"*

McGraw managed to speak, but his voice was querulous, womanish, and he appeared to be wringing his hands. "But I'm . . . I'm ascared," he said. "Whoever shot these fellers, maybe air waitin at at air farmhouse. Waitin for *me*. Waitin to tie my hands an stand me maybe against a wall . . ."

Sgt Patterson was gasping. He kept glancing toward the sitting corpses. He managed to bring his voice down, though, and he said to McGraw, voice cold, judgmental as death: "You're a fuckin coward, Clyde McGraw."

Quickly McGraw nodded. "Right," he said.

"You braggin on it?" said Sgt Patterson.

". . . might as well," said McGraw, shrugging.

"Suppose I was to shoot you with my pistol if you didn't go?"

". . . en I'd go," said McGraw.

"I'll count to ten," said Sgt Patterson.

McGraw began scuttling toward the road.

"At's more like it," said Sgt Patterson, and his arms flapped. And he hollered and danced. His feet slapped the grass and mud of that place. He called to McGraw to hurry back with the shovels.

McGraw turned and stared at Sgt Patterson for a moment. McGraw's sides already were moving in and out, and he was holding out his bandaged left hand, and he could have been some sort of inchoate supplicant pleading with God for a mad and hotly wobbly salvation.

"Don't stop now!" hollered Sgt Patterson. *"You're doin just fine! I'm real proud of you, you sonofabitch!"* And Sgt Patterson quickly brought his hands together in a brisk imperious clap.

McGraw ran off.

Up on the hillside, Boom covered his mouth. He had to, and never mind the horror and all the rest of what was happening.

Sgt Patterson and the man known (in Boom's mind, at least) as Appleton hunkered down out by the road, and they talked quietly, but now they were out of earshot, and anyway, there was an awful commotion out there on that road. The Yankees weren't exactly overpoweringly popular that morning, and men and women and children were hurrying along the road, in carriages and wagons, on foot, on horseback. Boom saw a little boy on horseback. A little boy wearing what appeared to be velvet britches and a fancy frilled shirt. The little boy was no more than eight or nine, and he was riding a great healthy roan gelding, and the animal was so healthy it almost appeared fat. The little boy was leaning forward and evidently was whispering into the roan gelding's ear, and at the same time he was whacking his legs as best he could against the animal's sleek flanks. He was the smallest horseman and the horse was the largest horse Boom had seen in months, maybe even goddamn years. Boom wanted to stand up and wave to the little fellow, but at the same time he didn't want to give himself away to Sgt Patterson and the other man, so he simply sat there and licked the roof of his mouth and wished he had a nice drink of springwater. He dredged up spit, rolled it across his teeth, swallowed, grimaced. Then he lay back and blinked and shooed away ants and flies and forgot to harangue the planet. There was a scum of purple sunlight clotted by smoke from the burning city, and it made Boom's eyes water. He rubbed them with his indexfingers, and then he sighed, dredged up more spit, sighed again, swallowed the spit. He closed his eyes, and he told himself that brave little fellow on the splendid roan gelding no doubt had been a child of rank and privilege, and he told himself the miserable little brat probably was more arrogant than the goddamn sun, if the truth were known, don't you know. And here, after rubbing his mouth and picking at his whiskers, Boom managed to sleep without dreaming, and he heard no voices, suffered no rattle of fear, loathed not a soul, even was tolerant of his scarred and tattered God. He was awakened by shouts from down below, and he opened his eyes, and McGraw had returned, and of course it was Sgt Patterson who was doing the shouting: *"No shovel? I don't believe you! You're goddamn funnin me! Who ever heard of a farmer who didn't have no fuckin shovel?"*

Said McGraw: "I wouldn't know . . ."

"What?"

"Nobody was to home," said McGraw. "The house was empty, an the barn was empty, an I couldn't find no shovel to save my fuckin life. I *looked*, though. Up an down. Inside an out. In the cellar, even. An air was an attic, an I looked *air*. An a lot of good it done me. Fuck. Talk bout chasin wild geeses . . ."

"Gooses," said the one whose name maybe was Appleton.

("Geese . . ." said Boom under his breath. And at the same time he managed to smile.)

"Geese, God damn you," said Sgt Patterson to McGraw. "I mean you're so iggerant it's a wonder you know how to piss."

". . . what?" said McGraw.

"Shit," said Sgt Patterson. He turned away from McGraw and began speaking to Appleton. Only he addressed the man as Appling, which meant Boom stood corrected, and fair enough; at least the mystery had been solved. Appling went trotting back toward where the rest of the company was waiting, and Boom figured Sgt Patterson had decided to bring the others to this place to help in some sort of burial of Pendarvis and Nelson before they went all rich and ripe. Boom was right. Less than an hour later, led by the one named Ratliff, the men came straggling up to that place of corpses and McGraw and Sgt Patterson. Directly they began digging the graves with the stocks of their rifles. Boom sat up and hugged his knees and winced. He kept glancing toward the dirty sky, and he listened to passing carriages and wagons, and he rubbed his knuckles across his lips. Boom watched the stream of wagons and carriages and walking refugees, and no one stopped to ask what had happened, to offer sympathy, to express outrage. No one even offered a shovel. Boom's eyes began to sting, and he wept. The wagons and the carriages had axles that squeaked and clapped. Tears or no tears, Boom was able to see women in pokebonnets, and he saw boys in caps, and he saw little girls whose hair slapped and streamed in the hot cindered air, and he saw coatless men who leaned forward and laid the whip to their horses . . . spavined slavering nags, most of them, with hot eyes and loose knees.

Finally the graves were dug. The bodies were lifted and carried to the graves. The fleeing wagons clashed and racketed, and a tallyho careened past, and a sound of female laughter shot up like the teeth of a saw.

Weeping, Boom stood up. There was no hiding from any more of this.

The bodies were carefully placed in the graves, and Sgt Patterson stood at the head of the graves. He said nothing, and neither did anyone else.

Boom ran down the side of the hill, and everyone looked up. No one spoke. Boom wept, and his nose ran, He snuffled. He sucked snot. He pressed his eyes with his knuckles. Now his afterimages were golden and purple. He coughed. His vision returned, and he walked to the foot of the graves and stood facing Sgt Patterson. He was wearing his top hat, and so he took it off and pressed it to his chest. Sgt Patterson's mouth was open but shadowed in such a way that he appeared toothless, older than stones and death. Boom looked around. No one spoke, and no one seemed about to speak. He squeezed his top hat with both his arms. His cock felt heavy, and he supposed he needed to piss. He kept glancing at Sgt Patterson, and he didn't suppose Sgt Patterson would last out the week. Then Boom, a proper Episcopalian who knew he hated God the way a rat hates joy and decency and clean breath, spoke in a measured voice, at once sweet and woozy and deranged, and he said: *"Man, at is born of woman, hath but a short time to live, an is full of misery. He cometh up, an is cut down, like a flower; he fleeth as it were a shadow, and never continueth in one stay. In the midst of life we are in death; of whom may we seek for succour, O Lord, who for our sins are justly displeased? Yes, O Lord God most holy, O holy an most merciful Saviour, deliver us not into the bitter pains of eternal death. Thou knowest, Lord, the secrets of our hearts; shut not thy merciful ears to our prayer; but spare us, Lord most holy, O God most mighty, O holy and merciful Saviour, thou most worthy Judge eternal, suffer us not, at our last hour, for any pains of death, to fall from thee."* Then, grunting, Boom bent down and scooped up a handful of earth and tossed half of it into Pendarvis's grave and the other half into Nelson's grave. Straightening, Boom said: *"Unto Almighty God we commend the souls of our brothers departed, an we commit air bodies to the ground; earth to earth, ashes to ashes, dust to dust, in the sure an certain hope of the Resurrection unto eternal life, through our Lord Jesus Christ; at whose comin in glorious majesty to judge the world, the earth an the sea shall give up air dead; an the corruptible bodies of those who sleep in him shall be changed, an made like unto his own glorious body; accordin to the mighty workin whereby he is able to subdue all things unto himself . . ."* And here Boom lost control of his voice. He lowered his head. He wept as loudly as he ever had wept. No one joined in. No one. Not Sgt Patterson. Not a goddamned soul. Boom wept into his top hat. He nearly choked on it. After a time he passed water in his britches.

LLEWELLYN

Tuesday, April 4, 1865.

Llewellyn was a big old bellerin harddrinkin mountain man who'd enlisted with a bunch of fellers from Harrisonburg just before the first fight at Manassas back in '61. He had a great tangled black beard that would have done credit to a J. E. B. Stuart, and he enjoyed killing Yankees. Not maiming them, and not repulsing them, but actually straightout *killing* the goddamn sonsabitches. He hated Yankees even worse than he hated niggers. He may even have hated them worse than he hated the man who'd run off with his sweet wife, whose name was Lucy and whose photograph Llewellyn carried with him wherever he went. The feller's name was Oswald G. Averill, and Llewellyn had sworn to kill Oswald G. Averill on sight. Whenever. Wherever. War or no war. He'd given his word on that, and it kept him going. He was a skeleton who walked around in a big man's frame, and he'd caught on with Sgt Patterson and his men not long after the battle at The Crater outside Petersburg.. He was one of what everyone figured were thousands of men whose units had been torn apart by the war, and he'd been faced with the choice of either tagging along with a new company or taking the long walk home. But was it really a choice? After all, anyone who took the long walk home was nothing less than a deserter, wasn't at so? Surely the war was lost, and surely Llewellyn wasn't so stupid and possessed by hatred at he didn't *know* the war was lost, but he wasn't about to stop killin Yankees. Not just yet. He didn't mind expressing his opinions to anyone who would take the bother to listen, and he was especially outspoken with his opinions when he was drinkin whisky an otherwise actin up. Not to make too fine a point of it, Llewellyn was meaner an a turd in a nest of wasps (or maybe a wasp in a nest of turds), and he figured if the war was to last until the year 1900, say, the Confederacy surely would win, since by at year surely Llewellyn personally would have kilt ever last fuckin Yankee on the face of the fuckin earth. And that was John T. Llewellyn's opinion of *that*, and no one really argued with him. He wasn't the sort of man who thrived on debate. He liked to tell people he thrived on bein *agreed with*, an what did anyone expect of him—to thrive on *not* bein agreed with? Shit, where would of been the sense to *at*? So John T. Llewellyn had blundered through nearly four years of this here war, and his hatreds had been his rod and his staff, and he figured he had kilt maybe two dozen Yankees, and he liked to say his memories of those killings helped him sleep nights and were sweeter than molasses and licorice and sugar tits.

The reasons for his hatreds were not particularly complex. In October of 1859, about a year and a half before the first fight at Manassas, Llewellyn made an eventful trip to Harpers Ferry to visit a sick sister, and he became caught up in a terrible history. In Harrisonburg, he worked as a postoffice clerk, and he'd been married to his darling Lucy for about two years, but he wasn't exactly the most peaceful feller in the world. To him, a good fistfight was a thing of beauty and an abiding joy forever and ever, amen and kindly pass the hat, and he never hesitated to use more than his fists. For instance, a good kick to the other feller's old nuts gave him considerable pleasure, especially if the other feller hollered or screamed or puked or otherwise carried on. With his Lucy, though, he was gentle beyond gentle, and he easily wept. His bones seemed to go all suety and absurd, and he heard strange frail music in the rear of his skull. Not a day went past but what he didn't tell her he loved her, and he even was gentle when he spread her and had his heavy conjugal way with her. Oh, he may have hurt her oncet or twicet, an oncet or twicet she

sort of whimpered an turned her face away, but he always apologized and told her how sorry he was to be the kind of man who
too often was more bull than human, and he kissed and licked her
fingers and knuckles and begged her to forgive him. Which she
did, of course—since any other sort of behavior would have been
unthinkable coming form a married woman there in the year 1859
in such a place as Harrisonburg, Virginia.

But Lucy and her delicate and pretty ways weren't always
enough for John T. Llewellyn. Which was why he didn't exactly
writhe in protest when the telegram came from his sister's husband in Harpers Ferry. Poor Edith, never a robust girl, had come
down with some sort of desperate fever, and maybe it would be
wise if John T. Llewellyn paid her a visit—just in case she didn't
last but a few days more. So he rode up to Harpers Ferry—by
stagecoach to Winchester and then north and east to Harpers
Ferry on the steam cars of the Winchester & Potomac. The trip
usually took the better part of two days, but that particular trip
took four days for John T. Llewellyn. He became quite friendly
with a widow woman named Minnie Bumpers while they were
being jostled and damn near bounced to death in the stagecoach,
and so they spent two days and nights in a room in one of
Winchester's lesser hotels, which had the nerve to call itself the
Shenandoah Palace. Minnie Bumpers was only twentyfour, and
she said to John T. her late husband had been slain in a duel with
a man who had criticized her personal honor. She said she came
from Louisville, Kentucky, and she insisted she'd been forced to
flee that city because the man who'd besmirched her personal
honor was the nephew of a Congressman and the grandson of an
Episcopal bishop. She was small, with red hair and glittering
green eyes, and she said her maiden name had been Minerva
Colleen O'Flynn—of the Shouting Springs, Pennsylvania, O'Flynn
family, don't you know—and she really didn't appreciate being
treated in such a cruel an outlandish fashion. John T. Llewellyn
of course was sympathetic, and he comforted her in his arms.
Two quarts of good old mountain 'shine were in his kip, and so he
and Minnie Bumpers did not lack for warmth and good cheer.
The stagecoach's other passengers all were women of middle age,
and their faces went all pale and oily with a sort of slackjawed

astonishment as they watched John T. and his pliant greeneyed Minnie tipple and laugh and tipple and sigh and tipple and kiss. Shamelessly. Right there in front of those women as the stage-coach slammed and hammered their dry old prissy hind ends and sent them hurtling crazily from side to side like indignant rag dolls. But then came a quieter time for John T. and his new friend . . . between the sheets of their lumpy bed in the Shenandoah Palace in Winchester. A quieter time, yes, but surely not a less energetic time. He rode that skinny little Minnie as though she were a rich man's snorting thoroughbred, and he flogged her bony flanks with open hands and spurred her on with his knees. The bed collapsed their second night in that place, and they sneaked out a back door. John T. ducked away from his ladylove in the darkness, and he paid no attention to her cries. There had been nine dollars in her purse, and he'd appropriated all of it unto himself. Ah, well. That sort of thing didn't matter. Knowing Minnie as well as he did, he had every confidence that she promptly would regain the nine dollars—and then some—on her pretty and enthusiastic back. So he skedaddled to the W&P depot and bought a ticket on the early train for Harpers Ferry.

He arrived in Harpers Ferry before noon, and this pleased him a good deal, for he was thirsty. He and Minnie had done away with all of the 'shine he'd been carrying in his kip, and he'd developed a substantial thirst. The first thing he did, then, was drink himself into insensibility in a saloon that carried a sign bearing the legend: O. O. OLDHAM Liquors & Beers. The proprietor was a nervous little bald fellow with mottled flesh and a withered left arm, and he said he knew both of John T.'s brothers, and he smiled and said they spent a great deal of money on his liquors & beers, which meant they surely were good boys indeed. The man also said he knew John T.'s sister, but not as well, of course. He'd heard she wasn't feeling so good, and he surely did regret that sad turn of events. What was it she had again—some sort of fever? Ah, God love her . . . she surely had O. O. Oldham's best wishes, and perhaps the Lord would save her sweet spirit. And John T. nodded. And he pounded the bar and bought drinks for the house, which wasn't too terribly generous a gesture, since only one other man was in the saloon at that particular time. He was thin, and he blinked a great deal, and he said his name was Harold St Xavier, and he said he knew that name made him out to be some sort of foul sneaky Papist, but he hastened to add he was a Methodist, by God, and he couldn't help it that his old dad had had a Papist surname, now could he? Harold St Xavier hiccoughed, and he said to John T. wellsir, if anyone didn't know I was drunk, they'd know it now, wouldn't they? Harold St Xavier laughed. His teeth leaked. He shook his head.

John T. looked away from this feller. He hadn't been up here to Harpers Ferry but about three times in his life, and it surely didn't seem to be a very lively place. Oh, well, as long as the liquors & the beers were available, he'd manage to beat his way through this visit to his sick sister. First, though, he might as well ease the heat of the day with a few drinks. Or more than a few. Whatever. So John T. Llewellyn drank. And so did O. O. Oldham and Harold St Xavier. They drank on into the night, and a good time was had by one & all. More or less.

John T. also had two brothers living in Harpers Ferry, and O. O. Oldham sent a boy to their homes to fetch them. They were older than John T., and they worked as millers for the North Virginia Grain & Feed Co, and they drank every bit as much as he did, and maybe more. Their names were Fred and Charley, and they believed in laughter and women and beer maybe even *more* than John T. did (if such a thing can be imagined), and they and John T. always had been close. So the three brothers, plus O. O. Oldham and Harold St Xavier, had themselves a fine high old time of it in that saloon, even after a certain curious commotion began outside. John T. asked after their sister. Fred and Charley told him she'd rallied a little, God bless her darling heart. In her brothers' minds, Edith always had been the family saint. She was married to a bilious and intemperate man named Horace Bevens, who operated a grocerystore and undertaking establishment, and she was every bit as fragile as John T.'s wife Lucy—and maybe even every bit as fragile as the adroit and athletic little Minnie Bumpers of recent lubricity. John T. just well ah ummm the liquors were warm & the beers tickled his nostrils & he knew his cheeks were red but that was all right

especially seein as how he by God wore a beard & a beard hid a
great deal of a man's cheeks didn't it eh huh right? He laughed,
and they all frowned at him the stupid shits a lot they know bout
the things a real man feels. Outside were shouts. Why would
there be shouts? This was a Sunday night, for Christ's sake, and
all good Christians went to bed early on Sunday nights so as to
face the new week refreshed and alert. Surely they didn't *shout*,
especially on a Sunday night. John T. didn't really know they was
a bank being robbed at this hour of the night ha ha? Was an army
of thieves and drunkards afoot, bent on violence & rapine? And
here John T. laughed and told himself he surely did *hope* so, don't
you know. Yes indeed, good old violence & rapine. Surely they
made the world go round, and they were a comfort to John T.'s
hard belligerent spirit. He wondered bout the noise though oh
you know well account of who was making it? They all somehow
beat their wobbly way to the door, and Fred was leaning on
Charley, and Harold St Xavier was belching, and O. O. Oldham
was humming a song having to do with true love and a girl named
Rosalie, and the first thing they saw was a couple of armed
niggers staggering outside in the dark. These niggers were toting
rifles, and they came to the saloon doors and said they were
soldiers in the service of a Captain Brown, and they brandished
the rifles and said all civilians were ordered to stay indoors now
that Captain Brown and his forces had taken over the town. The
niggers had soft voices, and they seemed uncertain and vaguely
astonished. John T. spoke up. He said he wanted to know who
the fuck this Captain Brown was, and one of the niggers told him
Captain Brown was a Messenger of the Lord come down to save
the colored people from slavery an all its evil works, sah. John T.
moved toward the niggers and told them they were full of shit up
to their goddamn darky eyeballs, an they'd better hand over those
goddamn rifles before he broke them over their goddamn picka-
ninny fuckin skulls. The niggers abruptly shook their heads no,
and one of them began poking John T. in the belly with the
muzzle of his rifle. John T. flinched. He blinked. He drew back.
The niggers still spoke softly, and they insisted they wanted no
trouble. Nodding, even smiling a little, they pushed John T. and
his brothers and Harold St Xavier and O. O. Oldham back inside

the saloon. Then they slammed shut the saloon doors and went away. John T. stood just inside the saloon doors and rubbed his belly. Fred and Charley began shouting words having to do with War and Insurrection. O. O. Oldham made fists. Harold St Xavier threw up. His puke was gathered up by the dirty sawdust on the saloon's floor.

Niggers, said John T.

At's right, said O. O. Oldham.

Jesus Christ, said John T.

I couldn't agree more, said O. O. Oldham.

Again Harold St Xavier threw up, and John T. told him to jam a cork down his throat and stop stinkin up the place, you poor sad sonofabitch you. Harold St Xavier lurched away a few steps, then fell in a dispirited heap on the dirty sawdust. It apparently had been spread across that saloon's floor along about The Year One or so, judging from all the dried hockers and dead bugs that were scattered around down there like citrons and raisins on a piecrust.

Niggers, said John T.

Right you are, said O. O. Oldham.

You got any sort of gun here on the premises? said John T.

No sir, said O. O. Oldham. I ain't at sort of feller. I wouldn't know one end of a gun from tuther, seein as how my eyesight ain't no good, an the only thing I'd be able to shoot would be maybe if I wasn't careful my pecker. Then, shrugging, O. O. Oldham went behind the bar and poured drinks for everyone—except of course the supine and unconscious Harold St Xavier. And O. O. Oldham told everyone he still valued his pecker no matter what, even over War and Insurrection and probably Judgment Day.

Fred and Charley glared at John T. and wanted to know whether he (John T.) proposed to let those niggers get away with whatever the hell they were up to.

John T. drank the rest of his drink, then slammed down his shotglass on the bar (after makin fuckin good an sure the glass was empty) and said something to the effect that it was a sad day for the good old American Republic when some fuckin cowardly saloonkeeper didn't keep no gun on hand just because he was ascared on account of his goddamn stupid miserable little old *pecker*, and whatever the hell had happened to plain old American manhood, did anyone know? So he and his brothers and the possessor of the goddamn stupid miserable little old subject of the conversation leaned against the bar and drank and tried to clear their heads and decide what they should do about the situation. Then there was a louder commotion outside, and they heard a sound of tough and peremptory voices that unmistakably belonged to white men. The door was pushed open by a tall man in a wrinkled blue uniform. A first lieutenant's bars were sewn on the shoulders of his jacket, and he was carrying a heavy longbarreled pistol. Fred and Charley and old O. O. Oldham knew this feller, and they introduced him to John T. as being Max Aswell, who worked as a foreman at North Virginia Grain & Feed and was an officer in the local militia. He said there was some sort of gang of thieves or lunatics (or maybe both) that had taken over the US Armory, and yes, the reports had said this gang included niggers and maybe even baboons and fuckin chimpanzees, for all anyone knowed. John T. asked this Max Aswell whether a man named Captain Brown was involved, and Max Aswell said he didn't know the names of any of those fellers. It was his understanding they'd recently rented a farm not far from town, but he didn't know why, nor did he know what sort of war it was they were fixin to fight. At any rate, the federal authorities in Washington had been notified, or they were about to *be* notified, and in the meantime the militia would keep watch on Captain Brown (if that indeed was the feller's name) and his ragtag cutthroat band. Then another tall man . . . this one wearing overalls and a cloth cap . . . came into the saloon, and he was introduced as Ed Perkins, and he said the insurgents (or whatever the goddamn hell they were) had seized both the armory and the nearby B&O enginehouse. Ed Perkins was an engineer for the B&O, and he said the railroad had effectively been cut. Or at least at was *his* opinion, you understand. John T. looked around. His belly was warm, but he wasn't about to puke. Not *now*. No *indeedy*. Why, this night promised to be even better than another night with the bouncy and inexhaustible Minnie Bumpers would have been. He shook his head, tugged his beard, pinched his cheeks. He told Max Aswell he knew how to load and fire a rifle, and he said he'd hunted a lot of deer and birds down air in the hills at clustered around his hometown of Harrisonburg (and this was true enough), an all you got to do, Lieutenant, is give me a gun an some powder an shot an point me in the right direction an tell me where the niggers are, you know?

Max Aswell had a large clefted chin and shrewd little gray eyes, an he smiled and told John T. why, thank you, neighbor, an don't you fret none; if your services are required, why, we'll call you up to fight shoulder to shoulder with our boys against those fellers quicker an a fart makes bubbles in a bathtub, don't you know. Then Max Aswell told old O. O. Oldham he thought it would be a good idea if he (old O. O.) closed down this here saloon, on account of well, it was unclear just how severe the fightin would be. And Max Aswell and Ed Perkins left without saying much more. Old O. O. shrugged, and he went to where Harold St Xavier lay and began kicking the poor sonofabitch, who came to in a sequence of shudders and yawns and cavernous belches. Harold St Xavier's shirt was drenched in puke, and he shook his head from side to side, and his wattles wobbled. Finally, though, he managed to stand up and lean against the bar and ask gummy questions having to do with whatever the hell was happening. And John T. got to yelling at him: *Armageddon is happenin, you fuckin stupid drunkard you! you fuckin taproom lizard! saloon shithead! beer barrel bastard!* And John T. carried on in that vein for several minutes before his brother Charley seized him by an arm and told him to be quiet; air was enough wind in the world, an the trouble with you, John, is at you don't know when to shut your yap an let a thing *go*. John T. grimaced. He twisted free of Charley, and he pushed his other brother, Fred, against the bar, and all the air whooshed from poor Fred's lungs, and he embraced his belly and sat down in the sawdust. Charley now began yelling at John T., and he took a wild whirling swing at John T., an John T. knocked him down in the sawdust with Fred. John T. stood over Charley and Fred and told them air was more to life an not doin nothin, and he said he felt sorry for em because it was clear somebody (maybe a nigger?) had made off with their sorry withered pathetic cowardly balls.

Then John T. went blundering out of that place, but not
before he seized a bottle of Kentucky whisky from the bar. He
shouted back to old O. O. that he'd pay for the bottle after the
fighting was done, an old O. O. had his word on it, an at was a
fact. He walked and groped through the hard autumn Harpers
Ferry night, staggering, grinning, bouncing off walls and an occasional hitchingpost, an they got em another think comin if they
see me as nothin more an a postoffice clerk who wouldn't know a
quail from a black bear an don't mind bein insulted by no niggers
who poke air guns in his belly like maybe I'm a cow or a horse or
my granddaddy's old dog, don't you know. And eventually, maybe
at midnight or maybe at four in the morning, after wandering
around Harpers Ferry for a period of time that seemed to him
longer than life but maybe a tad or so shorter than eternity,
John T. was struck a glancing blow and knocked on his back by a
horse that came galloping down one of the cold blank dark muddy
Harpers Ferry streets, and vaguely he heard someone shout at
him to get out of the goddamn way, and he supposed the voice
belonged to the rider of the horse, but right then John T. had a
mouthful of mud, and his eyes were clogged with mud, and the
mud ran down his face in clotted torpid streams that gathered at
the corners of his mouth and made him gag and spit, and he
couldn't quite form words. He rolled over. There was a pain in
his ribs, and it made him howl. The horse and rider were gone,
and he wondered whether he ever would be able to take them to a
court of law. The horse, too. Oh, yes. Absolutely the horse. For
the first time since the founding of the American Republic, a man
would sue a horse. Well, why not? Now John T. blinked away
some of the mud. He still was holding the bottle of Kentucky
whisky, and praise be. Maybe the Lord was looking after him,
and maybe the Lord also would look after Harpers Ferry and the
rest of the American Republic when the time came to do battle
with that Captain Brown and all those goddamn rapacious niggers. Then John T. yawned, closed his eyes, and dreamed of his
sweet Lucy, and she was gathering pansies in her apron, and she
walked toward him and strewed the pansies in his path, tossing
them gaily and delicately, giggling a little, showing her tiny teeth

and her gentle virtuous tongue. At the same time, though, fiery little Minnie Bumpers was coming up behind Lucy with what appeared to be a shovel, and she whacked Lucy on the head with the shovel, and Lucy's head scattered redly in various directions, and John T. Llewellyn, a man among men, a marksman and a lover and a drinker of fine whisky, covered his face with his sour and muddy hands and screamed, and then fiery little Minnie Bumpers danced away, and she jigged and jiggled and clapped and whooped, and o what's goin on here? when do they let me get away from all this here pain an craziness? how come nobody cares at I'm not ascared? And the words within him clashed and splintered, and his skull went all fisted and tight as though it were being squeezed between great merciless rocks, and he made weak wet sounds into a muddy fist. Then (maybe for want of anything better to do) he passed out.

He awakened to the sound of more of the peremptory shouts, and someone came along and kicked him in the ribs and called him a foul and shameful *tosspot* and suggested it might not be such a bad idea if he was taken to the nearest stone wall and put to death by a firingsquad. John T. whimpered a little, and his lips pooched. It was maybe midmorning before he was able to sit up and blink at the sky and rub his forehead and his temples. He'd lost the bottle of whiskey. He wandered in the general direction of the armory and the B&O enginehouse, but his way was blocked by two knobbed and adenoidal young militiamen who held their rifles at port arms and told him no *sir*, this way was out of bounds for civilians on account of some crazy feller named John Brown and a gang of crazy niggers an crazy Abolitionists were engagin in some sort of insurrection, an the talk was, you understand, at they was holed up while they waited for a general rebellion by all the niggers in all the South. The two young militiamen frowned at John T., and he supposed they thought he was something the dog had puked up. Their hands and fingers were all wormy and nervous on the stocks and the triggers of their rifles, so he turned back and went staggering away in the direction he'd come from. Finally he sat on a hillside and looked down at Harpers Ferry and the armory and the enginehouse, and apparently the militia had those buildings under siege. Militiamen were running back and forth, and they'd thrown up a skirmishline. But no shots were being fired, and John T. wondered what the hell those boys believed they were accomplishing. He kept clearing his throat and spitting. He embraced his knees and asked himself whether he believed there would be a general rebellion of niggers, or even if they would do anything at all. He tapped his tongue against the roof of his mouth. He shrugged. Damned if he knew *what* a bunch of niggers would do in this sort of situation. Himself, he'd always found them to be lazy and cowardly, but a person just never knew. Maybe they'd been promised liquor. Who the hell knew? The thought of liquor penetrated him and made him moisten his lips, and so, at nightfall, hungry and thirsty, he returned to old O. O.'s saloon. He supposed it would be closed, but it wasn't closed. This was the best news he'd had all day. Smiling, he went inside, and old O. O. took one look at him and told him he looked as though he'd stared old Death straight in the eye and was the worse for the experience. John T. shrugged. He admitted he'd had better days. Old O. O. grinned, and he gave John T. a quart of beer and a mess of hardboiled eggs and cold chicken. He and John T. got to talking about the events of the day, and old O. O. said he'd heard that a mess of US Marines were on their way to Harpers Ferry from Washington. In the meantime, that John Brown feller and his gang of crazy men had been surrounded by the militia, and they'd made no effort to get away. John T. snorted. He told old O. O. maybe they were waiting for the arrival of millions of angry rebellious niggers, and O. O. said don't laugh, my friend; at just may be what they *are* doin, waitin for the niggers to come here an arm emselves with armory rifles an raise almighty hell with the countryside, you hear me? I mean, at's what the *talk* is, an it surely sounds reasonable to *me*. In the meantime, though, everthin's more or less nice an calm, an at's why the militia let me open this here place. The thing is, they don't want to frighten an demoralize the general population, now do they?

John T. shrugged. He stood at the bar and had himself six quarts of beer and eight hardboiled eggs and he didn't know how many chunks and slices of cold chicken, and the rest of the day passed more or less warmly, and that night he finally got around to visiting his sick sister Edith and her husband, Horace Bevens, the bilious and intemperate grocer/undertaker. One thing about Horace Bevens, though—he hated niggers almost as much as John T. Llewellyn did. He was a skinny and liverspotted fellow, and he was something like twentyfive years older than Edith, and they'd been married maybe ten years, maybe more, and he had a way of talking that was like the voice of an oldmaid snapping off thread between her teeth. His union with Edith had produced no children, and this surely came as no surprise to John T. As far as John T. was concerned, a stone had a better chance of getting another stone in the fambly way than Horace Bevens had of impregnating poor Edith. The first thing John T. did was hunker down at Edith's bedside and hold her hand and squeeze it ever so gently, don't you know. She was awake, and she smiled at him and winked and told him golly, he surely did need a nice hot bath, didn't he? Where had he been? she wanted to know. Dancing with a passel of pigs? But then she pulled his hand to her mouth and kissed it, mud or no mud. She told him just the sight of him made her feel better, and that was a genuine fact. She spoke briefly of Captain Brown and the gang of lunatics. She said they frightened her. She said she didn't mind meanness, but lunacy was another story altogether, now wasn't it? A person just never knew how to deal with lunacy, wasn't that so? And anyway, why was that Captain Brown getting himself so fussed up over *niggers?* She was willing to wager he didn't even *know* niggers all that good . . . because, if he *did*, he surely wouldn't be leading them to rebellion, or whatever it was he and his crazy companions were up to. Then Edith smiled again, and she told John T. a person couldn't even take the time off to be *sick* without having to worry about . . . um, public violence, don't you know. She patted John T.'s hand. She told him he was a rascal and a rip and a bag of wind, but then she said shoot, nobody on this here earth was without fault or flaw, wasn't at so?

John T. made a sour face. He told Edith she surely did talk a lot for a woman who was supposed to be on her last legs. Then he kissed her on her cheeks and her forehead, and again she kissed his hand.

He felt muzzy and a little loosegaited when he returned to the front room, and he told Horace Bevens he surely could use a drink or two. Horace Bevens grunted with what sounded like exasperation, but he did fetch a bottle of Kentucky whisky, and he and John T. passed it back and forth as they sat on a couple of straightbacked chairs and toasted their feet in front of the fireplace. Horace Bevens said he'd heard that the Marines would launch an immediate attack on the lunatics. He spoke of treason and sedition. Then, grinning a bit, he said something to the effect that maybe there would be more than a little bloodshed, which just might mean business for his undertaking establishment, don't you know. After three or four drinks of the Kentucky whisky, Horace Bevens's tongue began darting and wobbling back and forth from cheek to cheek, and his mottled and wretched flesh actually began to glow and hotly leak, and his grin expanded itself, and his teeth gave off a yellowish aura that just about was goddamn endoftheworld scary. This aura—or glow, or emanation, or whatever the hell it was—put John T. in mind of masses of goblins and trolls and mounded snot. And this Horace Bevens told John T. well, by God, *somebody* had to attend to the dead, and if there was money to be made, ah, whoever made that money surely earned it, correct? Especially when violence was involved. Which meant terrible wounds and outright decapitations. Oh, it was simple enough for a man to create the terrible wounds and commit the outright decapitations, but the man who cleaned up the mess had to work a whole lot harder, didn't he? At everything—including the effort he needed to make in order to keep himself from puking. And Horace Bevens asked John T. whether *he* (John T.) wanted to volunteer to be the undertaker's assistant in case there was any carnage when and if the Marines attacked the insurgents the next day. John T. shook his head no. He sighed. He needed to take a goddamn bath and go to bed. He stood up and went out to the kitchen and heated his bathwater on his sister's castiron stove. It carried the legend: NONPAREIL.

In the front room, Horace Bevens apparently hadn't noticed John T.'s departure, and the miserable sonofabitch still was holding forth out there on the glories of the undertaker's calling.

There was a heavy tub—brass maybe—in a corner of the kitchen.
John T. stripped himself naked, filled the tub with water that was
hot enough to scald the sands in the desert, stepped into the tub,
yelped and danced, exhaled heavily, then quickly lowered himself
into the hellish water and gave a great blistered sigh and lay back,
stretching, linking his fingers and cracking his knuckles. Out in
the front room, Horace Bevens's voice was making slower and
more comfortable sounds, and John T. supposed old Horace was
about to drop off to sleep. Well, the sooner, the better, an at was a
fact. John T. had found a bar of grainy homemade soap on one of
the kitchen counters, and now he began scrubbing away his mud
and dirt and sweat. He told himself it had been good seeing
Edith, and he surely was grateful she wasn't as sick as he'd feared.
Lazily he grinned, and again he stretched, linked his fingers,
cracked his knuckles. He told himself he had to admit he *also*
surely was grateful he'd encountered his tough little Minnie Bumpers. It had been an interesting three or four days, and that indeed
was the gospel. He told himself it was good for a man to let a bit
of change and fresh air enter his days and clear his vision and
make him happy to be alive. Ah, whisky and beer. A good hard
enthusiastic redhaired woman. Niggers and lunacy and violence.
Drunkards and sawdust and peremptory shouts. Ah, God bless
God . . . life could be delicious, sweet as bare tits all splattery and
warm from sunlight and easy friendly winds. And here John T.
sniggered a little and soaped his crotch and closed his eyes and
played with his pecker and his balls and dozed off, and then
niggers were pounding on his door. He answered it, and his Lucy
hid in a closet, and the niggers told him times was changin, old
cappun, an you gots to stand aside now so's *we* can have *our*
chancet, don't you know. And John T. saw pink tongues and
purple gums, and now the peremptory shouts had gone all soft
and niggerish, and the niggers were telling him to bow down and
kiss their black asses, and he kept trying to tell them he was a
town feller, an town fellers didn't have hardly no truck a tall with
niggers, an he'd personally been real good to the niggers he'd
knowed, an he'd even lended em money when he'd had the money
to lend, and they'd always been grateful, and they'd been wise
enough never to look him directly in the eye, which meant they

knew the meanin of respect, o God damn air great wise eggy eyes, and Horace Bevens was hollering at him, and Horace Bevens was shaking him by the throat, and Horace Bevens shouted words that had something to do with death, and John T. reached out of the water and grabbed Horace's hand and jerked it free of his (John T.'s) throat, and why for the Lord's sake was Horace bawling? John T. thrashed, and the water had gone cold, and his flesh was bumpy and slick, and he pushed Horace away and blindly stood up in the tub, and Horace hollered hurry hurry hurry it's Edith an I don't expect she's breathin so good! (Which surely was true, seeing as how she wasn't breathing at all. The fever had taken away her breath, and she apparently had choked to death on fluid from her lungs, and that sort of thing was known as pneumonia, said a Dr Peavy that night to old Horace. This Dr Peavy was palsied and thin, and he appeared to be at death's door himself, and his breath had an odor of old wet cigars, and he told old Horace he was real sorry, just as sorry as sorry could be, don't you know.)

John T. sat with his sister's corpse until the gunfire began down at the B&O enginehouse. All sorts of stories were making the rounds, and the talk was that the militia boys were holding their own against the insurrectionists, thank you very much indeed. Most of the militia boys, it turned out, wore natty uniforms (unlike the informal and wrinkled Max Aswell) and took their bravery with them into the fray, standing firm against Brown's lunatics until the Marines arrived. It turned out that the lunatics had seized a number of hostages. The governor of Virginia, a man named Wise, was on hand to give advice and counsel to the militia fellows, and the lunatics did not hurt the hostages.

Several neighbor women came to Horace Bevens's place and washed Edith's corpse and combed her hair. Someone brought a pail of warm milk, and John T. drank from it. Someone else brought a platter of ham sandwiches, and he ate them all.

The Marines were commanded by an Army colonel named R. E. Lee, and they charged the B&O enginehouse behind a rash cavalry lieutenant named J. E. B. Stuart. The sound of the firing just about drove John T. around some sort of personal bend, and finally he had to run from Horace Bevens's house and go careening off in the direction of the fighting. He wept as he ran, and he told himself he wanted to do something heroic in the name of the late Edith. He ran blindly, and he staggered. Oh, if only he had even just a pistol. He'd by God scatter some rebellious nigger's brains from there to Baltimore. He told himself he'd never again go without a pistol. A man never knew when he would need one, and it was a wise man who learned from experience. John T. arrived at the B&O enginehouse just in time to watch J. E. B. Stuart lead the Marines in the assault on the B&O enginehouse. Small blossoms of smoke came from the enginehouse windows as the lunatics opened fire on the attacking Marines, but the Marines simply knocked down the enginehouse doors and invested the building in what seemed only a few minutes. John T. was standing just a few dozen yards from the fighting, and he stood straight and tugged on his beard and told himself maybe these Marine fellers would need reinforcement, and he by Jesus had the strength and courage of ten and was ready if it came to that. Dust and smoke rolled in a sort of scrim, and the sound of gunfire was flat and passionless, like a polite clicking clash of small round stones. It turned out the Marines had kilt ten of the insurrectionists and had captured eleven, including that goddamned seditious bastard of a Captain Brown. John T. caught a glimpse of Brown being led from the enginehouse. The man walked erectly, and he had a mad white Old Testament beard. John T. embraced himself, and his breath hurt. It turned out there was a grand total of four niggers fighting alongside Captain Brown's crew of zealot scum, and it turned out there was no general rebellion of niggers anxious to break the shackles of slavery. In point of fact, no niggers at *all* came flocking and jostling and hollering hallelujah to Harpers Ferry to help hold high Captain Brown's escutcheon, and that night there was a general celebration in old O. O.'s saloon, and John T. was taken by a fit of laughter just from thinking of all those invisible niggers who no doubt had broken Brown's filthy Abolitionist heart.

John T. spent the evening drinking with his brothers and with the fellow known as Harold St Xavier, and every so often the four of them even remembered to include the defunct Edith in the conversation. The funeral was held two days later. John T.

had wired his Lucy to come attend the services, but she didn't show up. Oh, well, maybe she was ascared on account of the fighting at the enginehouse. He didn't suppose he could blame her. The newspaper reports no doubt had been hysterical, and anyway, she'd never exactly been adventurous and robust. So his gentle and fragile Lucy was not at his side when Edith's funeral was held. It was a busy time for Horace Bevens and his undertaking business. In addition to burying Edith, he presided over the coffining and burial of two of the defunct John Brown niggers, and his grocerystore did a whale of a business. Apparently people liked to stuff away a great deal of food after there was an emergency and/or the shedding of blood. John T. remembered his own behavior with the pail of warm milk and the platter of sandwiches, and he told himself the ways of the world were passing strange and then some, and he only wished the Lord had blessed him with a better set of brains so he could understand more of what was happening. (He wished he by Christ had been able to kill a nigger and/or an Abolitionist, and he allowed as how it must be nothing less than a breathless and blazing goddamn pleasure to kill niggers and Abolitionists, and surely a man would be respected and held up as a happy example of bravery once he'd wiped out a nigger and/or an Abolitionist, and his life forever would be grand and profound.)

He started home the morning after Edith's funeral. Horace Bevens had been too busy with his grocery and undertaking business to pay much attention to John T., and so John T. had spent most of the night drinking with Fred and Charley and old O. O. and Harold St Xavier, which meant his eyes felt as though they'd been gummed shut, and his skull abounded with drums and cymbals and nasty tootling flutes. He sat in a Winchester & Potomac daycoach for the first leg of the trip home, and he struck up a nice little conversation with the man sitting next to him. This feller was bald and plump and fiftyish, and he sheepishly patted his pate and grinned and said his name was Robertson and he was a salesman of combs and brushes and various brands of pomades and hairtonics. John T. grinned right along with Robertson, and then John T. spoke of how he'd helped the Marines storm the famous Harpers Ferry B&O enginehouse, and he said it had been

71

a glorious experience he never would forget. Robertson tugged at his lower lip, and clearly he was properly impressed, and he gave John T. a number of combs and military brushes just as the train was pulling into the Winchester depot.

John T. arrived home in Harrisonburg just before nightfall the next day, and by that time he'd spoken of his heroism at Harpers Ferry with a retired farmer from Asheville, Tennessee, two maiden seamstresses from Roanoke, a railway surveyor from Charlottesville, a tailor from Lynchburg and a lawyer from New Bern, North Carolina. In point of fact, John T. Llewellyn had spoken so eloquently of his heroism that he just about was ready to believe he was speaking the truth. The two maiden seamstresses appeared to be particularly impressed. They introduced themselves as Ada Hartsfield and Emmy Parr, and they said they were first cousins, and they allowed as how they knew a poor woman who oncet in the Sweet Bye & Bye had been *touched* in a *private place* by a crazed and inflamed nigger who had . . . well, who had, ah, well, gone and, um, *waved himself* in the woman's general direction. Ah, but the story had a happy ending. The nigger's owner personally had shot that stupid darky dead, and surely the world was better off without such a . . . such a *monster*. The women asked John T. whether he agreed with them, and he told them no one in God's Kingdom agreed with them more. They smiled at him, and their lips were dry, and he didn't suppose either of them ever had been diddled, let alone fucked.

When he arrived home late that night, Lucy was gone. He had a splendid boner ready for her, but there was no sign of her, and her clothes were gone, as was her collection of little rag dolls that had been handed down to her by her late mother. There was a penciled note on the table in the kitchen, and it read:

> I have found somebody else—& about time. You are not
> a nice man & I rejoice in my freedom. Please do not try to
> find us. It will do no good. YOUR "FREE" LUCY

John T. seated himself at that kitchen table and began to tremble. He hugged himself. He didn't know what he needed, but he figured a great deal of what he needed had to do with the infliction of pain. He closed his eyes, and he suregod wished he had those maiden cousins here with him. They weren't exactly the youngest chickens in the henhouse, and he figured they probably had no experience at what he right then—what with his anger and his grief and all—had in mind for them, but they *had* been goodlooking in a narrow and crowsfooted sort of way, and he would show them the ways of men and women and passion and despair, and by Jesus they would thank him for the information, o surely yes. But now those women of course were gone, and John T. sat there with his goddamn boner, and he groaned and grimaced, and after a time he opened his britches and pulled his pudding and quickly took care of what ailed him. But he didn't take care of what *really* ailed him. Not then and not ever. Oswald G. Averill . . . ah, such a name to go resonating down the vast ceilinged corridors of perfidy and disgrace. It didn't take John T. but about half a day to learn that his Lucy had run off with that feller. O, and such a smooth one had been that Oswald G. Averill. For the past five years or so he'd been the headmaster and only faculty member of what he'd called the Blue Ridge Latin Academy, which usually had an enrollment of about a dozen boys. It was a claptrap little school located in a claptrap little building that once had been a claptrap little whorehouse until it had been closed as a public nuisance. John T. Llewellyn for one remembered that place with some fondness. Until their eviction in 1854 or so, the girls who'd held forth in that place had been notable for both their friendliness and their cleanliness, and their rates had been reasonable as well. But then they'd been thrown out, and they'd dispersed, and John T. for one had mourned their passing with all his threadbare claptrap little heart. ho ho. Oswald G. Averill's Blue Ridge Latin Academy was opened within a fortnight of the whorehouse's closing, and he was an impressive figure indeed. Lucy's younger brother Peter, a puley sort with pimples and too prominent an adamsapple, was one of the first boys to enroll at the Blue Ridge Latin Academy, and later she told John T. her dear little brother absolutely adored Oswald G. Averill. Well, maybe it was because of the man's size. Oswald G. Averill was at least six and a half feet tall, which made him even larger than the fiercely bearded John T., and he spoke

in a voice that was like doom and Judgment and hollow caves. He
said he had a divinity degree from Columbia University in New
York City, New York, but he preferred teaching Latin and read-
ing poetry and explicating the Napoleonic Wars. Such things
never changed the way religion did, he said, and they were not
ambiguous; they could be defined for once and for all, and a man
could go on from there. Averill said he hailed from Portland,
Maine, and he indeed had the flat Yankee accent of a born New
Englander, but there was no Yankee reticence to him, and he
liked to drink with anyone who had the price of a shot of whisky.
As a matter of fact, he drank a great deal, and sometimes he drank
a great deal more than a great deal, and sometimes he drowned
out the voices and laughter in some loud and raucous saloon or
other and sang gentle songs having to do with lost loves and
abandoned dreams. Just about everyone in Harrisonburg liked
this Oswald G. Averill, even if he was a Yankee . . . and anyway,
he kept his political opinions to himself and told his drinking
companions he believed in live and let live, and to hell with all
zealots and firebrands. He liked to ride horseback and carry on
with the ladies, and he said he was in truth a simple fellow, with a
little of the rascal thrown in for good measure, and he allowed as
how one day he would have to answer for his rakish transgres-
sions, but in the meantime he would grin and carouse and sort of
drift along with the tides and currents of his days, and he hoped
no one would be particularly damaged by his behavior. He spoke
prettily of the countryside, the whitely glassy Shenandoah and
the misted Blue Ridge, and he told anyone who'd listen how
deeply his spirit and his poor fussy academic mind had been
seized by the various rural glories that surrounded him. He had
his own horse, a black gelding named Prosperity, and he kept it in
a livery stable owned by a feller named Smoot, and he rode
Prosperity every Saturday afternoon and Sunday morning, and he
sat tall, and it didn't matter how much drinking he'd done the
night before; he rode easily, with lofty and remote grace, and
Prosperity's flanks twitched, and Prosperity gleamed, and the
picture presented by man and horse was strong, brave, unim-
peachable. John T. supposed he sort of liked Oswald G. Averill.
God knows, the man had bought John T. enough drinks to

cement a friendship guaranteed to last a thousand years, and damn if the feller's Yankee voice and his Yankee friendliness just about were enough to make the birds swoop down from the trees and dance across the earth while feverishly scraping away on tiny violins. O, Godalmighty damn, not even John T. Llewellyn, whose disposition wasn't exactly placid and who'd sooner hammer a man with his fists than engage in polite disputation, could resist Oswald G. Averill for very long, and John T. surely wished he could ride a horse the way Oswald G. Averill did and speak so smoothly and recite so goddamn much highsounding poetry, especially the sort that had to do with girls and their creamy breasts and whatnot. So it was safe to say he kind of liked Oswald G. Averill, and it also was safe to say his Lucy *more* than kind of liked Oswald G. Averill. She forever seemed to be making excuses to visit her brother Pete over at the Blue Ridge Latin Academy, and she kept telling John T. how much Pete admired Oswald G. Averill, and wasn't that a truly wholesome turn of events though? Why, Pete's pimples even cleared up, and he no longer mooned and brooded and felt sorry for himself, and he even began writing poetry, and he developed a certain talent for the describing of creamy breasts and whatnot.

But none of this is to say John T. Llewellyn paid a whole lot of attention to the tall and erudite Oswald G. Averill. And he certainly had no idea anything was happening between his sweet Lucy and Oswald G. Averill. Why, John T. and Lucy had a good life together, and no one doubted *that*. He had a steady job clerking at the postoffice, and he and Lucy attended church sometimes twicet a month, and by God she had to *know* he loved her, even on those occasions when he walloped her around a bit or hollered at her or called her names or ridiculed her stupid collection of little rag dolls. Jesus dear abiding *God*, she was his *wife*, don't you know, and wives did like they were told, by God, and they lay flat when they were told, by God, and they gave no sass, by God, and the last thing they did, by God by God, was create aggravation. Lucy had a small voice and a pallid shaky smile, but at the same time her tits were firm and her belly was sweet, and she had a good life, and surely no one could dispute *that*. She liked to kneel and grub in her vegetable garden, and she told

John T. she was moved by the earth and its odors and texture, and she brought him carrots and peas, tomatoes, onions and cabbages and chard and potatoes, and she smiled and hummed as she washed the earth off all those sweet things, and sometimes John T. would hold her on his lap and shyly whisper of devotion and fidelity. (O, now never mind Minnie Bumpers and the other women who'd seized his attention from time to time. They'd been nothing more than silly little *diversions*, and what sort of sissy was it who *didn't* require that sort of goddamn thing every so often when his flesh became a tad itchy for the warm touch of something new and adventurous?)

So why then had his Lucy run off with such a one as that fraud and smiling poetical windbag of an Oswald G. Averill? She belonged to John T. Llewellyn. She was *his* Lucy, don't you know. A holy oath had been subscribed to, don't you know. Couldn't Lucy see through that Oswald G. Averill? Had he maybe abducted her? Had he chloroformed her so she wouldn't wriggle, scream, kick or otherwise protest? Did all this mean the world forever would see her husband as some sort of great slavering witless *villain?* Her *husband*, who clerked at the goddamn postoffice so her belly could be kept warm and the chill could be driven from her pretty bones? Where was the justice or the sense in her betrayal of him? Godalmighty, such an ingrate the woman was, and had there ever been a woman who'd treated her poor husband so unfairly? And, as matters turned out, had there ever been a woman who'd *humiliated* her poor husband so *publicly?* For the truth of the thing was that she and Oswald G. Averill had left Harrisonburg in broad daylight, with the birdies chirping and the sun pounding down, in a wagon drawn by his fine glistening horse, Prosperity. Oswald G. Averill had closed down the Blue Ridge Latin Academy the day before, sending home the boys with notes to their parents, and the notes had stated that there was serious illness in his family up in the State of Maine, and he regretted having to go home so quickly, but a man was nothing more than a pile of pebbles and driftwood if he had no family loyalty. Surely his boys' parents understood that, didn't they? And so the next morning there was a brave and scandalous sight, and nothing was hidden, and no shame was displayed. It was,

some believed, a leisurely and arrogant sight, but no one raised a
hand to pull the lovers down from the wagon, and no one spoke.
Lucy wore a navyblue bonnet and navyblue dress, and she held a
burlap bag on her lap, and the burlap bag was all abulge with
little rag dolls, and she looked neither to the right nor the left.
Next to her, Oswald G. Averill sat erectly, and he idly flicked the
reins, and from time to time Prosperity nickered and snorted, and
Prosperity's shoes kicked up little shots and clots of dirt. It was a
hot tough benevolent loving terrible sight, and some people even
were observed drawing back a little, as though maybe that wagon
were carrying something dead and pestilential, wormy, slackly
wet, abounding with stinks.

John T. received all this information secondhand, of course,
and it came from people who appeared to be hunching and hun-
kering down just in case he decided to give them a walloping. But
he walloped no one. He did quit his postoffice job, though, and
he did snarl and scowl, and he did spend most of his time in one
saloon or another, and a great many men bought him drinks and
told him Lucy must have been a genuine bitch on railroad tracks,
right, John? And he . . .

"Hey . . ."

John T. Llewellyn felt something seize one of his shoulders.
He groaned.

"Come on now . . ."

John T. Llewellyn blinked open his eyes. He licked the roof
of his mouth, and it was gummy and sour.

"Sweet Jesus," said Tidwell, grinning, "you sleep like a goddamn what they call a felled tree, you hear what I'm saying?
Come on. It's dawn, boy, an somewhere in the world chickens is
crowin an hogs is sloppin and cows is givin sweet milk . . ."

". . . so?" said John T. Llewellyn.

"What?" said Tidwell.

"I botherin you?"

Tidwell spoke quickly, and a dark and frightened smile tugged
at the corners of his mouth. "No sir," he said. "No *sir*. You ain't
botherin me a damn smidge. I'm only doin what old Patterson
told me to do. We got to keep movin. Patterson says he talked
with some boys out on the road just a little bit ago, an he says em

77

boys done told him air's Yankee cavalry hereabouts, an we don't want no Yankee cavalry to cut us down, now do we?"

"I don't give a shit . . ." said Llewellyn, and now he was rubbing his eyes and spitting little dry gobs of he didn't know what.

"You was moanin . . ."

". . . oh?"

"An you was all sort of, um, all sort of . . . fisted up."

"I was what?"

". . . fisted up," said Tidwell, and his voice barely was audible.

Boom came walking toward them, and he was adjusting his top hat and tapping it. He squatted next to Llewellyn and said: "We've got to get out of here, an the sooner, the better, you hear me?"

Llewellyn sat up and said: "You tellin me what to do?"

". . . I don't tell anybody what to do," said Boom, and he nudged his eyes with a knuckle.

"You're the preacher, ain't you?" said Llewellyn to Boom. "I mean, you're the *weepin* preacher, the goddamn *bawler*, ain't at so?"

"I didn't mean to bawl," said Boom, and he put on his top hat. He adjusted it. He cleared his throat. The top hat was gray with filth, but he was the only man in the company who owned one, and maybe that meant something. "I just . . . I mean, the thing is, it all just sort of caught up to me. Hasn't it all ever caught up to you?"

"Not yet," said Llewellyn.

"What?" said Tidwell.

"Pardon?" said Boom.

"I expect I been dreamin," said Llewellyn.

". . . an so?" said Boom.

"An so," said Llewellyn, "the best is yet to come."

"Oh," said Boom.

"What's he mean?" said Tidwell to Boom.

"I don't expect he wants to tell us," said Boom to Tidwell.

"Right," said Llewellyn, and for the first time that morning he smiled.

PATTERSON

Tuesday, April 4, 1865.

At twilight they sloshed across a shallow creek, gray with mud and pointed stones and floating twigs, and their bare feet hurt, and they winced, and most of them staggered and tripped, and Sgt Patterson hollered at them not to stray off; there still was a war being fought, and someone was needed to fight it. Several of the fellers laughed sourly at what he'd said, but most of them didn't even look up, let alone laugh. Every so often there was a sound of distant artillery, but no one spoke of it, and several times that day some sort of tattered Confederate cavalry patrol went past at a bony dispirited canter, and Sgt Patterson figured only God in His mighty firmament knew where those fellers were headed. Some of the cavalry horses had bloody mouths, and they all had bald spots and appeared to be suffering from some sort of mange. Sgt Patterson felt sorry for the cavalry horses. He was a town boy, and he'd never learned how to mount and ride a horse, and he didn't suppose he ever would. Not now. It was too late for that sort of foolishness, and he didn't have much doubt but what he would die, maybe by tomorrow, maybe by the next day, but surely soon. He was walking alongside Coy, the onearmed man, and now Coy was speaking of his stump, and his voice was quiet and intimate, and he could have been revealing the next day's battle plans (he was short, and he was at least thirty, and at one time—before his skeleton days, of course—he'd been more than a little plump and downright loudmouthed and even cheerful), and he said: "It's like my arm still is air, you know? It's like I need to rub it . . ."

Sgt Patterson shrugged a little, but he didn't say anything. He was thinking of Pendarvis, and he was thinking of all sorts of men who'd died. He couldn't understand what sort of villainous sonofabitch could have ordered the execution of Pendarvis and Nelson. He'd always believed the Yankees were the villains here, and what had been the point in adding Confederate villainy? O, dear Savior, where was the sense in any of—

"It aches when the weather's damp," said Coy.

"What?" said Sgt Patterson.

"My *arm*," said Coy. "My goddamn arm at *ain't*."

". . . oh."

Coy idly rubbed the shoulder that had held his poor amputated right arm. "But don't get me wrong," he said. "I don't mind bein here. Not a bit."

Sgt Patterson nodded. "I know . . ." he said. And he did know. Both Coy and the other seriously wounded man (Miller, the feller whose shins had been slashed by that Yankee bayonet at Hatcher's Run back in October) weren't all that fond of their wives, and so they'd chosen not to go home. Lord knows, they *could* have gone home if they'd *wanted* to, but apparently they disliked their wives more than they disliked the war, and so they'd remained on duty . . . limited as it was by their wounds. And now, for the sake of something to say so his brain wouldn't rot and his tongue wouldn't fall out, Sgt Patterson decided he wanted to discuss the subject of marriage with this fellow Coy. "You're really all *at* unhappy?" said Sgt Patterson. "I mean, why did you marry her?"

"Shit," said Coy, and he spat.

"What?" said Sgt Patterson.

"I wanted to get fucked," said Coy.

". . . oh," said Sgt Patterson.

"At was fifteen years ago, an I was fifteen an old Dorothy was fourteen, an I was a virgin, don't you know, and I'd of done anythin, anythin a *tall*, short maybe of choppin off my tallywhacker, to get her to lay down an spread her legs an give me what I was achin to get."

". . . surely," said Sgt Patterson.

"You member *your* first time?" said Coy.

". . . surely," said Sgt Patterson. He then nodded, did this Sgt Patterson, this Sgt Patterson the virgin, and his nod almost was brisk, and he even managed to wink, this Sgt Patterson the liar and dreamy lusting Sodomite, o such a fine straightforward feller was he.

Coy was from up by Gordonsville, and before the war he'd worked in a tannery. (He was the only man Sgt Patterson ever had met who didn't particularly mind working in the stink and gag of a tannery. He liked to laugh and say the stink and gag of that tannery had more than prepared him for the stink and gag of this here war.) Now Coy was grinning. At the same time, he was tugging his empty sleeve and apparently even trying to scratch it. Then, finally, he dropped his sleeve and rubbed his chin and said: "She gave me a good fight, though. Like a wild Indian an en some . . ."

"But didn't at make it better?" said Sgt Patterson.

"I expect so," said Coy. He grinned. He nudged Sgt Patterson with his arm and said: "You got a point, you do."

"So tell me bout it."

"You really want to hear?"

"I surely do," said Sgt Patterson.

"You don't mind me passin the time this way?"

"Not a bit."

Coy chuckled deep in his throat. He exhaled. He moistened his lips. "Well," he said, "all *right* . . ." He looked off toward a distant ridge of hills, and he inhaled wetly, and now his voice went thoughtful—or at least as thoughtful as a feller such as this here Coy could make it—and he said: "I finally what you call had my way with her one night in the belltower of an old Methodist church out on the Fredericksburg road, an o, o, I tell you, I fancied myself to be the biggest little old loverboy between the Atlantic Ocean an the Tennessee state line, an it didn't matter none to me at Dorothy hollered an bawled a whole lot an scratched me damn near to ribbons. I figured she was just a little bit carried away, what with it bein her first time an all, an girls sort of hurt when its air first time, ain't at so?"

". . . yes," said Sgt Patterson.

"But even en I wanted to be a man of the world . . ."

"Oh?" said Sgt Patterson.

"So I . . . well, I told her to hesh up. I told her it didn't do no good for her to bawl an fuss. I told her some things was left for the woman to pass through alone, an no amount of bawlin was bout to do a bit of goddamn good . . ."

"You said at?"

"I wouldn't fib to you," said Coy, grinning.

"It's a wonder she didn't come after you with a hammer an a fryinpan."

"At came later," said Coy.

"Oh?"

"I got her in the fambly way, you see."

"Oh?"

"Yessir," said Coy. "An her an me was married on her fifteenth birthday, an at night she more or less trounced me with her feet, an she hit me on the goddamn *head* when she was done with trouncin me with her goddamn *feet*, an it was an old onyx clock at she hit me on the head *with*, an I was out colder an an oldmaid's asshole for somethin like ten maybe twelve hours, an when I came to she was settin on the edge of the bed, an her smile was like the smile of an angel, an she said to me: 'Now you listen here to me, Mister Coy. I don't like you, an I certainly don't *love* you, an I don't expect at situation will ever change unless I go crazy an start runnin naked in the pastures an leapin acrost the meadows with my tiddies flappin in the breeze . . . but I got no plans to go crazy, you hear me, Mister Coy?' An I nodded. An I rubbed my poor head. An I told at Dorothy of mine I understood her real good. An she nodded, an I expect she even kind of smiled. At any rate, she told me *good*, she was real *happy* I understood the truth of our situation. An I looked at her an asked her *what* truth of *what* situation. An she said the truth of our situation was real simple—she was the boss, an I was the nigger slave, an I'd better not be forgettin the way things was *en* an forever *would* be, world without end an may the good Lord bless

82

the collection plate. Well, I don't mind tellin you I stared real hard at her after she said all at stuff bout her bein the boss an me bein the nigger slave an all, but she didn't flinch, an she didn't blink a goddamn *eye*, no *sir*. So I said to myself, I said: Tom old friend, you just better lay back a little an let this here girl think she's gettin the best of you. Give her a chancet to calm down, an en you'll have her where you want her."

"How long did at take?" said Sgt Patterson.

". . . forever," said Coy, shaking his head. Now he again was scratching his right shoulder and his empty sleeve.

"Forever?" said Sgt Patterson.

"Yessir," said Coy.

"I expect I ain't surprised," said Sgt Patterson.

"Oh?" said Coy.

"Well," said Sgt Patterson, "if she'd of calmed down, you'd of gone home after you lost your arm, am I right?"

"I expect so," said Coy.

"How long's it been since you lost at air arm?"

"Last May. The Wilderness. Damn near a year ago."

"At far back down the road?"

"I expect so," said Coy.

"Jesus," said Sgt Patterson. "Time really moves along right smart when it's of a mind, don't it?"

"At it does," said Coy.

"What do you hear from her?"

"I ain't heard from her since Christmas of '63. We ain't got the greatest mail service in the world, you know. She sent me a little card back air in '63. She wished me many happy returns of the day. The card had I believe it was an etchin of a little baby, an the baby was smilin, an it all was so sweet I could of throwed up."

"Well," said Sgt Patterson, "maybe she meant well."

"Don't be too sure of at," said Coy.

"What you sayin?" said Sgt Patterson.

"What am I sayin?" said Coy. "What am I God damn *sayin?* Well, I'll *tell* you what I'm sayin. I'm sayin at air woman would as soon nail me to the fuckin outhouse wall as she would look at me. Oh, she's a woman now. A woman an en some. Last time I seen her, she was pushin six feet in fuckin heighth an she must of weighed two hunnert an thirty pounds, which is a passel of fuckin weighth an a whole lot of fuckin heighth, wouldn't you say? An she was just as mean as she was fuckin *big* and fuckin *heavy*, don't you know, an I ain't got no reason to believe she's got all soft an sweet in the years since I last seen her. Ornery is as ornery does, you know? An *big* is as *big* does, yes *sir*. I mean, the pig don't change its spots, you hear me?"

"What?" said Sgt Patterson. "What pig? Why we talkin bout pigs? Pigs don't have spots."

"Some do," said Coy, and his voice had begun to go all wounded and frayed.

"Pigs?"

"Take my word for her," said Coy.

"All right. I don't know much bout pigs. I mean, I worked in my daddy's drygoods store, an we didn't talk bout pigs all at often. Air wasn't all at much call for at sort of talk."

Coy chuckled. He didn't say anything.

Sgt Patterson shrugged. His shoulders hurt. Hell, all of him hurt. He said to Coy: "So tell me what you mean bout spotted pigs . . ."

"I was talkin bout *her*," said Coy.

"You mean your wife?"

"Right," said Coy. "Old Dorothy. Old Hell on Wheels an Greazzy Shit. We got four kids, you know at? Four kids an I . . . an I . . . well, the thing is, since the day we was married, I ain't had but maybe twenty times with her . . . in the way a husband is with his wife, I mean . . ." Coy looked away, maybe again at the sky, maybe somewhere else. Then he blinked in Sgt Patterson's direction and said: "All we got *here* is a little old *war*, an everybody seems to be dyin, an we're gettin whipped real bad. Well, I know all bout gettin whipped real bad. Listen, ever mornin when I went to work tannin hides, I was grateful for em hides. I even was grateful for the stink of em, for all the blood an all the nastiness. I mean, em hides took me away from *her* for ten, twelve hours a day, an praise God up air in the sky with His clouds an His angels an all for *at*. Listen here now. I'm goin to tell you somethin I ain't never told a soul. When this here war is over, an the Yankees ain't shot off no more of me, I'm goin far, far away, an I ain't never comin back. I'm goin to Texas or South America or Canada or someplace like at air. I'm goin to find me a nice big fat dark woman, a Mex maybe, or an Eskimo, an I'm goin to make goddamn sure she don't care if I was to hammer on her from time to time, an en I'm goin to set back an let the days curl round me like feathers an kisses, an I'm goin to love at woman, an whup her, an love her, an whup her, an love her, until the sun rolls away an the clouds turn to cheese, all right? You understand what I'm sayin?"

"I believe I do," said Sgt Patterson.

"You figure I got a right to em opinions?"

"I guess . . ."

"She's laughed at me for years. Laughed at me. At *me.*"

". . . oh."

"She tells the little ones I stink. She says I work in at air tannery on account of I can't get no decent white man's job. She says I *like* to stink. She says I don't know no better. She says I'm so iggerant she's surprised I can find my way to the outhouse."

"She must be somethin," said Sgt Patterson.

"Oh, she's *somethin,* all right," said Coy. "But en so are death an piss an rats."

". . . Jesus," said Sgt Patterson.

"Right," said Coy, and he hawked and spat, and some of his spittle smeared a corner of his mouth.

Sgt Patterson didn't say anything. He was tired of Coy's talk. He wanted to think about something other than goddamn Coy and goddamn Coy's goddamn wife. He looked away from Coy, and he hoped Coy would take the hint and be silent. Now Sgt Patterson was walking along in a skeletal hunch, and he felt as though his bones were about to fall down. He and the fellers were shuffling along a narrow rutted road that curved through a gathering of tall thin gray trees, most of them birches. He heard jays and cardinals, and he kind of wondered whether he'd soon be seeing a robin. He supposed he needed to see a robin. He'd never paid much attention to robins back in Suffolk before the war. After all, why would a drygoods clerk have paid attention to robins? The thought was enough to make a man laugh, but

Patterson was too weary to laugh—and anyway, he wasn't all that sure he was a man. Not a *real* man, at any rate. He couldn't get Pendarvis out of his mind. He kept inhaling, hoping to catch some sort of conjured flavor of Pendarvis's lips and mouth. But that was stupid. He'd never known Pendarvis's lips and mouth. Not really. He'd only dreamed them. He'd only wished them. And . . .

No.

Enough.

God damn it all, enough was enough, and enough was too much.

(Alvin Pendarvis, from Staunton. A preacher's son. Pretty, and he'd known it. He and his younger brother Lute had joined up only seven months ago, and they'd been greener than grass and bad teeth when they'd been shoved into the trenches at Petersburg, and one night not long afterward Sgt Patterson had found Alvin and Lute Pendarvis hugging one another and weeping and kissing, and their tongues were sucking and licking, and he kicked the two of them, and he bent over them and smacked them across their faces, and he told them they God damn made him want to throw up. But he didn't holler. He didn't believe it really was necessary that anyone else hear what he had to say. He squatted over them and told them he'd kill them if he again caught them doing one another that way, and he even spat on them, and he said something to the effect that thousands of good old boys weren't dyin in order at a couple of . . . a couple of goddamn incestuous *Sodomites* could diddle emselves like air wasn't nothin wrong with it an it by God was air *right*. Less than a week later Lute Pendarvis was sliced in half by shrapnel from a Yankee cannonball that exploded after bouncing into the trenches. His top part vanished in a spray of blood and bone. His brother embraced his bottom part and wept and screamed. In point of fact, Alvin Pendarvis wept and screamed until Sgt Patterson kicked him in the neck and the balls. Alvin Pendarvis gurgled, twitched, bleated, weakly kicked out his legs, and then of course Sgt Patterson wanted to embrace him, to kiss the pervert tears off his pervert cheeks and suck away the saliva that leaked from his filthy pervert mouth. And, tears and all, Alvin Pendarvis knew this, and so he reached for Sgt Patterson, but Sgt Patterson shuddered and backed

away from him. Alvin Pendarvis's fingers were all spidery and
blind, and for some reason they made Sgt Patterson want to cry.
The next day Sgt Patterson and Tidwell helped Alvin Pendarvis
bury what was left of the unfortunate Lute Pendarvis, and then he
crouched in a dugout with Alvin Pendarvis, who said to him: Our
daddy ain't goin to take this too good. He didn't want Lutey to
go, seein as how Lutey ain't but sixteen, but Lutey said to him
well if Alvin gets to go, en so should I. An he said somethin to
Daddy bout how the war could end any day now an he didn't
want to *miss* it, all right? So I expect Lutey didn't miss it. An *it*
didn't miss *him*, did it? One cannonball took itself a big bounce,
an look . . . no more old Lutey. Boom. Farewell, Lutey. Farewell, all the times you prayed. Farewell, all your kisses an all your
funnin around an all your love of the Lord. Boom. Farewell.
Boom. Boom. Farewell an farewell. And then, as might have been
expected, Alvin Pendarvis embraced Sgt Patterson and wept, and
Sgt Patterson's face and his shoulders and his arms went all tight
and stiff, and it was as though he was the one who'd been killed.
He'd more or less tried to avoid Alvin Pendarvis since then—
until the other night, when he'd spoken with Alvin Pendarvis and
then had had the shameful Sodomite dream about the feller, him
so pretty an sad an all, with his sweet kisses an all. O, God damn,
why did it all have to end this way? He knew a few things about
death, and he knew a few things about friendship and love and
grief, but he'd never known a goddamn thing about the ways of
the Sodomite, just as he'd never known a goddamn thing about
the touch and the texture of female flesh. Rufus Patterson, the
baby. Rufus Patterson, the Virginia Virgin. Rufus Patterson, who
didn't even know it was possible for pigs to have spots. Ha. Such
a wonderful feller was this Rufus Patterson, and why had the
Lord allowed him to survive when so many better men had been
taken? Pete Bell, for instance, an older feller who'd bought the
goddamn farm on the first day at Gettysburg back in July of '63.
Pete had been the best friend Rufus Patterson ever had had in this
here war, an older man, smart and quiet, a former brakeman for
the Virginia & Atlantic, married and a father of two, a careful
man who had bad teeth and a serene disposition. And he had a
calm wisdom as far as the fighting of the war was concerned, and

he seemed sure he would survive it and go home to his wife and his children. But then he was shot in the face by a band of dismounted Yankee cavalrymen on the first day of Gettysburg, and that was the end of Pete Bell, and Rufus Patterson found him layin on his belly with his fuckin face shot off. Then, for some reason, Rufus Patterson got to laughing, and within a few moments he'd passed out. The next afternoon, though, in a peach orchard west of a place known as Little Round Top, with no Pete Bell to suggest what they should do in order to stay alive, Rufus Patterson—who'd already gone through the battles at Sharpsburg and Fredericksburg and Chancellorsville—was carried away by all the blood and all the smoke and all the dying, and he decided he hated Yanks, o how he hated them. He set aside his grief for Pete Bell, and he screamed and howled with rage and triumph and joy too. He hacked Yanks with his bayonet and jumped on them where they had fallen; he screamed and screamed and screamed; he beheaded one man with one great sideways swipe; he laughed and laughed and laughed; he spluttered and gasped and wiped the dust from his eyes and looked for more Yanks, more Yanks that he could swipe at, and the Yanks finally went howling to the rear and Rufus and the others chased them, whapping them with the butts of their rifles, slicing them with their bayonets, never relenting, never giving them a chance to rally, chasing them, wave after wave and column after column, surging through the dust, grabbing, hacking, cursing . . .)

Next to him, Coy said: "You expect maybe we can take us a little rest? I mean, pardon me for sayin so, but my feet is bleedin . . ."

". . . feet?" said Sgt Patterson.

"Yessir."

"Shit," said Sgt Patterson.

Coy gasped a little and said: "Hey, I'm sorry I brought it up."

Sgt Patterson hesitated. He stared at Coy, and then he laughed, and then he whickered, and his hands plucked at his shirt, and his balls still were sticky, and God *damn*.

SNELL

Wednesday, April 5, 1865.

He awoke at about four in the morning by the watch his darling Marjorie had given him six years ago for his fiftieth birthday. There was a narrow and nervously white little creek that poked and gurgled just beyond a stand of dogwoods and maples, and he walked to that creek and made faces at its vicious rushing water, then stripped himself naked and immersed himself, and his teeth pounded and clacked. He heard nothing, not even the wind, not even a sound of insects. He supposed he should have awakened Pitt and had him sit on the creek's bank and keep watch for any Yankee patrols. After all, no matter what certain people wanted to believe, the war still was being fought, and Brevet Brig Gen Maynard Thomas Snell, commanding officer of the Hartstone Zouaves, would see that they kept that little fact in mind no matter how desperately they may have wanted to flee, to throw down their rifles and vanish into the darkness and skedaddle like cowardly thieves in the night, scurrying across the various pastures and cornfields of the sad battered Commonwealth of Virginia and never looking back, and to hell with honor and simple courage. (I am the abaslayman an the garlock, he told himself. I am able to bend time an cause the elements to dance within the earth. I am all these fellows ever have deserved, an no shame has been attached to our efforts. In Hartstone, Virginia, by

89

God, we have achieved respect, an we all are able to prack an flibble the slowest an most dignified trovers known to humanity.) Brig Gen Snell slapped riverwater across his face, and he beat himself across the chest, and he fondled his balls and for a moment tugged his icy submerged tallywhacker, and he shuddered and grimaced, but he uttered no sounds that might have made his men suspect he was experiencing any sort of discomfort. He knew he always had to create an example, and so a lot of squealing and gasping would have been improper and nothing less than a womanish betrayal. Oh, he was doing so very well indeed, and he only wished Marjorie still were alive. He would have impressed her. She would have been proud as the planet's next sunrise, and that was the truth of that. Brig Gen Snell smiled in the darkness. Water curled around his hips. Presently, smiling and humming, he went sloshing out of the water. His personal baggage had been lost a few days earlier when his regiment had been forced to abandon its position south of Richmond, which meant he didn't even have a towel with which to dry himself—and so, shivering and dancing, he dried himself with his shirt. Soon now, once there was a respite in the fighting and the Army of Northern Virginia had consolidated its positions, he would be able to replenish his personal baggage, and he would be provided with all the towels and trowels and ninepins and hairy fligs his position demanded, and his drewgels would carry the day with pride and chard. Now, though, he would have to make do with his shirt. Ah, the aggravations and inconveniences of the war. The pain that clustered around a man who had the courage to do his duty, no matter the slings and arrows of outrageous parp, brile and slime that forever tried to seize him by his ankles and his blistels and pull him down.

The regimental adjutant, Capt Pitt, came blundering out of the woods, and twigs crackled under his feet, and he went to where the naked Brig Gen Snell stood all pale and aslosh in all that gallant hastening water, and he said to Brig Gen Snell: "Yessir. Air you are. Wellnow . . ."

Brig Gen Snell was rubbing his crotch with his shirt, which he had squiggled into a tight wad. "At is correct," he said. "Here

I am, an here I shall remain until these ablutions of mine are completed to my satisfaction."

"Yessir," said Capt Pitt. He was a large and hairy fellow, and before the war he'd been a publisher of Bibles and hymnals.

Brig Gen Snell was small and pale. He was very small indeed—barely five feet tall and weighing (what with the deprivations of war and the incompetence of those who were charged with supplying the army with its food and ammunition and its soap and its towels and its trowels and its lilypads and its baby weasels) something no doubt less than one hundred pounds. Still, he knew something about the enforcement of discipline, and he had little doubt Capt Pitt was just as afraid of him as the soldiers in the ranks were. Now, rubbing his crotch and his buttocks and his chest, he said to Capt Pitt: "Are the men havin air breakfast? Is air plenty of fresh coffee? I like fresh coffee, don't you? It helps a man face the day, doesn't it?"

"Yessir," said Capt Pitt. "Absolutely."

"If a man is unable to face the day, Captain, he might as well cut off his testicles with a razor."

". . . yessir," said Capt Pitt.

"We shall prevail, you know."

". . . yessir," said Capt Pitt.

"What hear you from the pickets?"

"The pickets, sir?"

"The pickets. I ordered a line of pickets to be established north of this stream. What's the matter with you? Don't you recollect what I said? Is air some sort of discomatter with your earrin?"

"Earrin, sir?" said Capt Pitt. He shifted his weight. More twigs crackled under his feet.

"Hearin, Captain," said Brig Gen Snell. *"Hearin."*

"Oh," said Capt Pitt.

"Have they reported to you?"

"Yessir."

". . . and?"

"And they have nothin to report. They have seen nothin, an they have heard nothin. At's the truth, sir. I have air word on it."

"But do you trust em?"

"Yessir," said Capt Pitt.

Brig Gen Snell's head moved briskly from side to side, and his lips flapped, and then he said: "After all these defeats an betrayals and derelictions of duty, Captain? How can you believe a thing they say? Believin em is like trustin a pig not to steal your supper. It resounds of piffery an paffery an puppery, an you ought to know better. I mean, how many battles will they lose for us before we come to understand at we can trust em when it comes to nothin? I mean zero. Captain. Nothin a tall. Air afraid, Captain. Air afraid, an yet they say air tired, which is a stupid baldfaced frashood I mean falsehood, since it's air fear at makes em behave the way they do, so how are we supposed to trust em? how can we put air stones an air quilts an air frippery frappery frups in the right perspective? Do you expect you can follow me on all this what I'm sayin to you?"

Capt Pitt didn't reply for a moment. Then, his voice thin and shredded, he said: ". . . yessir."

"They could have done better, you know."

". . . I suppose, sir," said Capt Pitt.

"I'm tryin to do all *I* can, an so should they."

". . . yessir."

"We all need to pull together, an en victory will be ours. Such a sweet thing is victory, an it'll gain us such respect an love when we go home. We all need respect an love, don't we?"

"Yessir. I suppose we do."

"You suppose a lot, don't you?" said Brig Gen Snell to Capt Pitt. "You suppose This an you suppose At, an it's like you don't care maybe as much as you ought to. I mean, air's a chance you're too nonchalant, you agree?"

". . . maybe, sir."

"We can't afford to be too nonchalant, Captain. Point of fact, we can't afford to be nonchalant at all. This isn't a Sunday afternoon in August back home, an we've all been picnickin out at Mountainview Park, an maybe we've put away too much chicken an we're fixin to doze off, you understand? With ants an flies crawlin an buzzin, an the ants are carryin off grains of sugar, an

92

the flies are washin air hands? You member at sort of thing, my friend?"

"Yessir."

"Well," said Brig Gen Snell, "air you are. It all can seduce a man, can't it? Maybe it even can just bout make him want to love his enemies. Ah, but at would be very wrong, wouldn't it? A man who loves his enemies is a man who's got beanblossoms an moonbeams where his almighty godgiven soul an his certain perfect clapperleaves ought to be . . ."

Capt Pitt nodded. He coughed. He looked away from Brig Gen Snell.

Briskly Brig Gen Snell nodded. He finished drying his body, then quickly wriggled himself back into his uniform. It smelled terrible. He couldn't remember how long he'd worn the same britches, the same boots, the same tunic, the same goddamn stinking shirt. He seated himself with his back against a maple tree, and Capt Pitt helped him with his boots. Capt Pitt grunted, and Brig Gen Snell wanted to smile and perhaps chide the fellow, but, well, maybe for once Brig Gen Snell could go a little easy on poor Capt Pitt. Lord knows, the man always had appeared to *mean* well. And so Brig Gen Snell let it go. Instead, he stood up and cleared his throat and spat several times. He rubbed his hands together. He blinked at Capt Pitt and said: "I feel just fine. I don't even miss my sword an my pistol, do you know at?"

"Well, at's a good thing, sir," said Capt Pitt. At one time, this Capt Pitt had been a fine brave fellow, a hollerer and a hero, a leader of men, no matter how desperate the situation. Now, though, poor Pitt appeared to be yielding to the general air of fear and defeatism that had infected the Army of Northern Virginia. Now, though, poor Pitt barely held up his head, and he no longer was a hollerer, which meant he no longer was a hero, which meant he probably wasn't even worth the powder to blow him up, if the truth were known. This was a vexatious situation, to say the least. God knows, Brig Gen Snell had tried to do something about it, but he hadn't had much luck, and the truth was, sad to relate, he hadn't had *any* luck. The other evening, for example, when he and his men had encountered those two cowardly swine who'd

been looting that crossroads store, he had assumed that by execut-
ing those two an example would be established, and his men
would be more soldierly and enthusiastic. But, good God, his
men had been reluctant when he'd ordered them to form a
firingsquad, and some of them even had wept, and it hadn't
helped matters any when the prisoners had screamed to his men
that they'd had no *right* to—

The morning's first bird made a quick piping sound.

"Ah," said Brig Gen Snell, and he smiled.

Another bird joined in.

"Pretty," said Brig Gen Snell, and he began walking back
toward the regimental bivouac.

Next to him, Capt Pitt for some reason pressed his hands on
his shirtfront.

The dawn heaved up, and Brig Gen Snell sucked saliva and
told himself he needed to be brave and stalwart and full of brenk.

PATTERSON

Wednesday, April 5, 1865.

They stopped for their noon meal in a cornfield adjoining a farmhouse that someone had burned down. Sgt Patterson sat with his legs folded and chewed on a piece of hardtack that may or may not have held maggots. The question wasn't real important, though, seeing as how Sgt Patterson had every intention of eating that piece of hardtack even if goddamn moist squirmy maggots had been layered on it like fresh thick homemade butter. Or maybe jam. Or maybe both. Whatever the hell. So Sgt Patterson chewed and sucked, and his tongue rubbed the hardtack, and he decided it was more than time for him not to give a shit about much of anything.

Tidwell sat on the damp cornfield earth next to Sgt Patterson, and Tidwell was trying to create some sort of conversation, but Sgt Patterson wasn't paying him much mind. Right now Tidwell was speaking of his wife and eight children, and he said: "Soon as this here war's over an done with, Sergeant, you ought to go out an grab you the nearest little old gal an marry her an ream her night an day an day an night until the clouds blow up, you know?" Then Tidwell chuckled a little and said: "It's all good for what ails you. I tell you somethin—it's just bout guaranteed to make you healthy an wealthy an wise an grow hair on your nuts an give you a deep voice. I mean, it makes you proud, Sergeant.

Proud to be alive. Proud to of made babies. Proud to be in charge of a woman. Yes indeed."

". . . all right," said Sgt Patterson.

Tidwell frowned at him. "You don't sound like you heard what I done said."

"I heard," said Sgt Patterson. "I heard just fine. I ain't deaf. Not just yet."

"Well, you figure you're goin to find you a girl when this here war's over?"

"I expect so," said Sgt Patterson. Briefly he closed his eyes. They were hot. He rubbed his eyelids. When he opened his eyes, they were wet, but at least they'd been cooled off a little.

Tidwell's face narrowed. Slowly, carefully he moistened his lips, coughed, wiped his mouth with the side of a hand. Then: "We can't go on a whole lot longer, can we?"

"What?"

"This here war."

"What bout this here war?" said Sgt Patterson.

"Richmond's gone, you know at?"

"I expect I do."

"It was just a matter of time, an now the Yankees are marchin up and down the streets of Richmond," said Tidwell, "an how much more of this here Confederacy is left? At's what people are askin emselves, don't you know. This mornin I went down into a gully to take a piss, an I found two fellers down air who said they was from Tennessee an they'd walked away from air regiment day before yesterday. Air on air way home . . . all the way to Tennessee, come what God damn may. They ain't got but maybe half a pound of fatback between em, but they told me it was better an nothin, an they told me they'd decided to trust to the Lord to provide them with more to eat when the fatback was gone. They said air's a whole lot of fellers fightin down in the Carolinas under Joe Johnston, an they said the rumor was those fellers in the Carolinas wasn't about to abide by no surrender by any of us here in Virginia, up to an includin old R. E. Lee hisself, an en you know what em two fellers done? They both *laughed*, by Jesus. Air voices was all hoarse an full of splinters, but they laughed real loud, if you know what I mean, an they told me Joe

Johnston could kiss air rosy red bungholes, you hear me? Maybe they were wrong in what they said. You think so?"

"No," said Sgt Patterson.

". . . how long *we* goin to stay together?"

"What?"

". . . we'll stay together long as you want us to. I've talked with most of the other fellers, an we're pretty much in agreement. I mean, we've come this far . . ."

"Thank you kindly," said Sgt Patterson.

"I mean, whatever you say, it's all right with us."

Sgt Patterson swallowed the last of his piece of hardtack. Juices swirled in his belly, and gently he belched. He said: "I figure we'll know when the time'll come for us to quit. In the meantime, we ought to stay together. Yankee patrols and whatnot. We don't want to be killed by Yankee patrols. Especially by Yankee cavalry patrols. Those sonsabitches could wipe us all out in bout five minutes if we wasn't careful."

"You really think so?" said Tidwell.

"I surely do," said Sgt Patterson, grimacing a little, spitting, then rubbing his moiling belly.

"You think we're all goin to be kilt?" said Tidwell.

"I expect I don't know," said Sgt Patterson. "I mean, it ain't only *Yankees* we got to worry ourselves bout. It wasn't *Yankees* who stood up Pendarvis an Nelson and shot em down like they was dogs in the fuckin manger eatin all the sheepies an the calvies an the little chicks. It was Southron men who shot Pendarvis an Nelson. Sons of the Stars an the Bars. Wonderful. Under the command of some fucker who had army regulations where his fuckin heart should of been. I don't know. I mean, what's happened to hearts? I had one when I came into this army, an I just bet you had one, too. The preachers call it somethin along the lines of the showin of mercy, ain't at so? You ever . . . you ever stop to think at if we lose mercy, en it don't make no difference who *wins* the goddamn war, on account of both sides already have *lost* the fuckin thing? Maybe you've heard at sort of talk before— from sissies or old women or whoever."

Tidwell nodded. Shrugging a little, he said: "I've heard it before."

"You think *I'm* a sissy? You think *I'm* an old woman?"

"No sir," said Tidwell. "I surely do not."

"At Gettysburg on the second day," said Sgt Patterson, "a man name of Thad Manwell died after a big treebranch fell on him an tored open a hole in his belly a teamster just bout could drive a team an a wagon through. I was thinkin bout Gettysburg last evenin . . . an especially at second day. An the thing at sticks out in my memory is at while old Thad Manwell laid air dyin, all he done was worry bout how *ascared* he was. He wasn't *sad* as much as he was worryin bout bein *ascared*, an I don't know, but it seems to me at sort of thing ain't right. He was a good boy, old Manwell, an he should of had better things to do an worry bout an bein maybe a little afeared. He should of been thinkin bout his mama, you know? Or his girlfriend. Or peaches. Cheese. Cold water. A derby hat. His dog. Fiddleplayers an shortbread. You hear me, Tidwell? You foller my thoughts on this here subject? An at the end, at the *very* end, Thad Manwell asked me to kiss him, an so at's what I done—I leaned over him, an I done kissed him on the forehead. An en he was what they say Gone. An I keep askin myself how come. An the only answer I come up with is Politics. Never mind niggers an slavery an all *at* shit. I mean, do *you* care bout niggers an slavery all at much? Well, one thing is for sure—*I* don't. An I know Thad Manwell didn't. All he cared bout was his goddamn fear. Fear of what was settin out air in the goddamn Beyond. I don't know, a whole lot of the time I get to thinkin he's one of the lucky ones. At least he don't have to wonder no more. Maybe at's a blessin . . ." Then, abruptly, Sgt Patterson swallowed whatever else he'd wanted to say. He began blinking like a timidly astonished little bird, and he looked away from Tidwell. He picked at a scab on one of his feet. He used a sleeve to wipe hardtack crumbs from the corners of his mouth. Then, from Sgt Patterson, as he continued to look away from Tidwell: "So, yeah, all right, I did her. I kissed him. Ha. Funny I should call at time back to mind. I mean, I seen more old boys get kilt an you can shake a stick at. But somehow old Thad Manwell sticks in my mind. An so do Pendarvis an at other feller, at Nelson feller. Think on em two. An think on em who *kilt* Pendarvis an Nelson. We're all supposed to be on the same side, but we're killin each other. Like I done said before, where's the . . . where's the *heart* to any of this? Pendarvis an Nelson were good boys, an they only were tryin to keep body an soul together, an they . . . an they . . . hey, listen to me, they came here because they figured they was goin to be heroes, because they figured they had air duty to do, an a man's duty is a sacred thing, right? An I expect they was willing to die for the Confederacy even they didn't really know why. But not at the hands of some chickenshit sonofabitch leadin some chickenshit firinsquad made up of Confederate fellers like you an me. Oh, hey, how come those fellers let the chickenshit sonofabitch get away with it? I mean, how long had they been fightin this here war? Hadn't they had enough? Don't air come a time when a man stops hunkerin an suckin his thumb an worryin bout his asshole an just plain an simple *stands up* an *walks away?* You listenin to me, Tidwell old friend?" And then Sgt Patterson's head swiveled, and again he was looking at Tidwell, and his eyes appeared white, full of maybe paste or hard cold sour cream. He stopped picking at the scab on his foot, and he rubbed his hands across his shirtfront. He was smiling a little, and he said: "You don't want to think bout any of this, do you? Well, I can't say like I blame you. I don't want to think bout it neither. I just couldn't blame a goddamn soul if he decided to walk away an never look back, if he said enough's fuckin enough, an kindly don't be givin me no more words, Sergeant Patterson, seein as how you don't know nothin, an it don't matter none how many men you seen die, and it *surely* don't matter none how many men you *kissed* when they died. Oh, Jesus, Manwell, you poor fucker, I only wish I—"

"My name's Tidwell," said Tidwell.

"Oh," said Sgt Patterson.

"You called me Manwell," said Tidwell.

"Shit," said Sgt Patterson, "I'm real sorry."

Tidwell nodded. He didn't say anything.

Sgt Patterson closed his eyes. He hugged himself and saw the face of Pendarvis. He wondered whether Pendarvis and Nelson had wept at the end. He supposed they had. He watched Pendarvis's lips, and they moved sweetly, and Pendarvis was speaking in tongues, and his words had to do with love and sweet passion.

Sgt Patterson opened his eyes and swiped at them with his skinny dirty fingers. He heard a rude peremptory sound that was like a clicking of stones, and the back of his head vanished in a sort of crimson halo.

BOOM

Wednesday, April 5, 1865.

He'd been lying flat on his back, dozing a little, his top hat covering his face, when the shot was fired. Then he was on his feet and running away from the sound of the shot, and so were the others. He more or less embraced his top hat. He ran in a crouch, and so did the others. He ran in a zigzag, and so did the others. He did not holler, and neither did the others. They all scattered like small hunched urgent animals, beavers maybe, or lean and desperate rabbits. He needed to move his arms, and so he held his top hat by its brim, and his elbows churned, and his breath was hot—too hot. He heard shouts, and he even heard laughter, and he heard a sound of hooves. Cavalry. Yankee cavalry. Shit. (He remembered how he and his boys had been trapped against a bluff, and the Yankees hadn't done much much more than ride back and forth and yell and whack and dismember. He grimaced. He sucked spit. He did not want to remember any of it, but there it was, and it sat within him like boils and a particular crouching sort of eyeless and uncomprehending death.) He tripped and fell, and he rolled over old broken cornshucks from last autumn, and his hat rolled a few feet away. He retrieved his hat, and he scrambled to his feet, and for some reason he held his hat over his balls, as though he expected imps and trolls to reach up from the earth and seize his pathetic defeated balls and twist them off. He kept looking around as he ran, and he saw the one named Tidwell, and the fellow's face and shirt were smeared with blood, and it appeared to glisten. Also, Tidwell was screaming. Well, Boom supposed he really couldn't blame the man. Again Boom stumbled, and this time he dropped heavily to his knees. He leaned forward, and he swayed, and he crushed his hat to his chest. He felt as though the Lord had reached down and had knocked him to his knees with the flick of an immense Thumb. He looked around, and others of them hurried past, crashing over the cornstalks, which were altogether too noisy, and he only wished he had his Old Catawba with him again. Old Catawba surely would have carried him off to safety, correct? But he'd shot Old Catawba deader than hell, hadn't he? And he and the others had eaten that poor old nag, hadn't they? Where was Mr Tudor the tutor? What had happened to the sassafras tea, and where were all the scholars and gentlemen? Boom shook his head. Groaning, he got to his feet, and he beat at his hat until it had regained whatever remained of its battered shape. He resumed running. They all were headed toward a grove of small scrubby evergreens. He listened for more sounds from the Yankees, but he did not look back. He knew enough about rout and despair and retreat not to look back. One only looked back when one sought to surrender. If one did not seek to surrender, then one ran like the devil and tried not to think, waffle, weep or utter lonely pathetic cries. And so he and the others went crashing and blundering out of the cornfield and into the grove of small scrubby evergreens, and he and the others dropped to their bellies and turned their rifles (those who had rifles) in the direction of the goddamn shouting laughing Yankees and Yankee horses and the goddamn Yankee horses' fuckin goddamn Yankee *hooves* an all. Boom gasped and coughed. His rifle was loaded. He always kept it loaded. He'd taken it off the body of a boy he'd found lying dead in a barnyard. The boy's jaw had been shot off, and his eyes had been open. They were hazel eyes, and birds already had started pecking at them, and so they were bleeding. Boom had had to pound the boy's hands with a rock before he'd been able to pry loose the rifle. He'd broken a number of the boy's fingers with the rock before the boy reluctantly had relinquished the rifle. Then, off beyond a hill, a caisson had exploded, and so Boom had grabbed the rifle and had gone scurrying away from the dead boy and had hid behind a demolished corncrib for what he later figured had been more than an hour. The next day, dragging the dead boy's rifle and stumbling along a road that was full of refugees and retreating troops and fleeing politicians and weeping children and pale shushing mothers, Boom had found the top hat resting half in and half out of a scum of water in a ditch at the side of the road. He'd smiled. He'd retrieved the top hat, and he'd more or less wiped it dry with a sleeve, and he'd plunked the confounded thing on his head, and for a moment or two he'd felt almost jaunty and maybe even gallant. And since then it hadn't been out of his sight. It had become a crazed and he supposed incoherent personal talisman, but he wasn't about to do without it, and he knew he would defend it to the death. Which was absurd, and he was old enough to know it was absurd, but he also was old enough—and wise enough, by God—not to reject a thing simply because it was absurd. Why, shit, the planet nourished itself on absurdities, and there were worse places for a man to build his house and till his fields than the Kingdom of the Silly & the Egregious, and so he wasn't about to be ashamed of himself. And he lay on his belly and ate dirt as his mind conducted this numbskulled and Quixotic exploration of the Kingdom of the Silly & the Egregious, and at the same time he told himself he should be frightened, since surely those Yankee cavalry fellows were about to come after them. But no such thing happened. Not right then, at any rate. Boom craned his neck and watched a man named Ratliff crawl forward. Everyone was listening for sounds from the Yankees, but there were no particular sounds, and certainly there were no sounds of Yankees. Then Ratliff stood up. He shrugged. Off to one side, a small bespectacled fellow named Pearson or Petrie or some such also stood up. This Pearson or Petrie looked around, and then he helped the bloodsmeared Tidwell stand up. Tidwell was shaking and whimpering. Appling stood up, and so did McGraw and the onearmed Coy. McGraw went to Tidwell and embraced him. It was Boom's understanding that those two fellows were first cousins. He heard Tidwell say something to the effect that there'd been only five Yankee cavalrymen out there, and then he heard McGraw say that the cowardly sonsabitches probably had skedaddled after firing into the cornfield. Appling said something to the effect that the Yankees had fired just one shot—and that one shot had hit Sgt Patterson, hadn't it? Quickly Tidwell nodded, and he told everyone Sgt Patterson was dead and dead and deader than dead. Then Tidwell fell down and began to weep, and he rubbed his face, spreading more blood across his cheeks and his forehead and his ears. Boom wondered what his mother would have said about all this, and he wondered what his dead brothers would have said. No doubt Sam and Carter would have been logical about all of it, and no doubt they would have explained all of it in such a way that would have reflected great credit on the brave Confederacy. The crippled Miller stood up, and so did the huge bearded Llewellyn, and so did Pope and Goodfellow and Barber. So did a man named Vincent, and now all of them except Boom were standing. They looked at him, and Miller leaned against one of the small scrubby evergreens. Grunting, wiping moist dirt from his mouth, Boom stood up. Now they all were facing him, and he hoped to God he didn't know why. Pope smiled and began speaking slowly to Boom. He said he and some of the other fellers believed Boom was keeping some sort of secret from them. He asked Boom was he (Boom) maybe a preacher or a schoolteacher or some such thing? He said Boom had done a fine and pretty job of praying over the extinguished Pendarvis and Nelson. He said they all had been impressed. He said the praying had marked Boom to be a man of dignity and sweet humility. Pope was moistening his lips, and he looked around, and most of the men were nodding, and a few of them (Pearson/Petrie, McGraw, Vincent, Goodfellow) even were smiling and nodding, as though somehow they goddamn *needed* their good old Parson Boom. The others didn't smile, though, and big Llewellyn actually was frowning. At the same time, he was tugging on his beard. His hands were scabbed, and his nails were splintered and nubbed. Pope looked around. Now he spoke to all of them, and he said he was tired. He said he was so tired his bones felt as though they were about to turn to dust. He asked the others whether they were as tired as he was, and they all nodded . . . all of them except the large frowning Llewellyn. Who said to them that now he hated

Yankees worse than he'd hated them this morning. On account of
now, to add to all their other crimes, they'd kilt Sgt Patterson,
who'd been a fine sergeant, after all, and who'd always done
everthin he'd asked the rest of em to do, by Christ, don't you
know. The others nodded. Some of them even shrugged—except
Coy, of course, who no longer had that particular ability. Boom
rubbed his jowls and his throat. He scratched his balls, and
Pearson/Petrie giggled, and so did Vincent. (Boom should have
known better than to have led his troopers beside that river. He'd
been thinking along the principle of interior lines, and the principle of interior lines had to do with the unalterable fact that a
surrounded force had shorter lines and thus could repulse and
perhaps even defeat a much larger force that had long exterior
lines, and it was a principle he'd learned from R. E. Lee and the
late T. J. Jackson and his late friend J. E. B. Stuart, and they'd
employed it well, and it had created much glory, but the thing
about a principle was that it always had flaws. After all, if a force
was outnumbered five to one, it lost all the advantage of interior
lines, correct?) Now Pope and little Pearson/Petrie and most of
the others were standing smack in front of Boom, and Pope told
Boom he couldn't fool them; surely he'd once been an officer, and
surely he would know what to do. Boom frowned at them. Big
Llewellyn was standing twenty or thirty yards away, and he was
staring toward the cornfield. Boom asked Pope why this question
was being asked with Sgt Patterson so recently dead and still
unburied, and when the hell had they all met and come to this
stupid conclusion? Pope and little Pearson/Petrie and the others
(all except Llewellyn) made dry incoherent sounds, and then Pope
reminded Boom that yes, yes, surely they'd all regarded Sgt
Patterson just as highly as highly could be, but Sgt Patterson
wasn't about to be giving any more orders, was he? And, well, it
wasn't as though they hadn't discussed among themselves what
they'd do if Sgt Patterson was kilt. Boom nodded. And *he* told
them fine and dandy, and he told them he was a brevet brigadier
general of cavalry, and he told them he was about to desert and go
home, and what did they think of that?

PITT

Wednesday, April 5, 1865.

The small country church apparently had taken a direct hit from a bomb or a cannonball or some such device. The place had no roof, and its steeple had toppled forward, and two of its exterior walls had been blown down. Still, the two remaining walls did provide protection from the wind, and Capt Pitt (full name—Edgar Percival Pitt; age—fortytwo; peacetime profession—publisher of hymnals and Holy Scripture) was grateful. He'd never been fond of the wind. Large as he was, he still didn't believe he had the flesh for it.

There had been a sound of spring birds all day long, but now it was twilight, and the sound of birds was gone. Capt Pitt's wife, whose name was Eleanor, was fond of the sounds birds made, and sometimes they even made her weep a little and speak brokenly of the Lord's bounty and His generosity and His large abundant Heart. Now, squatting next to a small fire with Brig Gen Snell and the men who remained under Brig Gen Snell's command, Capt Pitt wished he knew whether he was as crazy as Brig Gen Snell was, and he wished he knew what to do about the present situation, which of course was intolerable.

Eleanor would tell me to clear out, said Capt Pitt to himself. She would say: You all are committin suicide—an for what? And

106

then Capt Pitt sighed. He shrugged. He plucked at the knees of his britches.

"You seem fatigued, dear old friend," said Brig Gen Snell to Capt Pitt, and the old fellow even appeared to be smiling . . . but crookedly, with jumbled teeth and a mouth that was too thin and razory.

Again Capt Pitt shrugged. "Wellsir," he said, "I don't expect the days are gettin any shorter, are they?"

"Ah, but we must not complain," said Brig Gen Snell. "Too much complainin diverts us from the gloon an the ecstamattin of our strauntin purpose, don't you agree?"

"Yessir," said Capt Pitt. "Long as you put the proposition at way."

Six men squatted by the fire with Capt Pitt and Brig Gen Snell. They glanced at Brig Gen Snell and grinned a little. Their names were Burns, Crabtree, Lillis, Ford, Lavelle and Shankland. Crabtree was a sergeant. The others were privates. They represented all that remained of Brig Gen Snell's command. Of course they all knew how crazy Brig Gen Snell was, but none of them appeared to care. For them, the time for caring about that sort of thing evidently had been lost somewhere back down the road. What road? Who knew? What difference did it make? Still, they weren't so confused and despairing that they'd lost their military discipline. Brig Gen Snell tried to bathe every day, no matter what, and so did the men—even Capt Pitt, who maybe was not as fond of bathing as arguably he should have been. And the men marched in cadence when Brig Gen Snell ordered it. Well, in a sense that was to be expected, since these fellows were the only ones who'd not sneaked away in the past two weeks. And the true and certain and final end of the war had come the previous Saturday, south of Petersburg at a place called Five Forks. Something like a hundred men had remained in Brig Gen Snell's command, and they'd withstood seven Yankee attacks before finally breaking apart and fleeing, and Capt Pitt had wept that sad day; o how he had wept, and his eyes had gone all hazy and hot, and Brig Gen Snell had staggered back and forth and had brandished his sword and had shouted hoarse and witless words having to do with Duty and Courage, and of course that poor sad demolished old man might as well have carried a large placard proclaiming: I AM CRAZY AS A BEDBUG!!!!! There had been final explosions that day, final glimpses of Brig Gen Snell's precious Duty and Courage, and Capt Pitt had watched men, exhausted men, skeletons all, wild and full of whoops and exhortations, go lurching off against the Yankees, grappling with the Yankees, even impaling and hacking the Yankees, moving on them with weary grinning grace, not giving a damn and not giving less than a damn, repulsing the Yankee attacks and launching wavering staggery attacks of their own, and Capt Pitt saw a man named Dobson pick up a great tall stringy Yankee twice his size and slam the fellow against a tree and break the fellow's neck in such a way that the fellow's head damn near fell off, and Capt Pitt watched three Yankees bayonet a boy named Ruggles and kick him and saw away his throat and probably drown him in his own blood, and then several of the remaining ragged rebels came crunching in on those three Yankees and slashed *them* into the proverbial ribbons and strips of hot crimson flesh, and Capt Pitt personally grappled with a young Yankee lieutenant who surely would have killed him if it hadn't been for the fact that he—the young Yankee lieutenant, whose eyes were blue, by the way, and whose breath was sweetly astringent, something like ammonia—tripped over a tough hard unyielding cluster of tree roots and fell flat on his face, thus enabling Capt Pitt to dispatch him with a single quick hot pistol shot to the back of the neck. So then another battle, and Capt Pitt had no way of remembering all of them, but he figured he always would remember that encounter at Five Forks, since surely it marked the end of the war. (The Yankees finally had carried the day, and there no longer were nearly enough—nor had there been for more than a year—bloody muzzy woozy Rebel skeletons remaining to hoist their rifles to their bony shoulders and give their holy yipping Rebel yells and make an issue of slavery or the rights of the states or any other of those windy foolish abstractions that had caused their blood to leak across so many towns and cities and cornfields and orchards and woods and roadjunctions and railroadyards of Virginia and the Carolinas, Tennessee, Georgia, Alabama, Mississippi, even Kentucky and even no less a place than the Yankees' precious

Commonwealth of Pennsylvania, by God.) And now Capt Pitt
had to rub his eyes and look away from the fire and the faces of
the other seven men (including the mad Brig Gen Snell) who were
all that remained of the Hartstone Zouaves, which hailed from
Hartstone, Virginia, a brave and cheerful force that had numbered four hundred seven when it had marched off for Manassas
four years ago to cheers and tears and applause and sturdy tone-
deaf bandmusic. Ah, the life of a Hartstone Zouave. The smiles.
The sense of comradeship. The absurd uniforms. Crimson panta-
loons. Belts with sashes. Jaunty fezzes. The wonder was that the
Yankees hadn't taken one look at those uniforms and laughed
themselves to death. Capt Pitt knew for a fact that in the early
spring of '61 Brig Gen Snell (who'd only been a major then) had
spent nearly ten thousand dollars outfitting—and arming—the
Hartstone Zouaves. But surely the then Maj Snell had been able
to assume such an expense. He probably had been the most
prosperous tobacco farmer between Hartstone County and the
Potomac River, owning some seven hundred acres of good plump
cleared land that was the envy of One & All. Why, there were
those who said the wonder was that old M. T. Snell didn't fall
down dead from the weight of all the money he forever seemed to
be carrying to the bank the morning after he auctioned off the
tobacco from his private warehouse. Ah, but all that sort of thing
had been said of old M. T. Snell back in '61. Now, in '65, no one
spoke of old M. T. Snell's wealth, and Capt Pitt supposed there
was a good chance no one even remembered it. Of the men who
remained in old M. T.'s command (all seven of them, if Capt Pitt
were included), probably none of them even particularly remembered their silly Zouave uniforms. The time for all that sort of
heavy clumsy nonsense was long since gone, and Capt Pitt for one
didn't even want to—

Brig Gen Snell, sitting frail and tiny and crosslegged with his
back jammed against an overturned and splintered pew, abruptly
spoke up. His boots were too close to the fire, and they gave off a
sort of slick leathered stink, and he blinked at the others and said:
"The tests all are yet to come. We are summoned by the milkbobs
an the power of our frightness. We must make certain the Confederacy remains as secure as a mother's tomb."

"Tomb, sir?" said Capt Pitt.

"Womb," said Brig Gen Snell, nodding, carefully rubbing his mouth.

"Yessir," said Capt Pitt.

The others didn't say anything. The survivors of the old Hartstone Zouaves had fought at Five Forks bravely and then some, and nine had been killed and six carried off with wounds that probably would be fatal. And so just eighty or so had remained. But that night . . . last Saturday night it had been . . . Brig Gen Snell had stood all small and whitely shaking in front of the slumped remnants of his command and had told them they all were cowards and rascals. He'd told them they lacked privvery, and he'd told them he was full of disgust and absalombic loadin praffer. He'd told them they all could go home to their loved ones and their animals and their varbs for all he gave a slam. He'd kept fiddling with his pistol, alternately waving it about and shoving it down into its holster. He'd waved his arms. He'd told those who wanted to get out to do so immediately. He'd brandished his pistol, and after a time he'd shot himself in the holster, and the holster had flown away in all directions, but he was uninjured. Then he'd got to waving his sword. He'd gone after a little fellow named Hamblyn with the sword, and Hamblyn had screamed, and Capt Pitt and two other men had rushed forward and had disarmed Brig Gen Snell, wrestling him to the earth while he'd clawed and hollered. It had been then that most of the remaining men of the Hartstone Zouaves had begun to drift away. Capt Pitt had sat on the chest of Brig Gen Snell, and Brig Gen Snell had wept, and Capt Pitt had grimaced. The men had drifted away, and no one had called to them to come back. Finally only the six remained, and later that night Capt Pitt asked them why in God's name they hadn't gone, and Sgt Crabtree told them he guessed he an the other fellers kind of figured shoot, one more fight or two wasn't bout to make no difference, an anyway, they had an obligation . . . even if, wellsir, you know, even if a whole lot of craziness was wrapped up in whatever it was. The other fellers . . . shit, Sgt Crabtree didn't blame em for walkin away, an he didn't think he was better an em because he *wasn't* walkin away, but this here old general, him an his tobacco farm an his money an all, him an his craziness, well, the thing was, where had the craziness come from? what was to blame for the craziness? did a feller turn his back on a man just because the man was touched? didn't loyalty matter a damn? And then Sgt Crabtree (a tall fellow, bald, maybe thirtyfive, who himself had been a tobacco farmer—but on a considerably smaller scale—back in Hartstone County) had shrugged and had walked away from Capt Pitt and had joined the five other men who'd elected to remain under Brig Gen Snell's strange deranged command. And those six soldiers had squatted and had lounged and had chatted quietly, and half a mile away had been fires and explosions, a hard screaming twilight. And now, here in this rubbled and ruined church, these men still were squatting and lounging and chatting quietly, and there was no strength to them, no substance, no finite definition, and they could have been ghosts, shadows, torn cobwebs. But, for whatever reasons, they still somehow were fighting this damnable war, and it didn't seem to matter that others had walked away from all the cruel lunacy. These eight fellows (and Capt Pitt included himself as well as Brig Gen Snell) still somehow needed to do their duty, no matter how fatally foolish their duty was. Why, Capt Pitt actually had commanded the fellows when they'd executed the two looters. Three of them—Burns, Lillis and Shankland—actually had wept. And of course both the looters had wept. One of the looters, a pretty fellow with blond hair and pale wet characterless blue eyes, actually had crawled on his hands and knees, actually had plucked at Brig Gen Snell's britches, actually had tried to tell Brig Gen Snell that he and the other looter had been *ordered* by some sergeant or the other to go out and forage the countryside for whatever they could find. And Brig Gen Snell had kicked the man across the throat. Shrieking, the man had seized his poor throat and had started to gag, and Brig Gen Snell had wrested Shankland's rifle from Shankland's astonished hands and had shot the pretty looter smack between the eyes. Brig Gen Snell of course no longer was carrying a weapon of his own. Ever since the night Brig Gen Snell had assassinated his holster and damn near had killed himself with his pistol, Capt Pitt wore Brig Gen Snell's sword and carried Brig Gen Snell's pistol, and Brig Gen Snell hadn't even appeared to have missed them. Capt Pitt had every intention of returning the sword to the general, but not right then, seeing as how . . . well, seeing as how Brig Gen Snell had owls and bats and great hooting swans flying around inside his skull, and obviously the sound of their wings had deafened him. After the first looter's head had vanished in blood and bits of bone, the second looter had tried to crawl away, but Brig Gen Snell had grabbed a second rifle (this time from the hands of Lillis, to be accurate about it) and had squatted over the second looter and had tugged at the fellow's shoulders, rolling him over so that he lay blinking upward while at the same time bawling and trying to cover his face. Then, grimacing, Brig Gen Snell had shot the second looter in the face, and some of the second looter's blood got in Brig Gen Snell's eyes and mouth, and he spat and shook his head, and no doubt the owls and the bats and the great hooting swans were colliding with one another in an explosion of mouths and feathers and outraged claws. Then Brig Gen Snell had straightened up and had glared at Capt Pitt and the others and had told them the vengeance had been achieved, but no thanks to *them*, wasn't that so? And he'd walked out toward the road, and Capt Pitt had followed him, and after a time he'd glanced at Capt Pitt and had nodded down at his bloody chest and had said something to the effect that well, by golly, he believed he needed a fresh shirt, didn't he? (Any shirt would do. The time of the fancy Zouave uniforms was long since past, and the chances were Brig Gen Snell didn't even have the most remote memory of them.) Capt Pitt had nodded when Brig Gen Snell had spoken of his need for an unbloody shirt, but none was available. Since Five Forks, the men had no clothing other than what they'd been wearing that day, and so it was a full night and the following day before Lillis and Sgt Crabtree came across the reasonably fresh corpse of a Yankee cavalryman whose body had been left at some flatly anonymous vacant rural crossroads about twenty miles west of Richmond. Lillis and Sgt Crabtree stripped the shirt off this corpse, and Lillis threw up. He simply lurched to the nearest ditch and bent over and let the vomitus leak from him in a slow tired despondent dribble, and he didn't say anything, and neither did anyone else. The shirt was dirty and smelled vaguely of shit, and it was far too large for Brig Gen Snell, and he had to roll up its sleeves and tuck great expanses of its tail inside his britches, but at least the damned thing wasn't bloody, and—to coin a phrase—beggars could not be choosers, could they? So, for a change, Brig Gen Snell had been properly grateful, and he'd told Lillis and Sgt Crabtree he surely did appreciate their generosity, and he'd present them each a box of good old Hartstone County cigars just as soon as they all returned home after giving the Yankees the inevitable whipping. *Inevitable.* The word was Brig Gen Snell's, and it had caused him that day to stand erectly and smile at all of them. All seven of them. Ha. He'd told them the Army of Northern Virginia had betrayed the Confederacy with its cowardice, its lack of energy and grit. He trembled as he spoke, and he kept pressing his palms against his unbloodied shirt. Then, frowning, he began speaking of matters that he admitted no doubt were beyond him. He spoke of death and funerals and graves, and he spoke of corruption, and he spoke of dust. He told the men nothing really mattered, nothing at all, if one inspected the state of the planets and the galaxies with a cool and unsentimental eye. He coughed, and he shifted his weight from leg to leg, and he linked his fingers and fastidiously cracked his knuckles, and he pointed out what he said were certain terrifying facts. He glanced in the direction of the good old Blue Ridge mountains, and he said he'd read somewhere that in thirty thousand years or so they would be gone. He smiled, but his eyes didn't smile, and his tiny oldman's body was too stiff and anxious. He said everything was vanity, and he said everything was vanity of vanities, and he said everything was shit. He said he had no more idea of Judgment and Eternity than he did of the cholers and the humours and the irrational whims of the female race. He tried to laugh, but he was unable to make any particular sounds. He told his men they all were failures, and he went on to say he was a worse failure. After all, he said, who was more of a failure than the man who was in charge of a failed group effort? He said he didn't know who—in this world or the next or the one after that—could explain any of this to him or to anyone else, and he said he no longer had the faith necessary to believe human beings really *deserved* such explanations. He said his wife was a dead fish, and he said he had a daughter who had three legs and a set of curved horns growing from her ears. Now he was able to smile, and he even giggled a little. He said he'd once owned a bay mare that had been able to dance the waltz. He said that if a man waved his wand in the right direction, he could effect remarkable changes, and tobacco would grow from the nostrils of sheep. He spoke for several hours, and one by one the men drifted away from him and lay down and curled themselves against the night cold and wrapped their arms around their chests and fell asleep. And then only Capt Pitt remained there, and Capt Pitt literally fell asleep on his feet, and the next thing he knew, he'd collapsed to the earth, and he was unable to move, and he didn't really care that he was unable to move, and so he went to sleep, and the devil take everything. That had been only three nights ago, but it had felt like decades and epochs as far as Capt Pitt was concerned, and now . . . as he sat with Brig Gen Snell and the others in this cold demolished church . . . he figured his bones never again would move; he figured he'd already died but no one had told him; he figured o, o, o, he never again would touch his Eleanor's timid flesh, and he never again would tend the roses in their dooryard back home in Hartstone, and he never again would breathe the polite and coddled Hartstone earth, and he never again would hear the music of fiddles and trumpets, and he never again would sing from one of the hymnals he'd published so successfully and so profitably over the years, and he never again would take up with an occa- sional hotly loose and liberal woman in some shabby backstreet crib in Winchester, say, or Staunton, or Richmond. He figured he should weep because of all this tragedy, but he just didn't have the energy for that sort of thing, and so he simply squatted there by the fire, and after a time—speaking so abruptly that Capt Pitt and the others actually flinched—Brig Gen Snell said to him: "I take it the pickets report no enemy probes."

"At is correct, sir," said Capt Pitt to Brig Gen Snell, "the pickets report no enemy probes. It is my belief at the enemy suffered heavy casualties today, and he's withdrawn to lick his wounds."

"Well," said Brig Gen Snell, "at's a pretty thing to hope for, isn't it?"

". . . yessir," said Capt Pitt.

The other men shifted their weight, and the sound was like the quiet strawfooted sounds of stabled horses. Capt Pitt glanced at them, but they all looked away from him.

"Is the artillery in place?" said Brig Gen Snell.

". . . artillery, sir?" said Capt Pitt.

"On our flanks, Pitt. Our *flanks*. We don't want to suffer an enfilade, do we? We might not be able to resist, isn't at so? I mean, keep your wits bout you, man. Always anticipate what those people might try to do."

"Oh," said Capt Pitt, speaking quickly. "The artillery is in place. Indeed it is. Two fresh batteries, in from I believe Tennessee. The batteries are commanded by a man named . . . Dibble. Yes. At is the name. Dibble. A large cheerful fellow he is, an he tells me he an his men are meaner an hell an rarin to go."

"Dibble?"

"Yessir."

"I know people named Dibble. Air from Roanoke. Fred Dibble used to be a tobacco auctioneer, an a damn good one. I used to hire him for my place, an he had a real, ah, musical way of callin out the bids, you know? But, ah, he's dead now. So I don't guess he's commandin a couple batteries of artillery."

"No sir," said Capt Pitt.

"He died because he got aggravated with his wife an tried to set her bedroom on fire. Trouble was, somehow he also set himself on fire. An so he died screamin, an at was the end of Fred Dibble."

"The poor feller," said Capt Pitt.

"The wife didn't think so," said Brig Gen Snell. "She came into an estate at was worth fifty thousand dollars at the least. The last I heard, she'd married a church organist up in Baltimore I think it was."

"Well," said Capt Pitt, "good for her."

Rubbing his mouth, Brig Gen Snell nodded.

The men all were leaning forward, and they were covering their mouths, but their shoulders shook, and every so often one or another of them released a terrible and splendid involuntary squeak.

BOOM

Wednesday, April 5, 1865.

At first most of them laughed, and Boom grinned and adjusted his top hat and told them go on an laugh; I don't expect I can blame you, And, truth to tell, he more or less laughed along with them. He looked at them, and they were shadowy, misted, like old men poking and groping through an enervated shapeless fog, and he just about wanted to weep in acknowledgment of their absurdity. But he didn't suppose that would do much good, and so finally he raised his voice and told them to settle down; there were certain things he needed to say, and he needed their attention. So he gathered them around him there in that evergreen woods and he leaned on his rifle and said: "I don't really know why you men think I know what to do, an I surely don't know why you've turned to me so quickly, an for the goddamn *life* of me I don't know how come you believed me to be an officer . . . but, well, the sad truth is at my full name is Edmund Aspinwall Boom, an until just a little while ago I was a brigadier general commandin three troops of cavalry attached to Pickett's corps of this Army of Northern Virginia, but you see . . . ah, the enemy has been houndin an harassin us an wearin us out an, well, last week they trapped us against the goddamn James River, of which I suspect most of you men have heard many times durin the course of the past year's fightin, what with the seige of Petersburg

116

an all, an anyway . . . well, air were maybe one hundred fifty of us facin seven or eight hundred Yanks all fat an sassy, an . . . well . . . the only thing at could have happened *did* happen, an we were put to flight. I don't know how many of us were killed, an I don't know how many were wounded, and I don't know how many just plain ran off, but it all comes out the same, doesn't it? I mean, I'm a general, boys, but I got nobody to general, an at's a pathetic state of affairs, wouldn't you say? But you mark me well. I am what I say I am, an I propose to do just exactly what I said I proposed to do—at is, skedaddle. But with dignity. So I can go home an be able to look my wife directly in the eye. Yes, boys, you heard me—skedaddle with dignity. You want to laugh, don't you? Well, go ahead, only just don't think I'm jokin. We're all of us more complicated an we like to admit, an I'm no different. I've been trying to think through all this . . . an a lot of other stuff . . . over the past few days, an I know goddamn well I don't have many answers, but one answer I *do* have is at I believe the killin ought to be declared over an done with, and if Jeff Davis an R. E. Lee an the rest of em won't admit the situation is hopeless, well, by God, we'd just better go ahead an do the admittin ourselves an get out of here. Maybe some of you think I'm a coward. Well, maybe I *am* a coward, but maybe at sort of thing don't matter anymore. Maybe we're all of us just done in, you know? So . . . hey, we need to do what's right, but for the first time in a long time I expect we need to do what's right for *us.* An never mind words an exhortations an appeals to the blood in us . . ." A pause. Boom glanced from man to man, from face to face, and most of the faces were dull, with collapsed flesh and bones that were too pointed. He knew damn well he'd talked too much, but if he didn't try to explain himself, where was the sense to any of this? Then, his voice shaky, he said: "We need to desert. We need to—"

Llewellyn, the big one, interrupted. "Bullshit," he said, and he folded his arms across his chest.

"I beg your pardon?" said Boom.

"I ain't run in the face of *no one,*" said Llewellyn. "Not never in my life . . . an I ain't fixin to start now. God damn it, I don't care if you're a general or the fuckin King of Siam, you're talkin

so much bullshit it's a wonder you don't slipslide in it an fall
down . . ."

"Aw, John," said McGraw to Llewellyn, "Christ's sake, stop
bein such a—"

"No," said Boom to McGraw. "He's got a right to be whatever he wants to be."

"Well, ain't *you* the kind one," said Llewellyn to Boom. And
now Llewellyn was standing straight, as though he expected all
the others to hurl their hollow silly bodies at him. "Standin up for
poor little John T. Llewellyn like at. I expect you think you're
doin me a big favor, ain't at so?"

Boom held up a hand. "Please. Just say whatever it is you
want to say. I want to hear it."

"I ain't bout to end it this way, *General sir*," said Llewellyn.
"I hate Yankees, *General sir*, an I don't appreciate hearin talk bout
desertin. As long as one of em fuckers still is breathin God's air,
en John T. Llewellyn wants to nail that fucker's ass to the nearest
fuckin tree, you hear me?"

"But we've lost the war," said Boom.

"Who says so?" said Llewellyn.

"Ask Sergeant Patterson," said Boom.

"*What?*" said Llewellyn.

Boom sighed and said: "Sergeant Patterson knows we've lost
the war."

"Surely he does," said Llewellyn. "Surely. Surely. Yes. Surely.
He's dead, an so he knows a whole lot. Surely."

"By bein dead, he knows everthin air is to know."

"How do you know at? He send you one of em telegraph
messages or somethin?"

"I just know," said Boom. He adjusted his top hat.

"Stop fuckin with at air hat," said Llewellyn.

"I beg your pardon?" said Boom.

"It makes you look like some sort of sissyboy. I mean—what
the hell sort of a name is Boom? You ought to call yourself Percy
an be done with it. Lordamercy, here comes Percy, the Prissy
Sissy. Or the Pissy Sissy. Whatever."

Boom shrugged. ". . . all right," he said.

"Percy the Sissy," said Llewellyn, grinning. Then Llewellyn spread his arms and advanced on Boom. "You want to dance with me, sweet Percy?"

"Not particularly," said Boom, and he did some grinning of his own.

Llewellyn plumped his lips and made kissing sounds. "You want me to fuck you? You want me to fuck maybe at stupid hat you're wearin?"

"I didn't really have at in mind," said Boom, and he still was grinning.

The other men were backing away. Coy was scratching his empty sleeve. Tidwell was embracing himself. Miller was rubbing his shins. Ratliff was chewing on what maybe was his tongue. Little Petrie was blowing on his spectacles and polishing them with a sleeve, and his mouth went hahhh and hahhh and hahhh.

Llewellyn dropped his rifle and said: "I'm a *man*, God damn you, an I ain't goin to let no fuckin fairy *Percy* tell me I ought to turn an skedaddle just because of fuckin *Yankees*. . ."

Boom carefully set his own rifle on the earth. He tapped his top hat. He placed his hands on his hips and rocked forward and back.

"I wouldn't have no trouble killin you," said Llewellyn to Boom.

"I believe you," said Boom.

"So get out of here," said Llewellyn. "Stop poisonin these here boys' minds. Do at little thing for me. Take your desertin talk an stuff it up your goddamn sissy ass . . ."

"I don't believe I want to do at little thing," said Boom. "I mean, I'd surely like to do you such a favor an all, but I'm afraid you're too much of a loudmouth an a bully, an I make it an act of faith never to give in to loudmouths an bullies. At sort of sissy behavior is bad for the heart, an more often not it makes a man's breath go all sour an awful. Myself, I got enough at's wrong with me. Probably too much. So maybe you just want to leave me be, all right?"

Llewellyn scratched at his beard and said: "Fuck you, Percy Prisspants."

". . . oh," said Boom.

Llewellyn lowered his head and charged straight at Boom, who stepped aside and tripped him. Llewellyn hit the earth on his belly, and most of the wind was knocked from him, and he made a succession of squealing sounds. Several of the men sniggered, and they included Miller and Petrie and Tidwell. Llewellyn rolled over on his back, and Boom kicked him across the neck, the shoulders, the side of his head. Llewellyn promptly began bleeding from the nose and an ear. Boom stepped back and tapped his top hat. His armpits stank, but they'd been stinking for he didn't remember how many weeks, and nothing really was new about their stink. Llewellyn crawled on hands and knees toward Boom, and Boom grimaced and cleared his throat. Llewellyn tried to seize Boom's ankles, but Boom dodged to one side. Llewellyn worked himself up into a sitting position. He glanced at the other men and told them this here *general* of theirs was nothing more and nothing less than a cocksucker. Boom went to Llewellyn and stood over him, and Boom still was smiling a little, and he bent over Llewellyn and seized the front of Llewellyn's britches and twisted Llewellyn's balls and prick and scrotum, and Llewellyn's eyes went a perfect white, and somehow his pain caused him to fill his britches with shit. Then Boom pulled a shrieking Llewellyn to his feet. Boom beat Llewellyn with his fists, knocking him down several times and finally rubbing Llewellyn's face back and forth across the earth until Llewellyn's cheeks and lips and forehead and neck bled. Boom breathed easily, and he was quite aware of his teeth and his crotch, and his crotch was more than a little engorged. He began kicking Llewellyn in the ass, and he finally kicked Llewellyn sprawling into a tangled cluster of weeds, ferns, underbrush. Llewellyn puled and groaned, and he crawled off somewhere, and the sound of his puling and his groaning went away, and he never was seen again. Petrie claimed his rifle, and Goodfellow sneaked out into the cornfield and took the rifle from the dead Sgt Patterson. It was an ill wind, et cetera. Boom rubbed his bruises and cuts, and at midnight or so he led the men back out into that infernal cornfield, and they quietly buried Sgt Patterson, and this time Boom said no prayers (he was afraid the Yanks might have heard anything he might have said), and then they walked singlefile to the banks of a narrow and foamy creek, where they drank and slept.

TIDWELL

Thursday, April 6, 1865.

They sat crosslegged on the earth, most of them, and they munched on hardtack and filled their canteens with water from the creek. Boom spoke to them, and the first thing he did was give them more information about himself. He said his family's name originally had been Baum, but his grandfather had changed it to Boom back in 1800 or so because most people *pronounced* it Boom, and the grandfather (a job printer just off the boat from Bremen and trying to scratch out a living in a tiny job shop in Georgetown) hadn't wanted to make trouble for anyone over such a trivial matter as the spelling and the pronunciation of his surname. Boom smiled a little as he told this story, and one of his lips had been split during the fight with Llewellyn, and it still was bleeding a little. Every so often he swiped at the cut with his knuckles, but otherwise he didn't bother with the damned thing. Then he told the fellers his old granddad had made a fortune in the lumber business, of all the peculiar things, and had transformed himself into quite the country gentleman . . . with his largest interest in his old age being the breeding of horses. His only son—Boom's father—became such a horseman that it was a wonder he wasn't an appendage to a horse, something like a second head, or maybe a second asshole, if the truth were known. But then Boom's father was killed at age thirtyseven when one of his horses tripped and sent him rocketing into a stone wall, where his skull was stove in and his brain matter was spread like warm clotted butter. Still, a tradition already had been established; this enthusiasm for horse-flesh already had been passed down to Boom and his two brothers, Sam and Carter. This no doubt was why all three of them became cavalry officers back in '61 at the outset of the war. Boom was married early, he told the fellers, to a sweet fragile little girl of seventeen named Lenore Highsmith, of the Highsmith family of Charlotte, North Carolina. The young couple took up residence in Alexandria, where Boom went to work as general superintendent of the family lumberyard and Lenore lost four babies in five years. Boom appeared to rock from side to side as he spoke of all this, and it made Tidwell wonder a little whether old Boom maybe was a little troubled in the head. What sort of man was it who said barely two words one day an en got to blabberin like somebody's crazed an gossipy old auntie the next? And Boom gestured as he spoke, and smile after smile flickered across his face, giving it a strange pale light that for some scarifyin reason made Tidwell want to hug himself . . . at least a little. And Boom kept glancing around, as though maybe he expected Yankees to erupt from the earth. But then he spoke of horses, the musculature of horses, the teeth and lips of horses, the legs of horses, and his voice softened a little, losing some of its tight urgency, and he told the fellers he and his Lenore often visited his widowed mother's fine estate down in Prince William County near a village called Freedom Ridge, an he had such good comfortin memories of at place, with its high ceilings an its beautiful table service an its ham dinners an its plump applepies an its grinnin obedient niggers, an he had such *especially* good memories of its stables an its horses an the good green earthy odors of its fields an its barns an the sweet honeysuckle at clustered around the kitchen door an most always gave the niggers a perfumy odor at they wouldn't otherwise have had, don't you know. And then Boom began to pace back and forth as he talked. He spoke briefly of his two brothers, and he said they were graduates of VMI, and he said Sam had been shot in the back and instantly killed when his troop had been ambushed by a regiment of Yankee infantry less than a week before the Sharpsburg fight in September of '62. The other brother, Carter, had died of jaundice in February of '64 after a long illness. Carter had been brought home to die, and his mother and a nigger woman named Clytemnestra were at his bedside when he expired, and his mother kept suggestin at he not be afraid. In a letter to Boom, the old woman wrote:

> He died well & nobly, did your brother. He spoke of you at the end, & he kept insisting his love for you was strong & profound.

Boom briefly visited the Freedom Ridge place over the Christmas holiday of '64, and he learned the real truth of Carter's death from old fat gleaming Clytemnestra, who told him yassa your mama did keep tellin Mister Carter not to be ascared, but he was ascared, all right, an he kep tellin her he didn't want The Old Nick to get him, an he kep tellin her he was real sad on account of he hadn't lived long enough an air was things he still wanted to see, an at the end . . . at the *very* end, I tell you . . . he kept tryin to hit your mama with his fists, only he couldn't hardly *make* no fists, you know? And then, according to what Boom told the fellers that cold wet savage scary morning by the side of that foamy creek somewhere west and maybe south of Richmond, Virginia, in the month of April and the year of 1865, he went to his mother's room, and she was sitting there in a wicker chair and hemming a dress while sunlight came in a quick spatter and outlined her old gray addled head, and he knelt next to her chair and embraced her, and she sighed and patted his head and his face and told him air, air, it's not any of it your fault, but go on an weep if you want to; I surely can understand. And then, smiling, she'd congratulated him on his recent promotion to general, and she'd told him he would bring great credit to his family and great glory to the cause of the South. And Boom had nodded. And he'd kissed his mother lightly on the crown of her head.

And now here he was, and it was the glum aforementioned month of April in the year of 1865, and he squatted for a moment at the edge of the foamy creek and splashed his face with water, and he shuddered, and he expelled his breath in a hollow rush, and then he said to the others: "I want us to get out of this. At's

all I want. I've known too many goddamn battles, an I expect
most of you have too, an at little fight yesterday is the last fight I
ever want to pass through, you hear me? Not much of a fight, was
it? I mean, all the Yanks did was fire one shot an en go skitterin
away while they laughed an hollered, an air only was maybe
halfadozen of em at the most, an the whole thing didn't amount to
a hill of beans, did it? Except as far as your friend Patterson was
concerned. It amounted to a whole lot as far as *he* was concerned,
isn't at so? It amounted to the sun an the moon an the stars an all
the fish in the sea, correct? It amounted to all philosophy an all
speculations on the nature of Heaven an God, not to mention the
mighty populations of angels dancin an shakin on the head of a
pin. Oh, I tell you, it was *profound*—at least as far as *he* was
concerned. So air's no such thing as a *little* fight or skirmish or
whatever, is air? You have the word of Edmund Aspinwall Boom
on at, boys. Edmund Aspinwall Boom, but for some reason the
men in my command called me Old Jack Boom. Jack. Jack Boom.
A tough an violent name, correct? Oh, I tell you, we surely do
drape an festoon ourselves with legends an lies, don't we? All in
the name of morale or whatever. Lord, this is such a war, isn't it?
Now. Well. Listen to me. We're goin home—those of us who
want to. At big loudmouthed gentleman, at Mister Llewellyn, I
expect he wanted to keep on fightin. Well, at's his right. I suppose
he's a brave man, although I'm past the stage where I can keep
brave an *crazy* altogether separate, if you know what I mean.
Remember, I'm Jack Boom—*General* Jack Boom, by God—an my
boys used to tell me I was the meanest bravest old goddamn
fuckin *cob* between here an the far side of the universe, an I
believe maybe I took what they said as some sort of gospel. So
talk bout *crazy*. Ah, but at least I'm not mean. I'm too dead to be
mean, ho ho. The thing is, you ever seen a mean dead man?
What's mean bout a bloated belly, bout stiff fingers pointin toward God an admonishin Him an askin Him how come He's so
almighty full of shit? Ha. Lord have mercy, listen to me. Listen to
the madman, the moron, the witless oratin fool. I ought to be
home droolin in my porridge with my Lenore wipin my mouth an
tellin me yes, she agrees; the moon indeed is made of snuff an
cobwebs an lightninbugs an cattails an bacon grease. Hey. Ah.

Now we have to get on home, don't we? I apologize for all my crazy talk. It's got no place at a time like this, an I am heartily ashamed. We *are* goin home, boys—all of us now at Llewellyn's chosen his footpath to Glory or whatever it is he's lookin for. An we're goin home more or less in a military formation. Why? Well, how else we goin home? One by one so we can individually be picked up an shot as deserters? No, by God in Heaven, we're a *military unit*, an we'll *remain* a military unit until we get where we're goin. At way, we'll be able to defend ourselves in case air are any provosts still on duty in this army, an maybe we'll even be able to talk our way out of a scrape or two by tellin the provosts we're marchin to the aid of General Snickleberger's regiment under orders of General Frothlehoof himself, by George by Heaven by gum. I mean, who'd *dare* mistake such as *us* for a gang of *deserters*, especially when I step bravely forward an tell em I'm no one less an the one an only General Jack Boom, leader of men an hero of heroes?" And here Boom laughed . . . and so did the others, but quietly, while glancing at one another and scratching themselves and plucking at their shirts. Boom told them he had a reasonably good sense of direction, and he'd decided they would head due west for at least two marching days, then wheel to the right and proceed north along the mountains. "An *en* one by one," he said, "you boys can drop out, just as soon as you're near your homes. An at'll be the end of it." And so, grunting, Boom adjusted his top hat, cleared his throat and suggested that now was as good a time as any for them to set off. They walked west and a little south along curving hilly country road. Tidwell walked alongside Ratliff, and they spoke quietly, and they agreed they were a little nervous about this *General* Jack Boom. But somebody had to be in charge, correct? Sure, Ratliff once had been a sergeant, but he'd had no real talent for that sort of thing, and anyway, he was too goddamn stubborn and ornery, and he was the first to admit those failings. So he simply grinned and shrugged and suggested he and Tidwell and the rest of them would be well served if every night from now on they prayed like hell.

Tidwell nodded. He watched birds and clouds, and he thought of his Rosemary. Specifically, the thought of her breasts. Oh, he also thought of their eight children, but first he thought of

Rosemary's breasts. It helped the day pass. It helped hide away questions and fears. So he moistened his lips and thought of Rosemary's breasts and thought of Rosemary's breasts and thought of Rosemary's breasts.

BOOM

Friday, April 7, 1865.

He sat crosslegged on the earth, and his back was propped against a tree, and he inhaled a fume of early lilacs. Dawn came in a soft swooning smear, and indeed it barely was more than a suggestion of dawn, and he kept rubbing his eyes and his face and his shoulders. His top hat rested on the earth next to him. He and his collection of weary shuffling skeletons were scattered along a road at the edge of a village he believed was called Boxerville—if his memory for the names of places on maps was accurate. He'd always been fond of maps. Sometimes . . . if he'd had enough to drink, say, or if he were thinking back on his grandfather and his boyhood and treefrogs and onions and his dad's fatly arrogant cigars and maybe even the mannered grace of Mr Tudor the tutor, or if he were remembering brave old horses and dogs and his fine tough wildly yipping and sweetly belligerent good old schoolyard companions, courageous fellows all, scufflers and brayers all, strutters and howling hooting rascals all, secure in their knowledge of their happy immortality . . . simply the touch of the maps, the dry uncommitted sounds the maps made when they were unfolded and spread on a table . . . why, that sort of thing caused his belly to clog and his vision to drift out of focus as all the handsome and civilized and sometimes even sort of downright goddamn *homely* names, the James and the Rappahannock,

Fredericksburg and Suffolk and Staunton and Boxerville and the
Blue Ridge, the Potomac and the Dismal Swamp, Harrisonburg and
Charles Town and Harpers Ferry and Alexandria and Manassas,
Isle of Wight County and Chittenden County and Gauley Bridge
and Sharpsburg and Vinton and Chesapeake and Front Royal and
the glassy and splendid Chesapeake & Ohio Canal . . . as all these
wondrous and forever honored names paraded inside his skull and
put him in mind at once of babies and graveyards, music and
grief, leaves and apples and hard dry clenched immortal smoke-
house hams, horse manure and chatty old women and cedarchests
and telegraphers and home brew and the anxious love of a good
woman whose belly was soft and whose arms forgiving and warm.

(He always had considered himself not complicated enough
to be serious, with a spirit not adroit enough to be profound nor
strong enough to cleanse itself of sentimentality. His wife, dear
sad Lenore, had believed otherwise, though. She'd told him he
didn't have enough respect for himself. Sometimes they would go
for walks along the clattery buzzing streets of Alexandria, and she
would link her arm with his and smile at him, and usually her
tiny teeth were wet and her great gray eyes would dart and blink,
and she'd tell him she found the idea of living without him
absolutely insupportable. And she didn't allow him to sass her.
She spoke of grandmothers and squirrels and cakes and Holy
Scripture and the sounds made by the whistles of locomotives and
steamboats; sweetly she pressed a crisp little elbow into his ribs
and told him nothing would have meaning for her if he didn't
exist, and at the same time she told him she would entertain no
words from him having to do with what she supposed he believed
was her gushing hyperbole. Such wild and immoderate exaggera-
tions, she told him, were common to women in love, but their
florid nature didn't make them any less true, correct? She walked
in tiny pattery steps, and now and again she nodded at someone
they knew, a maidenlady schoolteacher perhaps, or a tall and
horsy gentleman who owned a store that specialized in harness
and tack and whose very lank and bony frame was an advertise-
ment for his establishment, or neatly gleaming twin bachelor
brothers who operated a dancing academy and gave occasional

fencing lessons, or tittery girls hurrying off to some fine and proper Episcopal tea that also would be attended by a clutch of young fellows from one of the numerous stiffly formidable schools and academies that were clustered in Alexandria and Our Nation's Capital across the Potomac. On her good days, Lenore had bright quick comments on all those people, and sometimes she delivered the comments with a sort of humorous asperity, telling him that the only way to deal with blisters and wounds and carbuncles was to confront them directly and dismiss them with a sort of quick wounded laughter and go on from there and try to look at the happy side of life. That was what she called it—*the happy side of life*. The phrase at once made him wince and smile, and he told her she was the absolute confounded limit and then some. And *she* told *him* oh, *fiddlesticks*, you great slavering *brute* you, and sometimes she dug at him with quick busy fingers, making him inhale and blink and maybe even squeal a little. He loved her, and he'd never loved anyone else. He believed himself to be not attractive to women, and he'd never received any particularly persuasive denial of that belief. In other words, he was not accustomed to being besieged by shrieking flailing mobs of impassioned women and girls, and yet for some reason his Lenore loved him—even though she hadn't been particularly polite or sparing of his feelings when she'd discussed the question with him. He'd married her when he'd been thirtyfour and she'd been seventeen, and she liked to say to him he'd not precisely cut a dashing figure while he'd courted her, and she told him his suits had been rumpled too often, and his cravats had been askew too often, and his hats usually had been a bit too spotted from carelessly cruel attacks by the elements and perhaps even certain incontinent beaked and feathered creatures swooping and gliding up yonder in the heavenly cerulean blue, but then she invariably told him it was her opinion he was the kindest and the most generous and the most, well, *energetic* man she ever would know or ever goodness sakes' alive would *want* to know, and wasn't it just too awful mighty fine the way so many things worked out if a person just was smart enough to concentrate on pursuing the happy side of life? And of course he always sighed whenever Lenore spoke that way. And sometimes he would kiss her chin or allow one of his arms to brush her across her breasts. And she, the mother of his four children who'd never even been alive at their very goddamn *birth*, would blink wetly at him and tell him she never would be able to understand why she was so just plain lucky, don't you know. And she would try to say something about the dead babies, but invariably he would order her to be quiet, and he would lick and nip her ears and stroke her hair and do whatever else was necessary in order that she be distracted from her grief and what she saw as her shame. For years he tried to tell her there was no shame involved, but she didn't believe him, and she kept taking babyclothes from the cedarchest and touching the lacy hems of the babyclothes and pressing the babyclothes to her face and murmuring sad lost astonished words having to do with Death and Mysteries and all that sort of thing. Ah, such turmoil the human race was forced to pass through, and he never really had been prepared for it—until Lenore lost her four babies, and of course until this fucking stupid war began. But now he was well and forever blooded, and among other things he'd learned that interior lines weren't quite all they'd been cracked up to be, and it was not good for a man to lose his command because of time and exhaustion and his own lack of intelligence. The interior lines fiasco hadn't been his only miscalculation. No indeed. He had no taste or talent for this sort of thing, and why had so many goddamn windbag fartass *words* so abruptly taken hold of him? why his long speeches to these men who'd chosen him to command them, a request he couldn't reject, since maybe this time he'd have a chance to save lives instead of witlessly squandering them? why his dreary speech to his mother who wasn't there? why all the bleak thoughts that marched across his brain like an army with banners and cannon and wagons and muletrains and earnest bearded polysyllabic general officers? what had happened to the darkly taciturn General Jack Boom, the cavalryman nonpareil? And now this same General Jack Boom was shuddering, and he dusted off his top hat, picked it up and jammed it down over his ears. He supposed he was the biggest ninny this side of the Congress of the Confederate States of America. He shook his head, and he damn near laughed.)

BOOM

Now the sun was orange and relentless in the east, and it was time for all of them to be up and on their way, and to hell with these memories and speculations and gaunt haunting terrors. So he awakened the men, and they grumbled and hawked, but within an hour they indeed were on their way, and the first thing they did was enter what there was of Boxerville, which consisted of twelve empty houses and an empty general store and an empty Baptist church. The village was full of hollow banging doors, and the little Baptist church's belltower swarmed and sang with swooping nesting birds all full of themselves and proud of themselves, arguing and singing and in general *proclaiming* their existence in a universe that didn't necessarily give much of a damn about them or their songs or their nests or their eggs or their babies or much of anything else, and this place, this fabled and legendary Boxerville with its disuptatious birds and its broken windows and its goddamn hollow banging doors, appeared to have been abandoned months earlier, its residents dispersed by the fighting. No doubt all sorts of armies and outlaws and refugees and fleeing politicians had passed through Boxerville, and Boom was reasonably certain the village already had been thoroughly looted. At the same time, though, a person just never knew—and so Boom told the fellers they'd better search all these buildings, just in case. None of them argued with him about that (you just never knew, e&c, e&c), and they scurried away from him like anxious badgers or alleycats, clodhoppering into the empty buildings and in general finishing them off as far as destruction was concerned. Their search went on for an hour or so, and they tore away shelving, and they poked and dug in cellars, and they even leveled a number of walls, and it was little Petrie who found two tiny tins of sardines that had fallen behind a counter in the general store. He of course whooped for joy. Then, not more than ten minutes later, he found several boxes of rifles and amunition (both cartridges and powder) sitting in an abandoned wagon at the far edge of the village. A dead horse, still in it traces, lay in front of the wagon. The dead horse stank. It had been partially chewed to shreds in the belly and groin by wild animals . . . bears maybe, or dogs. Boom and the others wrapped their faces in rags and opened the boxes. Now everyone had rifles, and all the skeletons stuffed their pockets with ammunition. Boom got to smiling, and he said to himself: God damn it, maybe I love this. Later, as he walked along, he got to thinking of his Lenore's still remarkably firm breasts, and he thought of Lenore's breasts and thought of Lenore's breasts and thought of Lenore's breasts.

LLEWELLYN

Saturday, April 8, 1865.

He hobbled rather than walked, and every so often his legs gave way and he collapsed to the earth, scraping his shins and his knees and his face and at the same time uttering indignant cries that damn near were girlish. He kept telling himself he would rip at air Boom apart like some damn old stinkin dead chicken if he ever saw the sonofabitch again, him an his top hat an all his fuckin windbag *words*. Ah, shit, how Llewellyn did mutter and growl as he moved along, and how Llewellyn did wince and squeal as his sore ribs and his bruised face and arms and chest sent angry little shoots and splotches of pain through him, as he grimaced, as he spat, as he lurched from side to side and kept telling himself God wasn't no more an a Piece of Shit. He wondered whether God ever would receive His deserved comeuppance. He hoped so, and maybe God could take Boom and even the despised Oswald G. Averill along with Him—to Hell or wharever—when that glorious day arrived. Oh, the fact was that right then the one and the only John T. Llewellyn was occupying a great deal of his mind with visions and speculations having to do with good old Hell. He staggered along in he didn't know which direction, and he flopped down in ditches or abandoned barns or roofless farmhouses and sheds and tried to sleep whenever his bruises gave him too much distress, and from time to time he wearily munched on pieces of hardtack that had been in his pockets when that crazy fucker Boom had put him to rout, and sometimes his jaws were too stunned and heavy to let him do much more than move the bits of hardtack around with his tongue and soften them with his saliva before swallowing them more or less intact and hearing his belly wetly protest. He dreamed of Lucy, of course . . . and he dreamed of Oswald G. Averill, of course. The treasonous bitch and the unscrupulous Yankee. They danced naked in front of him, and Oswald G. Averill cheerily patted Lucy's cunt and allowed as how the meat was sweetest the closest to the bone, ha ha, and how come you were so almighty stupid as far as she was concerned, Llewellyn old man?

It all was enough to make John T. want to kick down the sky, and he twitched and threshed in his sleep, and his hands kept making huge fishbelly fists.

O, he had been too good to her, too kind and too decent, and surely that was the truth. So why had she run off? To be accurate about it, why had she run off with such a one as a *Yankee?* Especially a Yankee who was a fuckin *schoolteacher*, don't you know. John T. never had figured out the answer to that one, and he didn't suppose he ever would. Why had Lucy gone so earnestly out of her way to humiliate *him?* What the hell had *he* ever done? The thing was, he was a reasonable man, and if she'd only *spoken* to him, if she'd only been *straight* with him, why, everything no doubt would have been just fine, and the two of them would have continued their happy life, and in later years they no doubt would have joked about their troubles. But no, all she did was leave him that nasty note

(You are not a nice man & I rejoice in my freedom)

and then flee with that sonofabitch like a thief in the night—and never mind the fact that the two of them left Harrisonburg at the shank of a clear and sunny day with the whole town bearing witness to their treachery almost as though they were *proud* of what they were doing. Oh, life could be so fuckin heavy and grim, an what was a man to almighty *do?* Ha. How sad. How tragic. Shit. Why had the one and the only John T. Llewellyn been singled out for such unfair punishment? What the hell had *he* ever done? This was the one question that kept hammering and stuttering across his mind year after year, no matter how earnestly he tried to forget. The Bitch and her fuckin Yankee goddamn Friend, and all the beer in God's Kingdom, all the whisky and all the gin, couldn't wash away the shame of John T. Llewellyn.

At the time of Lucy's betrayal, back then in 1859, it seemed that all the heavens and all the elements and all the Imps of Satan were conspiring against him. Less than a week after coming home to learn his wife had deserted him, John T. awoke one morning itching like billybedamned, with several hundred—or maybe several thousand—tiny villainous companions dug into his belly and his crotch, thanks to his little redhaired friend Minnie Bumpers, whose ass he promptly decided he would nail to the nearest outhouse wall if he ever again saw her. So then the crabs, and he had to pay three dollars to a sniggering old doctor named McAlpine who treated his lesions and got rid of the little critters with various liquids and ointments the names of which John T. did not catch. Dr McAlpine pointed out to John T. that he (John T.) surely was running in a lot of bad luck, what with losing a beloved sister (poor dead Edith, up there in Harpers Ferry) and coming down with the crabs more or less at the same time as his (John T.'s) wife skedaddled with that goddamn Yankee school-teacher. A man just can't never know what catastrophe'll strike him next, isn't at so? said Dr McAlpine, rubbing his mouth and from time to time turning away from John T. and hunching his shoulders and thinly expelling his breath.

And John T. said to the old fart: You think it's all *funny?*

And (still hunching and shaking) the old fart said to John T. in a dry and bemused and almost farmerish voice: Yessir. At I do. You just better believe it.

And the thing was, the old fart's amusement was shared by just about everyone in Harrisonburg who knew Lucy had left John T. with the tall bearded schoolteacher who sat a horse so well and stole another man's wife at the drop of a pair of bloomers, a person might say. Tongues whirred, a person might say. Teeth clicked, and spittle was sucked and dredged and swallowed, a person might say. People actually laughed at John T. on the street, and children pointed at him and made rude yipping sounds, and a few niggers even, well, smiled at him. By the middle of November he'd had enough. He drank to forget what Lucy

(you are not a nice man you are not a nice man)

had done to him, and then he drank so he would be forceful and articulate enough to tell barroom strangers what had happened to him (of course leaving out the part having to do with fiery little Minnie Bumpers and the goddamn crabs she'd given him—as though maybe she believed he was fixing to celebrate a birthday), and his money ran low, what with the fact that he no longer had his postoffice job and he'd never really been renowned for his skill at saving money, and he barely had enough to eat, and he owed several saloonkeepers a sum in excess of one hundred fifty dollars, and so one crisp gray morning he visited the shabby spotted spittooned office of an attorney named Abner (Baldy) Leach, a longtime practicing rip and skillful drinking companion whose skull was so hairless it glowed like a beacon on a stormy night, and he sold his house and its furniture, bedclothes, cutlery, dishes and all its other traps and truck and accouterments and clutter to this Abner (Baldy) Leach for the vast sum of three hundred dollars, of which one hundred sixtyeight dollars and twelve cents went to pay his saloon debts. He gathered the remaining one hundred thirtyone dollars and eightyeight cents and that night spent more than seventeen dollars taking Abner (Baldy) Leach out drinking, and the two of them exchanged heated windy oaths of rascally and laughably spurious fidelity, and they grinned and honked all the while, and John T. accused Abner (Baldy) Leach of not being worth the powder to blow him up, and Abner (Baldy) Leach belched and said in an appropriately reverberant and lawyerish voice: You ought to know, my dear friend.

So did these noble companions part, and the next morning John T. bought for four dollars a swaybacked old fartbucket of a gray mare, saddled her up and left Harrisonburg, heading north and east up the Shenandoah Valley back to Harpers Ferry. It was his plan to find a job with his brothers' help . . . and maybe the help of his bilious and intemperate former brotherinlaw, Horace Bevens, the storekeeper and sometime undertaker. The journey up to Harpers Ferry took three days, and this time John T. found no Minnie Bumpers along the way, which may have been just as well, considering (ha! ha!) her crawly and abundantly itchy vale-dictory gift to him. His old gray mare (he'd named her The Wreck of the Hesperis) collapsed and died, probably of heart failure, about a mile and a half west of Harpers Ferry. Her forelegs gave way, and she pitched John T. forward, and he landed on his tailbone, and he hollered and flailed, and The Wreck of the Hesperis seated herself in the middle of the road, front to rear, with a sort of spindly slatted dignity, like a sinking steamboat perhaps, then gave a final exhausted nicker, rolled over, made a puddle of loose shit and went about the business of dying. John T. removed her saddle and left her there in the middle of the road. Hell, what else was he to do? Toting the saddle and a suitcase, he trudged the final mile and a half into Harpers Ferry, and he never told a soul he'd been the old shitbag's rider. Why, hell, for all he knew, he'd broken some sort of law having to do with public health and decency, and he already had enough troubles, which meant he didn't want to have to answer for the death of a fuckin *horse*. He walked to O. O. Oldham's saloon, and it was open, and it had only three customers, and of course those three customers were his brothers Fred and Charley and the famous pukey Harold St Xavier, enemy of all clean floors and scourge of all those who fancied themselves as having delicate sensibilities. None of those fellers knew of Lucy's defection, and John T. put away seven pints of beer, then blurted out the information, telling his brothers and Harold St Xavier and old O. O. he couldn't understand what he'd ever *done*.

(I rejoice in my freedom I rejoice I rejoice)

John T. wept. He embraced his brothers. He embraced old O. O. He even embraced a somewhat uneasy and greenish Harold St Xavier. He told them he really *was* a nice man, and he allowed as how anyone who believed different could go fuck a goddamn water moccasin. Then he shook his head and shuddered and told the others he needed to change the goddamn subject. He said he wanted to talk about that Abolitionist sonofabitch of a Captain Brown, the mad insurrectionist (whose Christian name also was John, God damn it all). He said he'd followed the John Brown trial in the newspapers, and he predicted it now was only a matter of time before the nation would be torn apart by what people were saying would be known as a civil war—and about time, too. He said the issue of niggers and slavery needed to be settled for once and for all. He said the South surely would win, since it had justice and the law on its side. He tugged his lower lip and tried to behave in a properly thoughtful manner, tried to make himself as wise and judicious as the day was long, and he said he suregod felt sorry for all the good men who probably would be kilt in the inevitable fighting, but if a man didn't stand up for principles, what sort of man was he? Oh, this John T. Llewellyn, surely the one and the only, surely a great and splendid fellow whose mind had the power to extinguish the sun and curl up the sky and cause rivers to evaporate, had a fine and certain way of getting to the heart of a knotty situation, and he figured many were the lesser men who surely envied him. And he pounded the bar and bought drink after drink for these here boys (as well as old O. O.), and she his Lucy his love & his inspiration & the light of his wretched days was gone & probably forever, & what had he ever done done *done?* As long as principles were the subject of the evening, surely the question became—why hadn't she allowed herself to develop some principles of her own? What was it about women, anyway? If they didn't betray a man with their goddamn affairs of their goddamn hearts, they betrayed a man with their fiercely masticating sonofabitching crabs (which old Dr McAlpine had called lice, and fuck *him*.) Oh, a man's pursuit of his destiny wasn't easy, was it, boys (you too, old O. O.)? Oh, shit, piss & corruption, a good war would be a refreshing diversion, wouldn't it? It surely would clear the air, wasn't that so? Yes. A good war, with issues that could be grasped and kneaded and thrown to the earth like mud and manure and old dead guts and goddamn *understood.* Ah, the flourishing beauty of it all . . .

John T. went home that night with Fred and Charley, and he dreamed of The Wreck of the Hesperis, and he actually breathed her dead shit in his damn dream, and her eyes were bloody, and she leaked purplish saliva, and finally he awoke with a great stabbing boner making a mound in the sheets, and he was forced to diddle and stroke the boner and pat and flick his bulging balls until he made a mess in his palms and had to go outside to the pump and wash himself in wellwater that was so cold it made him dance and wobble and exhale and even shriek a little.

The next morning was a Monday, and Fred and Charley tried to talk John T. into walking to the North Virginia Grain & Feed Co mill with them. He remembered Max Aswell, the mill foreman and militia officer, didn't he? Well, Fred and Charley were kind of thick with old Max Aswell (that is to say, each week old Max Aswell allowed them to buy him a good number of drinks), and they figured they wouldn't have too much trouble finagling a job for their poor little puny baby brother, ha ha. John T. supposed he had some sort of obligation to smile at his brothers' humor, but right then his head hurt too intensely, which meant he had no goddamn strength for smiling. So he lay around for a couple of days, and he barely was able to gather the strength to walk downstreet to old O. O.'s saloon and lift a few in order to wash the dust from his mouth, ha ha and *ha*.

A few days later several wagonloads of men journeyed to Charles Town, which was several hours' drive from Harpers Ferry, and stood in that town's public square and gave witness to the hanging of John Brown. The man sat on his coffin as he was taken in a wagon for his appointment with the hangman, and John T. kept waiting for the miserable niggerloving Abolitionist sonofabitch to swoon, weep, scream for mercy, wet his britches, drop to his knees and bellow his fear and remorse. But none of those things happened. The contemptible John Brown sat erectly, and he glanced around—apparently at the sky and the surrounding mountains—and he was heard to say that it was a beautiful country. John T. was standing close enough so that he was able to make out the old Abolitionist fucker's words, and he wanted to spit on the old Abolitionist fucker, but nothing was in his mouth except feathers and eiderdown. A few minutes later John Brown was dead, and John T. and his brothers and the rest of the fellers who'd come over from Harpers Ferry gave a cheer, but the sound of their cheering wasn't all that loud, and for some reason the one and the only John T. Llewellyn briefly needed to look away . . . at the mountains and the sky, at the brown and gray December trees, at his own hands, his knuckles, the split places in his fingernails. A few minutes later he and his companions repaired to the nearest saloon and got down to a lot of solemn drinking. But the thing was, John T. didn't *feel* particularly solemn. The way he saw the situation, this business of John Brown and Harpers Ferry and now the hanging of John Brown was the first battle of the war that was bound to come, and he licked the roof of his mouth, and now the feathers and the eiderdown were gone, and he tasted syrupy liquids, and they had a flavor of brass. He drank beer. He drank whisky. Back & forth. Beer & whisky. Whisky & beer.

There were several fistfights that day there in that saloon in Charles Town, since not all its customers believed John Brown had been a villain, and Yankee sentiment was stronger than a person might have expected, and John T. gave a hard drunken foggy thrashing to a wiry little fellow who had quick fists and wore a derby and gave a good account of himself, delivering a cluster of snappy and punishing blows to John T.'s belly and his balls before finally collapsing bloody and unconscious to the saloon's floor, there to receive a number of kicks from John T., kicks that caused the wiry little fellow's friends to jump astride John T. and kick him and whack him on his head and his arms and his shoulders and pound him down to that same floor, where those cowardly bastards smashed him across the face and the neck and made him gag and puke. Ah, ah, the joys and fruits of political disputation. For several hours John T. really didn't know where he was, not until he somehow had been bundled back aboard the wagon and was rocking and flopping from side to side as it bumped and creaked its way back to Harpers Ferry and loud gray remorseless winds were tearing at his flesh and his lungs and sobering him up whether he wanted to be sobered up or not. He managed to make fists and grin into the night. He was remembering the sight of John Brown sitting on the coffin that had been provided courtesy of the government of the United States of America. The coffin had been nothing more than an unadorned box, farmerish and without color, and it appeared to have been hastily hammered together by people who didn't particularly give a damn about its contents. Ah, ah, such a grand and perfect coffin it had been . . . a shitbox for a shitbox lunatic whose politics and whose morality were themselves nothing but shit. John T. supposed he would remember that homely and probably downright ugly coffin all his life, and in point of fact he did.

Three days later he went to work loading boxcars with bags of grain at the North Virginia Grain & Feed Co mill, and the good old sweaty heavy exertion stretched and toughened his muscles and—perversely—helped him get rid of his aches and bruises. He and his brothers lived in two rooms over a harness and hardware store there in Harpers Ferry. The rooms were ratty and cluttered, and every so often John T. would get to hollering at his brothers for living in a fuckin pigpen, but all they did was grin at him and tell him why, shucks air, little brother, it's your pigpen too, you know, an you surely got our permission to take soap an a broom an a mop to it whenever you're of a mind, by God. This sort of thing almost always enraged John T. so deeply that he would go storming off to old O. O.'s place and get to drinking with such a thirst a person would have thought he'd swallowed a railroad engine . . . boiler and smoke and sparking flanged wheels and all. Usually Fred and Charley came after him, and they bought him drinks, and everybody apologized to everybody else, and usually they lifted toasts to poor dead Edith, their sweet and sainted late sister, and usually these toasts led them to weep, to rub their eyes and sniffle and speak of brotherhood and loyalty and John T. didn't quite remember what all else.

He and Fred and Charley didn't have much to do with Edith's widowed husband, the testy and liverish Horace Bevens, and they weren't any of them invited to the ceremony in January of 1860 when old crabby Horace took unto himself a girl named Millie Baggott as his second wife. John T. had heard of this Millie Baggott, and it was said she was something of a little redhot pepper when it came to haylofts and grassy nooks and warm mattresses, but he didn't set eyes on her until about a month after her marriage to Horace, when he and Fred and Charley stopped at Horace's place to go through a box of Edith's personal papers that Horace didn't have any use for—which of course meant they didn't have a smidge of monetary value, seein as how otherwise at greedy fucker of a Horace Bevens would of made off with em, an a feller could wager his ass an his nuts an his very life on *at*, o yes *sir*. Millie Baggot Bevens was baking bread in the kitchen when the Llewellyn brothers arrived, and John T. took one look at her and promptly began digging at his crotch with curved fingers. She had red hair, and her smile was saucy and brilliant, and he'd known her under the name of Minnie Bumpers. She actually staggered a little when she came into the front room and saw him, and old Horace reached for her and asked her was she havin a faintin spell an was she maybe in the fambly way, you expect so, my darlin? Millie/Minnie Baggot/Bumpers Bevens managed to smile at her anxious husband, and she managed to shrug and say well, one way or tuther, the Lord will provide, won't He, dear Horace? She shot narrow anxious little glances at John T., but all he did was smile comfortably as though he were the greatest and most steadfast friend she ever would have in this or any other world. He kept making benevolent sounds in his belly, and at one point he called her Sister Minnie, but then he sniggered and corrected himself, calling her Sister *Millie*, while at the same time explaining to the others that he'd once known a girl named Minnie, you see, and this Minnie hadn't been quite as good as she should of been, you see—but, well, the world had a need for girls who weren't as good as they should be, wasn't at so, ha ha? There was general laughter . . . from John T. and his brothers, that is to say. Characteristically, the miserable Horace Bevens did no more than frown, and of course Minnie/Millie was unable to do much more than make distracted little movements with her hands and absently pound her palms together, sending off aimless little screens of flour.

John T. and his brothers stayed on at the Bevens place for something like three or four hours, and Horace Bevens had Minnie/Millie feed their guests little ham sandwiches using her homemade bread, and the sandwiches were tasty, and John T. in particular made a fuss over them and told Horace Bevens what a lucky man he (Horace Bevens) was, and wasn't he (Horace Bevens) fortunate to have found such a pretty and gifted new wife to take the place of poor old Edith, who no doubt was looking fondly down from

Heaven and blessing this new and fortuitous union? The next morning John T. rolled and groaned in his bed, and he regretfully told Fred and Charley he was too ill to go to work. He managed a brave little smile and said something to the effect that old Horace's new wife maybe had poisoned him with her goddamn fresh bread and all. But then he turned down the corners of his lips and exhaled in a sort of a deprecatory puhhh. He waved a hand and said he was only funning, but at the same time he told Fred and Charley to skedaddle, to go on to work and give his regrets to the boss, old Max Aswell. Fred and Charley shrugged, nodded, then left for work, and a moment or so later John T. was out of bed and pulling on his britches. Ten minutes later he was walking toward the Bevens place, and his hands were in loose anticipatory fists, and his breath came in easy wavy wintry jets, and his step was heavy as torture and plague and vengeance. He walked into the Bevens kitchen without bothering to knock on the back door. He found his fair and wondrously sweet Minnie/Millie dusting a rockingchair in the front room. She looked up at him and started to scream, but he cracked her across the jaw, and that was the end of that. Her dustcloth went fluttering from her hands, and she sat down in the middle of the floor. He kicked her across the chest and the belly and the throat, and he smiled, and she tried to cover herself, but he kept bending over her and pulling her arms away from her thin little body, and of course he kept smiling, and he was grateful to her for giving him the opportunity to vent himself this way. He hadn't had so much real enjoyment since he didn't know when. He knocked her bloody and unconscious, and then he went out back and pumped the pump and filled himself a pail of good old cold wellwater. He carried the pail of good old cold wellwater into the house and marched briskly into the front room and poured it over his beautiful Minnie/Millie. She sat up, and again she started to scream, and this time he broke her jaw and caused her mouth and nose to bleed. Now she wasn't quite so beautiful, and his very goddamn bones clapped and clicked with the good old holy joy he felt. Now she rocked from side to side, and her eyes had drowned, and he squatted next to her and began speaking to her, and his voice was lazy and maybe even slurred, and he told her of the crabs she'd bestrowed on him, and he used his thumbs to spread blood across her mouth and her cheeks, and he even forced blood back into her nostrils, and he even squeezed and lightly tapped her broken jaw, and she made a number of fragile yipping sounds, and he smiled, and he slapped her, and he told her she ought to be grateful; he told her he figured she'd from now on be a whole lot more peaceful; he told her he figured she'd from now on be a better wife for old Horace Bevens, that prince among men; he asked her whether she'd given her fuckin crabs to old Horace; he asked her whether old Horace had eaten her pussy and thus maybe had gulped down a mouthful or two of the little buggers; he laughed, and he ripped open the front of her dress, and he slapped her tits, and he said this was maybe more fun than the slaughtering of hogs, or the cutting off of a stallion's nuts. He told her he supposed she'd have to do some fancy explaining to old Horace. He bent over her and grimaced and showed his teeth and nippled her nipples until they bled. She screamed through her blood, but her jaw wobbled, and so the scream didn't amount to a whole lot. Then, whistling, grinning, snapping his fingers, he straightened up, gave Minnie/Millie a number of tight happy farewell kicks and left that place. His sister had died in this house, and Horace Bevens had spoken anxiously of the undertaking business in this house, and John T. Llewellyn, the incomparable John T. Llewellyn, this John T. Llewellyn of the implacable fists and the enormous wrath and the efficient vengeance, gave himself a number of warmly sweet and comforting hugs.

He walked back to the rooms he shared with his bothers. He lay down, and he shuddered, and then he opened his britches and pulled his pudding for a faretheewell, and he gasped and grimaced and laughed, and he squeezed his prick as though it were a plump plum. He smiled. He shook and threshed as he released his wad, which was tough and quick. He smiled. He even laughed. This had been just, and it had been perfect, and for once in his life he felt no need to celebrate his good fortune with a lot of loud drunkenness. He never did learn what happened when Horace Bevens came home that afternoon. According to Fred and Charley, Horace was telling people his bride had fallen down the stairs, and Fred and Charley said Horace looked as though he'd lost his best friend—provided, of course, the goddamn old sonofabitch ever had *had* a best friend. Minnie/Millie stayed on with old Horace for about six months, and then one night she went out back, ostensibly to visit the privy, and she never returned. Old Horace was desolate, and he even hired an inquiry agent from Baltimore to try to find her, and a great deal of correspondence was exchanged, but Minnie/Millie Bumpers/Baggott Bevens never was seen again, and in March of 1861 old Horace Bevens sawed the lumber and then hammered out a fine plushlined coffin (the plush was purple, and the coffin had a pillow that was made of a nice matching yellow plush . . . with tassels) and put on his most elegantly black and dignified suit and lay down in the coffin and jammed a pistol into his mouth and blew away a good part of his skull, making a considerable mess on the plush.

By that time, though, John T. had returned to Harrisonburg, and so he received all his information on old Horace's death in a number of letters from Fred and Charley. Actually, since Charley barely knew how to write his goddamn name, Fred did all the writing, and he said there'd been quite a turnout for Horace's funeral, and he said the people in charge had done a fine job cleaning the blood from Horace's fine plushlined coffin, and he said it surely had been a shame Horace never had learned what had happened to Minnie/Millie. Wrote Fred:

> Horace nevar wazz the saim you know. At the end he wazznt even to mean & nasty & I achualley seen him smile oncet in a wile. Whitch sureley wazznt like our Horace now wazz it????? Oh ha ha what lifes we leed. Do you wonder like I do what hapened to at litle wife of his????? Dear Jesis wear all mizzerabel siners aint at so????

John T. figured he should have been amused by Horace's way of dying, just as he figured he and Minnie/Millie were the only two human beings on earth who knew why she'd been beaten up and why she'd finally sneaked out of Harpers Ferry like a fucking nigger thief scuttering along in the dark while toting a burlap bag full of bemused murmurous chickens. This image sort of made John T. smile a little, but not a whole lot. In those days, he wasn't much for smiling. He didn't really know why he'd returned to Harrisonburg. Oh, he knew why he'd left Harpers Ferry, but the two things weren't the same. He'd left Harpers Ferry because he hadn't much liked loading boxcars with endless bags of grain, and he hadn't much liked the fact that Harpers Ferry didn't exactly abound with hotly liquid whores and anxious maidenladies and unsatisfied wives, and he'd become weary unto the sonofabitching *death* with his brothers and the pukey Harold St Xavier and the boring old O. O. Oldham and their barroom talk and their barroom dreams and the sawdust stink of them. So he'd finally shut Harpers Ferry from his life, and fair enough. After all, he was a warmblooded bucko whose tastes were a bit too quick for such a place as Harpers Ferry, and fair enough indeed—but why the hell had he returned to *Harrisonburg*, of all places, which wasn't exactly the Pit and the Sinkhole of the universe, now was it? Did his return have something to do with Lucy and her treachery? Maybe so, and God damn her anyway. And God damn Oswald G. Averill. And, for that matter, and as long as the goddamns were being passed around, God *double* damn Oswald G. Averill's goddamn *horse*—Prosperity, the gleaming black gelding that reportedly had carried both Oswald G. Averill and Lucy off for parts unknown while her poor trusting clodhopping husband had been paying an innocent visit to his saintly sick sister. Why was there so little justice or even simple fairness in the world? What should John T. have done with that woman? Should he have

you are not a nice man & I rejoice in my freedom

chained her to a tree? Well, he supposed he'd been stupid. He not only should have chained Lucy to a tree; he should have flogged her with a goddamn whisking whistling blacksnake whip, and he should have by God kicked her in the belly. Shit, the trouble with him was he was too sentimental, and he'd been altogether too willing to give that woman the benefit of the doubt. So all he really did was mope around Harrisonburg, doing yard work and other odd jobs and occasionally lending himself to some serious barroom drinking with his friend Abner (Baldy) Leach the lawyer, who tried to tell him what the hell, John old friend, the planet keeps revolvin away, an the sun keeps risin in the east, an a pussy an a boner go together like cheese an crackers with maybe a little homemade butter, an the next boner you get is likely to be like the last boner you had, an pussy is like at too, wouldn't you say? All more or less alive, isn't at so? You take your average pussy an you turn out all the lights an you go sniffin an grabbin an kind of get your fingers wet, haw haw, an can you tell at average pussy from Queen pussy or Princess pussy or whorehouse pussy or even pussy from one of em Catholic convents where the women wear peculiar dresses an moan an mumble all the time air prayers or whatnot? Shit. I don't expect I have to tell you the answer, do I? Not *you*. Not good old John T. Llewellyn, the scourge an the terror of the Shenandoah Valley. No *sir*. So be of good cheer, boy. Like the feller said, it's always darkest before the dawn. Either at, or you're dead, you hear me? Haw. (I really can be a sketch when I'm of a mind, wouldn't you say?)

And John T. almost always made it a point at least to smile when Abner (Baldy) Leach got to talking along those lines. That way, Abner (Baldy) Leach usually would buy him a fresh drink, and this was important, seeing as how the next day, likely as not, John T. was trimming hedges for some rich sonofabitch who paid him maybe seventyfive cents a day, or he was cleaning some widow's fuckin cistern for maybe half a dollar, or he was sweeping and mopping the floor of some Baptist church or Masonic hall for maybe a whole entire big fat dollar, and he knew for a fact that there were free niggers who made more money for the same sort of work, but then—praise God! praise Him in His eternal Kingdom! praise Him with stringed instruments and organs and upon the loud cymbals!—the war finally came along, and quickly he joined a company of volunteers that marched east toward Manassas.

It was July of '61, and the talk was that a federal force commanded by a general named McDowell was headed straight for them and had every intention of putting down what the Yankee politicians and press said was nothing more than a stupid jackleg little rebellion. John T. Llewellyn marched with a persistent grin pasted across his face, and from time to time he and the other fellers waved at farmers and their wives and especially their

daughters who would gather behind fences and applaud and holler, and several times John T. actually went so far as to gather
wildflowers for the farmers' daughters and bestow little bouquets
on them with a heavy bow and a warm and he hoped absolutely
annihilating smile. The battle turned out to be a good one, even
though he actually didn't have much of an idea what was happening. He saw a place called the Henry House, and someone said a
Mrs R. E. Lee, wife of the man who'd commanded the federal
troops against John Brown at Harpers Ferry in '59, was held there
as a prisoner of old McDowell, but he only saw that Henry House
in passing, since he and his company and the whole goddamn
regiment was rushing to reinforce some boys who'd somehow
gotten themselves enfiladed by a battery of Yankee artillery, which
gleamed blackly in the wildflower sun that July afternoon as they
all hoofed and huffed from pillar to post and back again, and he
saw the Turnpike, and he saw Bull Run, and he saw Chinn
Ridge, and some of the other fellers kept hollering at him to
hunker down, since he was so fuckin big an all, and he grinned at
them and stood up straight and made fists and waved his arms and
hollered at the sun, and by the end of the afternoon there was a
godawful crush and commotion, all dusted and smeared with
confusion, with death, with a flat peremptory sound of artillery
and riflefire, with the shrieks of riderless wounded horses streak-
ing and wildly lurching across the sweetly violated Manassas
pastures and cornfields and the little farm roads while leaking
ropes and clots of blood from their sides and their bellies and their
necks, and late in the afternoon the one and the only John T.
Llewellyn killed himself a sweet little old Yankee boy he found
hiding and whimpering under an overturned ordnance wagon.
The sweet little old Yankee boy had sandy hair and sweaty
fishbelly wrists, and he didn't appear to be more than seventeen
or so, and he'd curled himself into a skinny whimpering ball down
there under that overturned ordnance wagon. John T. stood grinning down at the boy, and the boy covered his head (he was
hatless, and his hair was long, and he kept digging at his scalp
with frightened fingers that moved like worms), and John T.
carefully squatted next to the little sonofabitch, and the little
sonofabitch howled, and John T. had an image of John Brown

and a certain wagon and a certain coffin and a certain gallows, and the little sonofabitch rolled over on his back, and the little sonofabitch's legs twitched, and he'd already made a shy little boyish mess in his britches, and John T. had an image of the corpse of The Wreck of the Hesperis; he had an image of the bloody and demolished Minnie/Millie, and all his images came quickly, and they all were colorful and ennobling and abrupt, and he jammed the muzzle of his rifle against the little sonofabitch's wet and miserable neck and pressed the trigger and promptly was drenched in blood and hot liquefied brains and bone. His rifle had a kick that knocked him back, and he fell on his ass, and he grimaced, and he was aware of blood spreading across his eyes and his teeth.

(You are not a nice man you are not a nice man o & that is the truth & I should have left you the mornin after we were married you loud & vulgar pig)

It wasn't until maybe noon the next day that the rebel forces really believed they'd won the battle. Until then, everyone more or less had become lost in all the dust and swelter, and John T. for one had believed the whole goddamn situation had been nothing less than a goddamn mess. All the running back and forth and up and down . . . all the shouting . . . all the explosions, the brandishing of flags and banners, all the hollering that came from the engorged throats of urgent officers, all the shrieks of dying horses and dying men, the bleats and howls of the thousands of fleeing Yankees who'd skedaddled across the torn and gutted landscape as though The Old Nick himself were pursuing them . . . the whole fucking *thing* had put John T. in mind of nothing less than sheep desperately stumbling back and forth and banging themselves against fences as they tried to escape some farmer's implacable and merciless ax that already was all slopped and caked with blood and already was matted with hair and crimson bits of sheepflesh. Yah, such a business. Such blind and craven foolishness. It all was enough to make a real man's eyes roll upward in shame and disgust, and John T. Llewellyn for one surely was ashamed of the human race.

149

He passed through the fights that came to be known as Second Manassas and Sharpsburg and Fredericksburg and Chancellorsville and Gettysburg, and he went slogging and slugging across The Wilderness as the Army of Northern Virginia fought on the same violated ground where it already had fought the Chancellorsville fight that had cost it the hard mad brave brilliant T. J. (Stonewall) Jackson, and John T. Llewellyn for one told himself he always would think of that fight as the Battle of the Skeletons. And then John T. Llewellyn made his stand in the Petersburg trenches, and he'd begun hearing talk that the war was lost, and why didn't the generals and politicians face the truth of the situation? John T. Llewellyn didn't listen to that sort of talk. He more or less had kept to himself through the four years of the war, and he was grateful to God Almighty for giving him the strength not to need that overrated commodity known as companionship. He'd tried companionship and had found it wanting. After all, hadn't he expected companionship from that bitch on buttered toast he'd once called his wife? Well, now he knew better, didn't he? And he told himself the best thing he could do was take fuckin *advantage* of this here war and root out Yankees for the goddamn killin. He no longer was interested in wildflowers, and he no longer remembered how to laugh, and God save anyone who tried to touch him. He had hotly sanguinary dreams having to do with The Wreck of the Hesperis, and he kept seeing a tall old unrepentant bearded man sitting on a coffin. The other men in his company every so often went home for plantings and harvests, but the one and the only John T. Llewellyn didn't bother with any of that sorry shit. In his view, a true soldier was a soldier *all the time*, and a true soldier didn't go gallivanting off to work on his crops twice a year as though he was some homesick nigger fieldhand, and anyway, what the hell did he have to go home *to*? He had no wife, and he had no home, and in the spring of 1863 he learned he had no brothers either.

His company was bivouacked near a Virginia & Atlantic railroad bridge over a creek south of Fredericksburg, and a train stopped to take on firewood, and who should step off the train to stretch his legs but Harold St Xavier, the famous puker of Harpers Ferry song and legend, and he was wearing nothing less than lieutenant's bars, and he just about swallowed his back teeth when he saw John T. come lurching toward him. He reached out to shake John T.'s hand, but John T. wasn't bothering with that sort of polite shit. He no longer had the time for polite shit. He asked Harold St Xavier straight out whether he (Harold St Xavier) knew what had happened to Fred and Charley. I ain't heard nothin from em since this here war done began, said Jonn T., an I expect maybe at's a little bit strange, don't you?

Said Harold St Xavier: I'm real sorry, but you tellin me you don't *know?*

Said John T.: Know what?

Said Harold St Xavier: I don't expect I want to be the one to tell you.

Said John T.: You listen here to me, Mister Big Important *Lieutenant*, I don't give a good goddamn what you *want*. You tell me what you *know*, you puley pukin sonofabitch, or I'll break your fuckin back for you. And John T. seized Harold St Xavier by the neck and lifted him high and then higher than high and shook him and buffeted him as though he were a small floppy puppy. Then John T. slammed Harold St Xavier to the earth, and Harold St Xavier fell down and rubbed his neck and began to speak. And Harold St Xavier spoke and spoke. And Harold St Xavier didn't much bother to pause for breath. He reported that Fred and Charley (and Ed Perkins too—did John T. remember Ed Perkins, who'd been at one time an engineer for the B&O back in Harpers Ferry?) had vanished shortly after the Sharpsburg battle back in September of '62. Oh, yes, Fred and Charley—and of course Ed Perkins, who'd been a member of the Harpers Ferry militia—had been serving in the Army of Northern Virginia ever since the beginning of the war (and it was a wonder John T. hadn't run into them after either or both of the two Manassas battles, but then the army was a mighty large animal, wasn't it?), but for some reason the Sharpsburg fight had been a mighty brutal one, hadn't it? Those Harpers Ferry fellers had taken part in the fighting at the goddamn Sunken Road, and apparently it had squeezed the starch out of John T.'s brothers and old Ed Perkins, and they'd simply walked away. And this was all Harold St Xavier knew, and John T. had his oath on that. Then there was a toot from the locomotive's whistle, and Harold St Xavier scrambled to his feet. John T. grimaced. He grabbed Harold St Xavier by the shoulders and spun him around and kicked him in the ass. Flailing, Harold St Xavier went lurching forward, and John T. called after him that he was a coward and a disgrace. Harold St Xavier neither stopped nor looked back. He simply ran for the train, which already was moving, and he grabbed hold of a daycoach platform and swung aboard. The train sparked and creaked, and couplings clattered, and there was another toot from the locomotive's whistle, and then the train lurched and grumbled off into the cloudless and exhausted wartime Virginia night, and John T. Llewellyn, unquestionably the one and the only, at least as far as John T. Llewellyn was concerned, seated himself at the edge of the creek and removed his boots (he wasn't barefoot in those days) and held his rifle against his chest and thought of Fred and Charley and said aloud: Fuck em. And he thought of Lucy and said aloud: Fuck *her*. And he went through the rest of his litany of hatreds, including Oswald G. Averill and Prosperity and the late The Wreck of the Hesperis and the late Horace Bevens and of course Minnie/Millie, the undisputed crab & lesion queen of the universe, and he said fuck *him*, an fuck *her*, an fuck *all of em*, an fuck air dogs an air kittycats an air hoops an air kites an air bicycles an air foot treadles an air dollbabies an air balloons an air little wooden trains. He saw Lucy that night in his dreams, and he saw Oswald G. Averill, and they both were smiling, and she said to John T:

> I rejoice in my Oswald's body, & he takes care of me better an you ever did, you foul & repulsive pig. He knows somethin bout compassion, & he's not afraid to weep in my presence, especially seein as how most of his weepin is joyous & free. We sit together in front of open fireplaces, & we share all the warmth, & we discuss God, & we do not laugh, nor do we scoff. We read poetry, & Shakespeare is a cause for joy & lovin humility, & o God damn you, John T. Llewellyn, such a vile villain you are, & are you pleased with what you did with at Yankee boy at day at Manassas? are you

pleased with all the other Yankees you've kilt? are you
pleased with your loudness & what you like to believe is
your bravery? O, I could feel sorry for you, but I just
don't seem to have the time, you piece of shit.

And of course John T. groaned in his sleep, and he embraced
his rifle, and in the morning he awoke with a boner, but it was
nothing more than a piss boner, so it didn't count for a damn. He
pissed into the creek, and later that morning he beat up on a feller
named Belknap because the stupid sonofabitch had expressed an
admiration for redhaired women. Several dozen men formed a
circle around John T. and the unfortunate Belknap, and they
made few sounds, and John T. didn't have to be hit on the head
with the board plank to know that most of them were rooting for
Belknap but were afraid to make any noise, for fear the one and
the only John T. Llewellyn would take it out on each of *them*, one
by one, with the implacability of famine and hemorrhoids and
death. So he marched alone, did the one and the only John T.
Llewellyn, and he didn't give a damn. Gettysburg, The Wilderness, Petersburg . . . it all was the same to the one and the only
John T. Llewellyn, just as long as there were Yankees out there to
be demolished, and just as long as he could dream of getting even
(and then some, by God) with Lucy and her windbag poetical
professor. So he marched on, and he fought alone, and his thoughts
often kept him warm on nights that otherwise would have been
intolerable, and he truly didn't give a damn who liked him and
who didn't like him. That sort of concern was trivial and stupid.
That sort of concern marked a man as a sissy and made him
nothing more than a frightened puking Harold St Xavier, the
nemesis of all the world's barroom sawdust.

But then, for no real reason the one and the only John T.
Llewellyn could understand, he was given a severe thrashing by
a man who wasn't only a windbag but probably a sissy in
the bargain, a man who wore a top hat and talked too much and
kept insisting he was a fucking *general*, and it all surely would
be funny if only the one and the only John T. Llewellyn could
remember how to laugh. But he no longer had the slightest idea
how to laugh. All he knew was pain and hatred, and they

sustained him; he sucked on their sour tits, and they nourished his dreams

(does my existence help keep you alive o my darlin?),

and he figured he was grateful for them. And now, if only he could reclaim his war, maybe everything would be better. So then what was the Now of this *here* situation? Well, for one thing, it was afternoon, and he was sitting at the edge of a narrow little stream that was all noisy and quick with fresh springtime water. His rifle lay next to him, and he was soaking his bare feet in the water. He was grimacing. He snapped his toes. The water rolled over his insteps, and they tingled, and from time to time he caught himself holding his breath and making fists. Every so often he cleared his throat and shook his head. He was hungry. Hell, these days he always was hungry, and it was a wonder to him the sounds of his belly didn't rout the birdies from the trees. He wished he could look for berries, but of course this was the wrong time of the year for a man to be looking for goddamn berries. He sighed. He leaned forward and began splashing water against his ankles. Eight men gathered behind him, and one of them tapped him on a shoulder. He flinched. He reached for his rifle. Someone kicked it away. He looked back, and a small grinning old man stood over him and asked him whether he was lost. Six men with rifles stood behind the small grinning old man, and a heavy fellow wearing captain's bars stood next to the small grinning old man, and the small grinning old man asked the one and the only John T. Llewellyn why so few men understood the fact that this war could not be escaped. Then the small grinning old man said the war was nothing more than a prison, especially if a man were cowardly and didn't foo his footy. The heavy fellow glanced at the small grinning old man and loudly exhaled. The small grinning old man introduced himself to Llewellyn as Brevet Brig Gen Maynard Thomas Snell, commanding officer of the Hartstone Zouaves, an we ask you, young fellow, what is your reason for bein here? And now the small grinning old man no longer was grinning. Instead, he was squinting, and his eyes were moist, and somewhere robins were calling, and somewhere wildflowers already had sprung from the earth, and somewhere calves were ambling and switching along behind their mothers, sometimes running a little to keep up, and a flavor of fresh milk began laying itself across the one and the only John T. Llewellyn's tongue and the roof of his mouth. He needed to retrieve his rifle, but he didn't suppose right then was the time, and he told the strange little general he'd somehow lost touch with his company, and right now . . . not to make too fine a point of it . . . he believed he was lost. He needed moisture, and so he rubbed his tongue acrost his front teeth. Noisily he swallowed. He supposed he needed to smile, so he tried to smile, but all he really did was stretch his lips a little. The captain and the little general backed away a few steps, and the little general told John T. to stand up. John T.'s chest hurt, and maybe he knew why, but of course he hoped he was wrong. He stood up. His face was loose, and his beard itched, and he swayed from side to side. He rubbed his stupid lips, and they hurt. The little general asked him did he have any proof he wasn't a deserter. John T. looked around. He scratched his neck and asked the little general did *he* have any proof *he* wasn't a deserter. Then John T. sniggered a little and said something having to do with turnabout being fair play. A man stepped forward and told John T. to be properly respectful of the little general, and then the man lifted his rifle and clubbed John T. across the side of the face with it. The blow knocked John T. to his knees, and he rubbed his face and shook his head and allowed as how none of this seemed too awful fair, you know? He summoned moisture from deep in his throat and spat out two teeth. They were red and stringy, and he blinked down at them. Slowly his head moved from side to side and he said: Shoot now. Lookit air at what you done. Now several rifles abruptly were lifted against him, and down came the butts of those rifles, and John T.'s nose was broken, and it made a sound that was like a pistolshot, and he was knocked flat, and he screamed into the earth, clogging his mouth with it. He rolled over on his back and spat earth and blood, and it emerged from his mouth as a sort of drool. He blinked shut his eyes, and Lucy and Minnie/Millie joined hands and danced naked around him, and they sang and whistled, and they stuck out their tongues and made wet sounds, and they told him they wouldn't piss on the best part of him, whatever *that* might be. He sat astride The Wreck of the Hesperis, and the Wreck of the Hesperis was bloody and desperate and kept screaming at him, and the buildings of Harrisonburg clustered and teetered around the edges of his vision, and his brothers sat in a saloon, and the saloon was in Philadelphia, and the saloon was in Boston, and the saloon was in Paris and Cairo and Timbuktu and the jungles of South America and the furry frozen wilds of Canada, and his brothers were toasting one another because they'd had the sense to put this goddamn war behind them, and to hell with the Confederacy, right? to hell with duty, right? to hell with decency and bravery and the joy of killin, right? O, God damn it all, he was the one and the only *John T. Llewellyn*, and how *dare* these fellers treat him the way they were treating him, and how in the name of God Almighty would he ever restore the two teeth they'd knocked from his mouth? Could the poor bloody muddy things be hammered back in? sewn back in? gentled back in? glued back in? He rolled from side to side, and he heard the others talking quietly, and the little general was speaking of logic and reason, and the rest of them apparently were grunting some sort of muted and yet strangely heartfelt agreement, and it was as though they'd all passed through a bent and crazy religious conversion. He shuddered. He bit a wrist, and he didn't know why. Then he sucked the wrist, and he still didn't know why. He heard the captain say well, we can prop him against a tree an so at least he'll have a chance to see us an condemn us or holler at us or do whatever else he might have in mind. The little general made a sharply disapproving sound, and it apparently had originated with his teeth and his tongue, and he said dignity really wasn't the point here, now was it? Why do you believe this deserter should condemn *us?* said the little general, and his sibilants were all soppy with spit. And then John T. heard himself say: God damn yall, I want my teeth. His words had emerged all spittled and indistinct, but he did hear a thread of quiet laughter, and he tried to smile so he could show these fellers he appreciated their enjoyment of his remark. He figured well, shit, maybe he could show them what a fine and humorous feller he was, and maybe then they wouldn't no more want to shoot him—or do whatever else it was they had in mind. He was sitting on his old dad's lap, and the year was 1835 or so, and his old dad was telling him dishes were dear, and his old dad was telling him it was necessary that his hindquarters be spanked in order that he not break any more dishes, and so his old dad called to his mama to bring one of her hairbrushes. She made some sort of protest, telling his old dad she didn't want the hairbrush to be broken. And his dad said never mind bout broken, Missus Llewellyn. So she brought the hairbrush, and it was sturdy and blunt, and little Johnny's old dad rolled him over and tugged down his britches and spanked him until he screamed his remorse, and his old dad had him gather up all the shards from the broken plate from the floor, and then his dad said to him: Put em in your mouth, boy. Suck em a little. Run em acrost your tongue. At way, you'll member em, won't you? So the boy stuffed the shards in his mouth. So the boy's dad smiled and said: At's my good little Johnny. And George Lammers was capering and hooting in front of little Johnny, and George Lammers was maybe a foot taller than little Johnny and fifty pounds heavier, and George Lammers said to him Your mother's a whore your mother's a whore whore whore! A few minutes later George Lammers and two boys named Frank Pell and Lee Venable jumped on little Johnny and turned him upsidedown and stripped him naked and dropped him headfirst into all the shit and mess of the pigpen on the old Chesley farm just east of town. The pigs came snouting toward little Johnny, and one of them tried to nip his little wizzle, and he tried to call for help, but his mouth was full of pig shit. A month or so later, his mother left home, and she never again was seen. His old dad gathered the three boys together and told them yes, their mama indeed had been a whore, and Fred and Charley wept, and little Johnny stared at a far wall and did not blink. And now, as he opened his eyes, the little general said: "Are we all in agreement?"

The men nodded.

John T. wanted to ask them whether they would care to hear him sing or dance. Or maybe they would want him to kiss them. He tried to sit up. Maybe it would please them if they saw him moving. He groaned. He cleared his throat. He sat up. The little general came to him and stood over him and told him his conduct had been unsatisfactory. "You do not have the proper plumptitude," said the little general, pooching his lips and exhaling as though he were trying to inflate a balloon. He then bent over John T.'s face and slapped it. Briskly. Once. Twice. A third time.

John T. whimpered.

The little general straightened, but now he was smiling, and he said to John T.: "Well, at least you appreciate the seriousness of the situation."

John T. nodded. He had to. He rubbed his eyes with the heels of his hands. Then he said: "I well I wasn't wanted I was throwed out of my company on account of *I* wanted to fight this here war but all the *rest* of em wanted to fuckin desert I mean I been a good boy an I'll eat the shards if at'll prove to you my heart is pure."

The little general turned to the captain and said: "The nerve of this chap. He says *he's* the loyal one and his *companions* are the deserters. Can you imagine such a perversion? Pah. Such a pig he is. The sooner he is disposed of, the better off we'll all be."

"Yessir," said the captain. He may have been smiling.

So John T. was dragged to a tree and propped against the tree. He closed his eyes, but the captain pinched his cheeks, and he couldn't help but blink open his eyes. He wept and he pissed, and all the words were out of him. Then they shot him, and for a moment he saw Lucy, and she gleamed, and she was sniggering, and somehow he managed to call for her to save him, and she grinned a glorious grin and said:

No.

COY

Sunday, April 9, 1865.

Coy and Miller squatted over a morning campfire and drank coffee. Coy still wasn't used to having just the one arm, and he was annoyed with himself because, for instance, he had to set down his tincup before he could pour coffee from the pot. He didn't suppose he ever would get used to that sort of thing, but what the hell, he still was alive . . . and that surely was more than he could say about a lot of men he'd known. (And at least chloroform had been available that night the doctor had amputated his arm. He figured he never would have been able to stand the pain if there'd been no chloroform. He figured he no doubt would have God damn died.)

Miller rubbed his shins as he squatted. He noisily sipped his coffee, and then he glanced at Coy and said: "How long you figure it'll be?"

"Before we're shut of all this?" said Coy.

"Yessir," said Miller.

"Not long," said Coy.

"You know at for sure?"

"I don't know *nothin* for *sure*," said Coy, "but it seems to me either it'll all be done soon or we'll all be dead. I mean, look at old Patterson. I figured he'd outlive us all, but *now* look at him, right?"

"I don't want to look at him," said Miller.

"Shit," said Coy, "you know what I mean."

Carefully, biting his mouth, Miller rolled up the legs of his britches. His shins had gone all purple and even yellow with bruises and scabs. Some of the scabs had worked themselves loose, and Miller dug them out with his fingernails and flicked them away.

(Coy abruptly exhaled into his coffee, and his breath caused it to bubble for a moment.)

Miller pressed his palms against the bruises and the scabs. He grimaced, but at the same time he sighed. "Air warm," he said. "My hands, I mean. It's a good feelin, the warmth. The thing is, half the time I like to freeze to death, an tuther half of the time I feel like my fuckin legs is bein boiled off."

"You an me," said Coy, "were a fine couple of crips."

". . . amen," said Miller, and he squeezed his ankles and his toes.

Coy shook his head. He glanced down at his empty sleeve. God damn but what his missing arm didn't itch. He had no idea how such a thing could be, but then the Lord was supposed to work in mysterious ways when it came to His miracles, wasn't at the truth of the matter? Now Coy shrugged. He rubbed his empty sleeve, and of course it had to be his *right* sleeve, seeing as how he'd been righthanded. Oh, wonderful. Wonderful an grand. Wasn't life such a fine pail of shit a man just about could cut his throat from the contemplation of it?

"Well," said Miller, "you know, it's an ill wind . . ."

Coy looked at him

"Yessir," said Miller, rubbing and scraping. "An ill wind indeed . . ."

"An ill wind what?" said Coy.

"I'm talkin bout old Ruthie. I've talked bout old Ruthie before, ain't I?"

Coy rolled his eyes in the general direction of God. "Yeah," he said. "Right. Old Ruthie. Hooray for old Ruthie."

"Well, you don't have to be so goddamn snooty bout it. I mean, after all the talkin *you've* done bout at Dorothy of yours, at

Dorothy who don't hardly fuck you none cept on days at end in the letter Z."

"All right. All *right*. But what's all this talk bout an ill wind? How come you're bein so, um, so *mysterious* with your words?"

Miller hesitated for a moment. Then, smiling a little, he looked up from his sorry shins and said to Coy: "What I mean is, it's an ill wind at don't blow *nobody* no good. Maybe now, what with me bein sort of hurt an all, old Ruthie'll keep her hands off me."

"Sure," said Coy, grinning. "On the days at end in the letter Z."

Miller shook his head. He chuckled, and then he winced. He rubbed his bruises and his scabs. Finally he rolled down his britches and cleared his throat and said to Coy: "You don't know nothin bout what I'm talking bout, do you?"

"I expect I don't," said Coy, swallowing a mouthful of coffee. It was sour, and it wasn't as hot as it should have been, but what the hell, at least it was a sort of *memory* of coffee, which was as much as could have been expected of it. "I mean, your Ruthie an my Dorothy, they didn't exactly come from the same heavenly peapod, now did they?"

"Not hardly fuckin likely," said Miller, sniggering. He rubbed his palms across his shirtfront and then, again wincing, he stood up. He teetered for a moment, but he did manage to retain his balance. He sucked his breath, and for a moment he exposed his teeth. He spat into the fire, and it went pish. His face was lean, and he had enormous eyebrows, and now those eyebrows did a wicked little dance, and he said: "I got a riddle for you—how come all cunts is alike an all women is different?"

"You sure bout at?"

"Sure I'm sure."

"I mean, myself, I ain't got at much experience."

"Well, you can take my word for it."

"All right," said Coy.

"So answer my question," said Miller.

"Sorry, but I done forgot what it was."

"Shit," said Miller.

"Absolutely," said Coy.

Then Miller and Coy laughed more or less in concert. Boom hollered for the fellers to fall in. All of them—even Coy and Miller—were carrying brandnew rifles that had been taken from the abandoned ordnance wagon. Not that they planned to take up arms against anyone, but evidently the fuckin Yankee cavalry was everywhere, and it was good to be prepared in case those people wouldn't listen to reason. At least this was what they'd all been told by that, ah, *General* Boom, and his words maybe had been crazy, but they hadn't been any crazier than this here war had been, so the fellers had opened the boxes and had gathered up new rifles and had stuffed their pockets with bullets and the little papers that held gunpowder, and they'd joked a little, and some of them even had said they were trapped in some hitherto unknown circle of Hades, a place where they were condemned to fight Yankees until the goddamn universe blew up and all the churches fell down. Coy carried his brandnew rifle at a trail. Miller had loaded it for him, but he had no idea what would happen if he ever had to fire the damn thing. How would he reload? Would Miller be there to help him? He surely hoped so. He really did like old Miller, by God. Of all the sad ragged wrecks in this here little ragtag band of skeletons and silly shambling fools, he and Miller were the most obviously wrecked, and somehow their stupid emptysleeved limping pain made them special. The others seemed to go out of their way to talk and joke with Coy and Miller, and they never yelled at Coy and Miller for not keeping up. Now, walking along with Miller, slowing down every so often so as not to drift too far forward, Coy smiled at the high uncharacteristic April sky (it was too bright, and it didn't seem to hold any particular hint of rain) and thought for a time of Miller's wife, the legendary Ruthie, who was everything Coy's Dorothy wasn't—and then some, o you betcha. According to Miller, Ruthie was seven years older than he, which meant she never would see forty again, and before the war she'd baked Miller a pie of his choice whenever he'd allowed her to wriggle under him and accept his seed. Which was more than a little amusing, especially when a person stopped to think on how almighty skinny Miller was. The war really had little to do with Miller's skinniness, though. According to him, he'd been something like ten years of age before he'd weighed even fifty pounds, and his mother had insisted he would die of the consumption before he was fifteen if he didn't put on a whole lot more weight. Well, it was Miller's mother who died of the consumption before Miller was fifteen, and he got to laughing at her funeral, and his father slapped him and knocked him down and called him a disrespectful little shitter, and Miller couldn't help but agree. But usually he was respectful as hell, and he was enormously respectful as far as Ruthie was concerned, especially when she began feeding him all those wonderful pies. They caused him to gain weight, but her conjugal demands caused him to lose an equal amount of weight and maybe a little extra, and so he spent a decade of married life more or less desperately trying to hold his own. He worked in a hardware store up near Fredericksburg, and the fellers who lollygagged around in the hardware store gave him a good ragging because of old Ruthie and her demands, but all he ever did was grin and tell those fellers at least he didn't have to find his lovin in his fist, now did he? And he'd passed along all this information to Coy, and *Coy* had told *him* all about the implacable and grimly frozen Dorothy, and then Miller and Coy had laughed, and ruefully they'd spoken of Jack Sprat and Mrs Sprat, and they'd decided they would be friends for a long, long time. It was a good feeling as far as Coy was concerned, and he—

"Coy?" said Miller grunting.

"Yessir?"

"We goin to make her?"

"You bet your goddamn Fredericksburg ass we're goin to make her."

"Fredericksburg ass?" said Miller. "What's a Fredericksburg ass?"

"Skinny," said Coy.

"Get out of here," said Miller, laughing.

Coy snorted. He frowned down at his brandnew rifle. He couldn't hardly hold the rifle and help his friend, and so he flung the rifle off into a ditch and emptied his pockets of all his bullets and gunpowder papers. Miller watched him, and now Miller's laughter was gone. Coy used his good old loyal left arm to squeeze his limping friend, and he told Miller everything would be just hunkydory, you got my word on her.

BOOM

Sunday, April 9, 1865.

By rights, he said to himself, nothin more needs to happen to me—or to these boys walkin along here with me. Enough has happened already. Enough an en some. Ha. Oh yes *sir*. And then Boom shook his head. It was late in the Sabbath morning, and wasn't today Palm Sunday? Christ was entering Jerusalem in all His glory, correct? By God, Boom and these men should have been hearing churchbells, and they should have been hearing the secret splendid shush and sweep of gentle churchy skirts and petticoats. All this craziness needed to be over and done with. Boom wanted to go home. Nothing more needed to be proved. He wanted to go home. He told himself now was a time for tits and tears and laughter and warm food. He wanted to go home. But all he heard was a rude sound of jays. All he heard was the weary uneven shuffle of these barefoot skeletons. He poked at his eyes with his thumbs. He patted his top hat. He grimaced. He was hungry. He wanted to go home. But why then were they all toting brandnew rifles and fresh ammunition? Did he or anyone else really believe they could put up much of a resistance if the Yankees attacked them? Especially if those Yankees were on horseback? Boom shuddered. He was holding his brandnew rifle at a trail, and its butt bumped along the road, and every so often the jays swooped down, but he didn't look up, and neither did anyone else. He wanted to go home. He wanted to suck one of Lenore's nipples while thumbing the other. She always had enjoyed those times when he'd paid close and fastidious attention to her breasts. Sometimes she'd bit her lips until they'd bled, and she'd always told him yes, yes, kindly do not stop, my darlin. Now, remembering, Boom almost was ready to smile, and he almost was ready to admit the possibility that a boner of sorts was blossoming inside his britches. He grunted. He told himself he was a pig and a pervert. He shook his head. He wanted to go home.

A boy named Goodfellow was walking beside Boom. The boy's flesh was gray, and there was too much of it. He wasn't fat, though. He simply was gray. His full name was Jay W. Goodfellow, and he'd told Boom the W stood for Worrall, and he was only seventeen, yet he'd been in the Army since June of '63, just before Gettysburg. He'd given Boom a great deal of his personal history that morning. He was from Front Royal, and his daddy had been in the harness business before the war, but then his poor old daddy had upped and volunteered for infantry service at the age of fortyfour and had perished in the Battle of Cedar Mountain in '62. Jay Goodfellow had enlisted on his fifteenth birthday even though his mother had told him his late daddy really wouldn't have wanted him to do such an impetuous thing at such a young age. Jay simply had smiled at his dear mama, and he'd kissed her, and quietly he'd told her he had to do what he figured was right, and he said he hoped she wouldn't be too aggravated with him. He told her shoot, she still had his two younger brothers and his little sister Emmy, and so it wasn't as though she'd be all alone in the world, was it? He smiled as he spoke, and his teeth were rotten, and his breath stank. It was as though great hairy old rats had died inside his mouth. Rats and polecats and maybe a pig. Boom tried to keep his face averted as Goodfellow spoke, but he did manage to nod from time to time, and anyway, he liked the boy. As far as he was concerned, it was hard not to. And now, as the jays swooped and the wind was high and hot and they all walked and sometimes tottered through that sweet flat uncommitted Sunday morning, Goodfellow got to talking about—of all the goddamned things—railroad locomotives, and he said: "In Front Royal we're on the Manassas Gap line, you know, an just bout ever day I'd take me a little walk to the enginehouse an . . . well, just stand air an look at one engine or tuther. An I suregod was taken by the whole kit an kaboodle of em, you follow me, sir? You ever look at one of em real close? You ever *smell* one of em? I mean, the *oil* an the *woodsmoke* an all? Jesus Christ, sir, they ain't just *machinery*, no *sir*. They by God in Almighty Heaven *breathe* . . ." And Goodfellow allowed himself a languid and knowing nod. Then, narrowing his eyes and lowering his voice, he said: "Air's been times . . . well, air's been times when I've stood next to one of em big shiny engines, and it's been huffin an hissin ever such a little bit, if you know what I mean, an sort of waitin to let everthin *rip* an *roar*, an I just bout was in love . . . an I mean like in love, ah, with a *girl* . . . an if at makes me . . . strange, well, strange I am, an strange I'll always be, an the world can go to hell . . ." Then Goodfellow hesitated. He coughed. His lungs rattled. He bent forward a little and rubbed his belly. He looked up and smiled a little and said to Boom: "Yessir. I'm strange, all right. Surely." And he blinked at Boom. And he nodded. He rubbed the loose flesh of his face. "Yessir," he said. "Yes *sir*."

Boom shook his head. "You're not strange," he said to Goodfellow. "I've seen em too."

". . . engines?" said Goodfellow.

"Many times. An you're absolutely right. Air the . . . well, forgive the cliché, but air the stuff of dreams . . ."

"Back air in Richmond, when we was guardin em yards, I seen lots of engines, but they all was wrecked."

"Well, the war and all . . ."

"I don't like seein wrecked engines," said Goodfellow. "They make me real sad. I mean, engines shouldn't ought to have nothin to do with no war. They should take people from here to air, an they should take freight from here to air, an they shouldn't ought to be bothered with no *war*."

"I couldn't agree more," said Boom.

"But em dead engines still smelt good . . ."

"Oh. Yes. Well, I expect they did."

"They was dead but they wasn't dead, you know?"

"I believe I do," said Boom.

"I mean, they wasn't *all the way* dead," said Goodfellow. "Some of em . . . I swear to you, some of em still was warm."

"Really?" said Boom.

"I wouldn't lie bout a thing like at," said Goodfellow.

"No," said Boom. "I don't suppose you would."

"Thank you kindly, sir," said Goodfellow, smiling, exposing his wretched teeth to full view. He blinked furiously, and Boom supposed the poor boy was on the edge of weeping. "It all really means a whole lot to me," said Goodfellow. "It keeps me goin, you know?"

"I believe I do," said Boom.

"I thank you kindly, sir," said Goodfellow.

Boom nodded. He would have smiled, at least a little, but he didn't want to hurt Goodfellow's feelings. Goodfellow was altogether too close to weeping for that sort of thing.

Goodfellow cleared his throat. He blinked. He rubbed his cheeks and his chin. "You're a good man, sir," he said. "We should of had more like you. More officers, I mean . . ."

". . . well," said Boom, hesitating.

"I ain't complainin though," said Goodfellow, speaking quickly, his words all spittled and imprecise. He wiped moisture from the corners of his mouth. Absently he sucked a knuckle. Then: "It wouldn't do no good to complain, would it? I mean, I been gettin by all right, ain't I? I'm alive, ain't I? At ought to count for somethin, correct?"

"Correct," said Boom.

"But so many of the officers in this here Army, well . . ."

"Well what?" said Boom.

"An officer, your average officer . . . well, your average officer gets shot too much."

"I beg your pardon?" said Boom.

"I don't know why at is," said Goodfellow, and he plucked at his throat and then scratched an elbow, "but it's like they ain't got the sense the Lord gave a milkcow with a corncob up her ass, if you know what I mean . . ."

"I'm not all at sure I do," said Boom.

Goodfellow's loosefleshed face narrowed, and he appeared to be trying to give an impression of substantial good old soldierly

168

wisdom, and he said: "You know, sir, the thing is . . too many officers think it ain't enough for em to be brave as we are . . . they think they got to be goddamn *braver* an we are. An so what happens? Ah, but you know what happens, don't you, sir? What *happens* is, like as not the old officer ends up with a big red mess where his head ought to be, ain't at so? An for what? For nothin. For tryin to live up to somethin we don't none of us give a shit bout. What do em officers want—fancy words on air goddamn headstones? Jesus, sir, give me an my days to come . . . my future or whatever . . . a good old locomotive any time; it's human as hell but at the same time it's got its good sense . . . you follow me?"

"I believe I do," said Boom, and he decided it really wouldn't knock the heavens out of alignment if he smiled. So he did smile, and Goodfellow's ruined mouth returned the smile, and Boom damn near wanted to hug the boy. A horseman appeared on a far horizon, and the man's animal . . . skinny, limping, bleeding from a number of cuts on it sides and its legs . . snorted and gasped. The rider was plump and middleaged, and he was waving his arms. He was hatless and dusty, but he wore the tunic of a Confederate cavalry major, and he yipped and howled as he rode toward Boom and the skeletons. He slowed down as soon as he was close enough to recognize Boom. He reined up and saluted. Boom returned the salute. The man was grinning. His name was Slocum, and at one time he'd commanded a troop under J.E.B Stuart. His voice was hoarse. He told Boom the war officially would end tomorrow. General Lee was making final preparations to surrender to old U.S. Grant and to disband the Army of Northern Virginia, said Slocum. It all was as good as accomplished, said Slocum, and he still was grinning, and his words were fogged with sprays of spittle. He and Boom were not children, and they both knew the cause was lost, and they both also knew they didn't have to tell one another what was obvious. The skeletons began to cheer. They jumped up and down, and they embraced one another. They threw away their rifles. The rifles spun end over end. They made a good deal of racket when they struck the earth. Slocum was on his way to notify his regiment, which was bivouacked down near the North Carolina line. He leaned down from his saddle and shook hands with Boom. He told Boom they had nothing to be ashamed of, did they? Boom had trouble inhaling. He watched the rifles slam against the earth. Next to him, Goodfellow was shouting happy words having to do with locomotives and such.

SNELL

Sunday, April 9, 1865.

He strolled along, blinking and grinning, on this splendid Palm Sunday morning, and he wondered how some people could *not* believe in the existence of a benevolent and surely logical Creator. Pitt walked next to him, but Pitt was something of a ninny, and so he paid no attention to Pitt. Somehow Pitt had been tested on a balance wheel and had been found wanting. Somehow they all had been found wanting, from Jefferson Davis on down to the most humble and quaking private in the ranks. Say, by the bye, whatever had happened to the dear old Hartstone Zouaves? Why had their flanks not been shored up? Why had cavalry so seldom been summoned up to help out? Snell really had little use for those arrogant cavalry bastards with their *plumes* and whatnot. Their *plumes* and their *rhetoric* and the way the newspapers doted on them. If the truth were known, the cavalry was little more than a bunch of vainglorious fools, and somehow its clanking clicking leatherstinking Ibedamnangotohell posturing was enough to make Brevet Brig Gen Maynard Thomas Snell, who liked to think of himself as The Little Whirlwind, want to jam his fingers down his throat and express his opinion of those men with a hot remorseless spray of nothing less than his golden and unvexed very puke of very puke. Now he frowned as he strolled along. He was seeking some sort of insight. He needed to believe that war was a logical extension of the affairs of men. He tried to summon

171

a sort of chronology of attitudes and behavior. He said to himself the first chapter of the chronology had to do with parades, music, the anxious cheery kisses of girls . . . pretty or otherwise. The second chapter had to do with jokes and laughter and comradely boasting while the fellows squatted around campfires and blinked innocently and as yet had tasted no blood. The third chapter had to do with the fighting itself and the astonishment the fellows felt because no neatness was involved. The fourth chapter had to do with fear, and they all were afraid, no matter what they might have said. The fifth chapter had to do with the realization that no one in charge really knew what in the name of God was happening. The sixth chapter had to do with ultimate boredom, and hunger, and complaints about the slow delivery of the mail. The seventh chapter had to do with cynicism and despair, a weariness of the bones and the spirit. The eighth chapter had to do with hunger and amputations and grief. The ninth chapter had to do with guilt. The tenth and probably the final chapter had to do with madness. The Little Whirlwind supposed he indeed was mad, and he knew he didn't need for his men to form a committee to tell him that grim little fact, and he also knew he rather rejoiced in his madness, since it enabled him to fight this war the way he knew it needed to be fought. For the first time since the war's beginning, he really was quite pleased. His flanks were protected, and his men obeyed every crook of his eyebrows, every curl of his proud commanding lip, and steadfastly he gissled his pracks and with unfailing élan he mistigated his walipers and axeringlated the matteghios of his blups. These procedures were important; they were jewels of rare worth; no general worth his talwebbers could afford not to exercise them. And so he figured he walked in righteousness, and he wielded the weapons that struck down all those who shirked their bounden duty, and he believed he had the full support of the fellows who served under him. Oh, it was a pity he no longer had his pistol and his sword, but his fellows still obeyed him, didn't they? Their vengeance was grand to behold, wasn't it? Those looters and that great foolish bearish deserter indeed had died, hadn't they? So all right. So the principles of The Little Whirlwind's philosophy of command were as intact as the croils of virgins, correct? And he wrapped himself in his madness as though

172

it were great comforting leaves that carried a wondrous odor of
Green. It protected him from all betrayals and disappointments,
all anger at those who hadn't responded well when their courage
had been challenged. It gave him breath and laughter, and he had
no idea what he would have done without it. It exalted his soul. It
protected his flanks. It provided pickets who warned him when the
enemy was up to some sort of nasty business. It provided his Rod
and his Staff, and joyous, o warmly joyous, were the chambers of
his lart and his floomers. He wished he had a cigar, in particular
one created from the wheat and the barley or maybe the oats on his
farm back home. Ah, but the best cigars in truth came from corncobs and the necks of chickens, didn't they? Just as the most tender
beefsteak came from sheep and frogs. When was the last time he
and his school chums had gigged a pig? Gosh, such wonderful
fun, he and his school chums—all ten thousand six hundred ninety-
two of them—sneaking and whispering in the dark in pursuit of
unwary croaking pigs, and maybe tomorrow I'll go callin on Carl
Rossiter an Borden DeWitt an talk em into accompanyin me tonight,
an we'll carry nets, an we'll drink cold tea, o yes. It'll all be—

Pitt abruptly spoke up, and Snell flinched a little. Pitt usually
was a melancholy sort of fellow, but right now he was smiling,
and he said: "Sir, I do believe I've come to a conclusion . . ."

"Ah," said Snell, "but we *all* come to conclusions sooner or
later, wouldn't you agree?"

"I believe I'm talkin bout another sort of conclusion," said Pitt.

"Well, good for you. Good for you an your conclusions. God
bless you. God bless your conclusions."

"I'm serious, sir," said Pitt.

"So am I," said Snell. "I may be a great many things, but I
am not . . . trivial."

"Nor am I," said Pitt. "Or at least I don't believe I am. Not
any more, at any rate."

"Fine," said Snell. "You are to be congratulated. Perhaps I
can arrange a promotion for you. God knows, you may not be
much, but you're all I have, aren't you?"

"I'm not talkin bout a promotion, sir."

"Oh?"

"I'm not interested in a promotion, sir."

Snell glanced at Pitt, and Pitt's eyes were flicking from side to side, and Pitt's mouth was open, and he appeared to be having difficulty with his breathing, and Snell said to him: "Have I offended you in some way?"

". . . no sir."

"En what is it you want to say?"

"I want to speak of comedy, sir."

"Comedy?"

"Yessir."

"You did say comedy, didn't you?"

"Yessir," said Pitt, and his eyes kept flicking, flicking, and it was as though he were expecting regiments of crazed Yankees to come erupting from the very earth while yelling their hooty hollow Yankee yells and giving off their desperate Yankee stinks.

"Air somethin you lookin for?" said Snell.

"Yessir," said Pitt. "I'm lookin for Satan in a jester's suit, sir. I'm lookin for hyenas an jackasses an roaches an puppydogs an Abolitionists an politicians, sir. I'm lookin for the Alpha an the Omega, sir, an all the foolishness in between. I'm lookin for things at maybe'll make me laugh, sir. I'm all ready to laugh, sir. I'm all primed for it. I'm like a pump at's bubblin over, sir. I need windmills, sir. Windmills an maybe sheep, an you can be old Quixote, an I can be the little fat greazzy one. Yes *sir*."

"You're talkin bout at Spaniard's book, am I correct?"

". . . yessir."

"An you're talkin bout *comedy*, am I correct?"

". . . yessir . . . you surely are."

"You believe this war's a laughin matter?"

". . . wellsir," said Pitt, "it's bout at time . . ."

"At time?" said Snell. "At time for what?"

". . . wellsir," said Pitt, "in my opinion, it's bout at time for us to have a hoot or two . . ."

Snell smiled. At the same time, though, he shook his schoolteacherish finger at Pitt and said: "You forget one thing. You forget, ah ha, madness. You forget brains full of cobwebs, an you forget mouths at speak in tongues no one can decipher, an you forget all the brubjams and pettiflaps at parade acrost a man's mind when he's sort of, ah, let the reins slip from his hands . . ."

"Oh," said Pitt. "Yessir. I expect you have a point."

"You can have your Satan in a jester's suit, though. I expect you're entitled to him. I expect we all are."

"Thank you, sir."

"Just because I'm crazy," said Snell, "at doesn't mean I've got no sense of humor."

"I appreciate at, sir."

"Good," said Snell. He was wearing dentures, and now he clicked them, and he swallowed a heavy gob of pasty spit. He shook his head. His mouth was crooked and probably naughty. He said to Pitt: "Are we amusin enough for you?"

"Yessir," said Pitt. "Just bout."

"Do we die in amusin ways?"

"Sometimes . . ."

"You know, Pitt, I thought *I* was at the end of the road, but I was wrong."

"Sir?"

"*You're* the one who's at the end of the road, Pitt. You've gone beyond craziness, haven't you? You've gone maybe what's the *real* final step. Now, for *you*, everthin is *funny*, an maybe *at's* the final step, don't you agree?"

Pitt scratched his chin. Then, shrugging, he said: "Perhaps I do, sir . . ."

"So we must persist, don't you agree?"

"Yessir," said Pitt.

And Snell said: "We must play it out. An we must punish those who disobey the rules of the game."

Speaking gently, Pitt said: "You mean the rules of the comedy, sir."

At twilight they came to a deserted little town called Boxerville. They found an abandoned ordnance wagon that had a sprawled and stinking dead horse in its traces. The wagon had been partially looted, but a great many brandnew rifles and boxes of ammunition still remained, and Snell danced back and forth and up and down, and he told Pitt ah, such grand luck, and he assured Pitt the comedy probably would continue until all the sweet stars and the mighty flogarellas came crashing down.

TIDWELL

Monday, April 10, 1865.

Tidwell and his cousin McGraw and tough old Ratliff, the former sergeant, lay on their backs and blinked up at the constellations and spoke quietly of how grateful they were that they'd been spared. It wasn't much past midnight, and they should have been asleep, but the excitement had been too much for them, and their eyes were as bright and snappy as the eyes of hungry mice. They and the other fellers were bivouacked (or whatever) in a flat and silent pasture, and Tidwell for one couldn't understand how the other fellers were able to sleep. Now they all were on their way home for good and for fair; the war was finished, and all they had to do was place one foot in front of tuther foot and walk on home and maybe find the strength to reassemble themselves and go on from wherever they'd been before that Fort Sumter business back in '61. Tidwell grinned into the darkness. He surely did hope his Rosemary and their eight children would be happy to see him—*and* he surely did hope she would permit him to have his way with her darling plump body. It was the least she could so, wasn't it? He inhaled. He rubbed his teeth with the side of a finger. His rifle lay on the earth next to him. It had an odor of some sort of fresh oil. Boom had told them they'd be welladvised to keep their rifles and their ammunition until they received official word that the war was done, and so they'd retrieved their

176

rifles and what they could find of their ammunition . . . all of the fellers, that is, except the onearmed Coy, who'd thrown his away a number of miles back down the road. Ah, but no one really blamed him for that. After all, what the hell good was a rifle when a man had only one arm? How was he supposed to reload? Coy had been righthanded, and it was his right arm that was missing, and so his rifle had been nothing more than your tits on your boar hog, and Coy had done the wise thing . . . he'd thrown the stupid rifle away. Tidwell and McGraw and tough old Ratliff, though, could understand why Boom had pointed out to them that they might still have need of their rifles. For one thing, maybe they would run acrost a rabbit or two, and it was easier for a man to shoot a rabbit than to chase it acrost some farmer's cabbagepatch and kill it with his bare hands, strangling it maybe, or beating its head against a rock. For another thing, a rifle just might come in handy in case they were attacked by Yankees who hadn't been told the war was over. These arguments, delivered quickly and easily by a grinning Boom, who at the same time told the fellers he for one agreed with them and was just as happy as they were, had been enough to make them wander back and forth across the road—however reluctantly—and pick up their rifles and scrabble around for their discarded ammunition. And so it meant that the war at once was over and not over. Once the Yankees were notified, well, then these skeletons could throw their rifles away. Boom had reminded them, though, that they had a long journey home, and there wasn't much likelihood that the general populace was equipped to lay out great steaming feasts for their returning heroes, and so the returning heroes probably would have use for the rifles if a stray deer or squirrel happened to cross their path. Oh, it all made sense, all right, and Tidwell for one was grateful that such a smart feller as old Boom more or less was in charge of this here bunch. And he'd said so to McGraw and Ratliff, and they'd both agreed. Now, though, he was talking about how tired he was, and yet at the same time he still felt a sort of pride, and to hell with his tiredness, and he said: "Maybe we're worth more an we think we are . . ."

"How's at?" said McGraw.

Ratliff looked at Tidwell but didn't say anything.

Said Tidwell: "We ain't none of us sayin *surrender*. We're sayin *end of the war*, but we ain't sayin *surrender*. I expect at means somethin, don't it?"

". . . maybe so," said McGraw, and he swiped at his forehead with his bum hand. The one wrapped in the rag. The one that had been mashed by the runaway horse in the trenches at Petersburg. He coughed. He spat. "It's good to have pride, ain't it?"

"Shit," said Ratliff.

Tidwell and McGraw hunched forward a little, as though maybe they expected Ratliff to hammer their skulls with his brandnew oil rifle.

"Pride's what done got us into this," said Ratliff. "You can take pride an stuff it up your old bunghole, for all *I* fuckin care. It's on account of fuckin pride at we're laying here an jackin ourselves off because we think we're so goddamn *happy* . . ."

"Well," said Tidwell, "I'm not so sure I—"

Ratliff interrupted him. "Listen here. You just pay attention. How long's this here war been going on? Just bout four years, correct? Wellnow, you take me as an example. Back home in Winchester, well, maybe you wouldn't know it to look at me now, what with me bein so skinny an all, what with my bad teeth an all, but before this here war I cut a certain figure with a . . . well, with a certain class of woman an girl. I ain't never been married, but back in em days I didn't lack for no female companionship, you betcha I didn't. I kept myself busy with my fuckin. Air was Mabel an air was Laura an air was Marybeth an air was Jeanette, an they wasn't from the *best* class, understand, but they was good enough for the likes of *me*, you hear what I'm sayin? An I got fucked at least twice a week no matter goddamn what. Now listen to me. Air's fiftytwo weeks in a year, right? Which means each year back home I was gettin fucked bout one hunnert times. Multiply one hunnert by four years an you come up with *four* hunnert. Which means this here war's deprived me of four hunnert fucks. Which also means I don't feel too kindly toward this here war. An I know I *surely* don't care bout a lot of bullshit havin to do with whether we say *end of the war* or whether we say *surrender*. An as far as *pride* goes, well, pride didn't make us *win* the war, now did it? Come to think of it, pride didn't make *nobody* win the war. Maybe the Yankees think they've won the war, but at sort of thinkin is as stupid as a goat dancin the waltz. Nobody's won this here war. Except maybe the undertakers. Ha. The undertakers. Right."

Said Tidwell: " . . . well, I don't know."

Said Ratliff: "You don't know what?"

Said Tidwell: "You're bein awful . . . dark."

Said McGraw to Tidwell: "Listen, Jasper, maybe we all of us got a right to be what you call dark. I mean, we sure enough have seen a whole lot of dark *things*, ain't at so?"

Said Tidwell: "*You* listen. You an old Ratliff here, maybe you're speakin the truth. I expect I don't know one way or tuther. But at don't mean I got to go along with you. I'm thinkin bout my Rosemary along bout now, you know? Rosemary an the children. I love Rosemary an the children, an I just want to go home, an I don't need a lot of *dark* talk, you hear me?" And Tidwell's hands were shaking, so he linked them and began licking and sucking his knuckles.

Said McGraw to Tidwell: "Hey air, Jasper, we're just talkin. Don't pay us no mind."

"At's right," said Ratliff, and his voice was softer, which meant it probably was more open to soft thoughts and opinions. He glanced up at the sky, and then he said to Tidwell: "I get carried away sometimes. Sure enough I do. I get to feelin like somebody's beatin horseshoes together inside my skull. Clang, clang, bang, bang, an my brains want to pop open an sort of, ah, well, sort of slide out my nose, *you* hear *me?*"

". . . I expect so," said Tidwell.

"But we shouldn't count on *too* much," said Ratliff. "Boom was right bout us keepin our rifles. Nothin's over until it's really over, you know?"

Tidwell nodded.

"How's at?" said Ratliff.

"I agree," said Tidwell. "I've done already nodded."

"When a man nods in the dark," said Ratliff, "he might as well not be air."

". . . oh," said Tidwell.

179

Ratliff made a number of rumbly amused sounds. He was sitting crosslegged, and he kept glancing up at the sky, and now he said: "Ah, Tidwell. Good old Tidwell. You want to cut my throat an roast me over a fuckin spit an maybe drink my blood, don't you?"

". . . you can forget the part bout roastin you on a fuckin spit an drinkin your blood," said Tidwell, sniggering. "But the part bout cuttin your throat . . . well, let me think on it."

Ratliff and McGraw laughed.

A little later Tidwell managed to fall asleep. He dreamed of crickets and tobacco and cornbread and tits and moonshine. He dreamed of his wife, and he dreamed of his four sons and his four daughters. He hoped none of them would be ashamed because the South had lost the war. He saw them all running toward him in the dooryard, and he heard himself tell them to mind the flowers, and a thin white cat butted his shins, and he remembered the thin white cat as being an ornery old tom named Beelzebub, and he scooped up Beelzebub and kissed the old sonofabitch on the whiskers, and his wife and his four sons and his four daughters laughed and danced. Then Beelzebub was gone, and Tidwell heard an indignant blatting sound, and surely the indignant blatting sound came from a goat. Strange. Hadn't Ratliff said something about a goat dancing the waltz? Ah, but Tidwell was home now, and Ratliff's opinions were of no interest to him. He sat at the table with Rosemary and the children, and he opened the front of Rosemary's dress and thumbed her tits, right there in front of God and the children an maybe all the angels High Above. Rosemary blushed, and the children laughed and applauded, and he ate bread and gravy, and Rosemary said she was about to fix him some nice roast goat, and she said she only wished she had a crabapple for the roast goat's mouth. He wondered whether the goat would be roasted over a spit. He wondered whether he would be called upon to drink its blood. He heard footsteps. He heard another indignant blatting sound. He opened his eyes, and they were gummy, so he rubbed them. He heard someone shout something having to do with stray goat. He heard shots. He seized his rifle and stood up and staggered toward the place where the shots had come from. The meadow was sweet with dew. He saw the goat. It was white as Beelzebub. He fired at the goat, and Goodfellow was standing by the goat, and Goodfellow's head vanished.

RATLIFF

Monday, April 10, 1865.

The goat ambled off and disappeared over a hill, and that was the last any of them saw of the goddamn stupid animal, it and its fucking blats. Tidwell wept and screamed, and Ratliff embraced him and tried to comfort him, but his comforting didn't have much effect. He'd never been much good at comforting people, and anyway, Tidwell wasn't ready to pay much attention to that sort of thing. All Tidwell seemed able to do was weep and scream and after a time get to telling Ratliff hey, God damn it, saynow, at feller ain't dead a tall is he? it's all some sort of funnin ain't it? the war's over an I didn't mean to do nothin an surely the Lord knows at don't He? Tidwell's rifle stank. It lay next to the place where he'd collapsed after killing Goodfellow, and now Tidwell was kneeling, but he kept falling forward on his face, and Ratliff kept pulling him back into his kneeling position and embracing him and telling him come on come on you're supposed to be a *man* God damn you. Tidwell kept reaching toward his rifle, and finally Ratliff kicked the rifle away. McGraw, Tidwell's cousin, stood off to one side and made no effort to say anything to Tidwell. Nor did anyone else. Not even Boom the *general* said anything to Tidwell right then. Birds whistled and trilled. Ratliff shook his head. He'd never eaten goat, but he sure would have admired to have tried some that morning. Hell, he hadn't eaten

182

anything warm since a week ago yesterday, when he'd prepared the supper of mule haunch back there on that hill at Hollywood Cemetery in Richmond. Tidwell had slaughtered that mule, and now Tidwell had slaughtered Goodfellow. (Ratliff hardly knew Goodfellow except to say howdo. Oh, he'd heard Goodfellow occasionally talk about trains and locomotives, and he supposed Goodfellow had liked trains and locomotives a whole lot, but that wasn't much to know about a man, now was it?) And then, abruptly, his voice clear and dry, the miserable ravaged Tidwell said to Ratliff: "I'm a father, you know."

"At's real nice," said Ratliff. "Good for fuckin you."

"I didn't do it on purpose."

"Good," said Ratliff.

"What was he doin out air anyway? How come he was just standin air? How come, if he was so close to at air goat, he didn't shoot it?"

"Maybe he wanted to be its friend," said Ratliff.

". . . shit," said Tidwell. "Don't fuck at me. Please don't fuck at me. I'm a *father*. Rosemary an me got four boys an four girls, an a *father* wouldn't do what I just done . . ."

"But you done it, boy. You done it, an you can't change it, an anyway, it wasn't like you done it on purpose."

"I was asleep, an I didn't know what was goin on, an en I seen at goat, an I figured I needed to kill it."

"At's the truth," said Ratliff. "You're tellin the truth, all right, an I'd swear to it in a court of law."

"He was a nice little old boy," said Tidwell. "Kept to himself. Didn't fuss at nobody. Never was nasty or nothin like at."

"Well, the thing you got to do is stop thinkin bout him."

". . . how'm I supposed to do a thing like at?"

"Work at her," said Ratliff. "Be a man. Tell yourself you got to keep movin on. Tell yourself your wife an your children need you. Tell yourself your dog needs you. Your fuckin cat. Anythin."

Tidwell looked up at Ratliff, who still more or less was embracing him. Tidwell was blinking, and he coughed several times before he spoke to Ratliff. "You love me, don't you?"

"Love you?" said Ratliff, and he worked himself free of Tidwell and slid back on his rump. "*Love* you? Fuck, no. What you think I am?"

". . . no . . . no . . . I didn't mean nothin bad . . . only, well, God damn it, I'm . . . well, I'm so lonely I want to blow fuckin up, and how can you or anybody fuckin else expect me just to walk away from here an say to the world well, lah de dah an kiss my ass, I kilt one of our boys by mistake on account of I didn't aim so good at a goat, which surely would of tasted good if only my aim had been a sight better, an the goat got away, an we're all still hungry, and what did at sonofabitch have in mind for at goat? did he want to put it on a fuckin *lead* an make it a fuckin *pet?*"

"Maybe he wanted to fuck the fuckin goat," said Ratliff.

". . . at ain't funny," said Tidwell.

"I didn't mean it to be," said Ratliff. "I don't never joke when it comes to fuckin."

Tidwell frowned at Ratliff and said: "I don't expect I understand whatever it is you're tryin to say."

"The thing I'm tryin to say is," said Ratliff, "you shouldn't think too hard on it."

"What?" said Tidwell.

"It's simple," said Ratliff.

"You mean simple like simple stupid?"

"I expect so," said Ratliff.

". . . what?"

"I'm sayin to you, you stupid piece of cow flop," said Ratliff to Tidwell, "at we might as well think the poor sonofabitch wanted to fuck at air dumb lost goat an let it go at at. The thought, I mean. It ain't the kind of thought at leads nowhere, so we might as well not bother with it, all right?"

". . . I don't understand."

"Fuck you don't," said Ratliff to Tidwell.

Tidwell nodded. He shrugged. His eyes were eggy, outlandish, the eyes of a bewildered cow. He closed them. He pressed both his hands to his face. He squeezed his face. He moaned. He rocked from side to side.

Ratliff stood up. "You want me to tell you I'm sorry?"

Tidwell's hands came away from his face. He opened his eggy eyes, and they were gummy at the corners. He tried to speak, but all he managed was a sort of wheeze. So he nodded up at Ratliff.

Quickly Ratliff spoke. He felt a little frightened, and he didn't like the feeling. It lay clustered in his chest right smack between his nipples, and it was like a balloon, and he had no idea what to make of it. So, until he made up his mind about it, he decided he needed to speak. "I'm sorry," he said. Then he was silent for a time. Finally, after rubbing his hands together and blinking furiously in no particular direction: "All right now? Did I do good? Now maybe you ain't so lonely, you think so?"

". . . I thank you," said Tidwell, choking.

"I'm real sorry this here has happened," said Ratliff. His face (dark, tight, beetled) softened a little. "Shit, my friend, I ain't no good at this here sort of thing. I expect I'm too ornery, you know?" And then Ratliff tried to smile, and his face moved in various spasms and twitchings, but nothing much happened. He was not tall, but at one time his body had been tough, and most people had been wise enough not to—in Tidwell's words—fuck at him. But the war had done a job of work on Ratliff, just as it had done a job of work on the others, and he'd felt himself softening, giving way, wanting nothing so much as to lie down and watch all the knotted hastening clouds pass by and try to make a quiet peace with all the shit that had flowed over him for the past four goddamn years. He was a bachelor, and he thanked the Lord for that. Before the war he'd worked in his dad's brewery over by Winchester, and he'd been in charge of the books and the hiring and the laying off. He was thirtyeight years of age, and he loved his dad and his mama, but he didn't suppose he loved anyone else. He didn't love this here goddamn Tidwell, and *that* was for *sure*. He'd never had much use for men who whined and whimpered. Such men were too weak and womanish, and they made him want to pelt them with stones. He'd never been subtle, but he figured he was honest and straightforward—sort of like a fart in church. As far as he was concerned, those who didn't like him could go sit in another pew. So why then was he wasting so much time trying to show Tidwell a little sympathy? Well, the war was supposed to be over, and maybe the sympathy for Tidwell was Ratliff's way of saying he'd changed and was willing to admit his new softness and his new giving way. And so, shrugging, turning down the corners of his mouth, Ratliff again seated himself next to Tidwell, and he embraced Tidwell, and he spoke calmly into Tidwell's ear, his syllables measured and his voice easy and maybe even friendly, and he said: "We're all lonely, God damn it. Don't nobody hold it against a man who's lonely. An don't nobody hold it against a man who maybe makes him a mistake or two. At air Goodfellow, he just sort of was at the wrong place at the wrong time, an you ain't no more responsible for nothin as you are for this here war an niggers an all. Now come on with you. Let's you an me . . . let's you an me stand up now. You're goin to want to help us bury old Goodfellow, ain't you? I mean, we can't just leave him out air in at meadow, can we? Come on with you. Say somethin. This ain't no time for the cat to make off with your tongue, now is it?"

Tidwell wept against Ratliff's shirtfront.

"Right," said Ratliff to Tidwell. He stroked Tidwell's head, and gently he kneaded Tidwell's cheeks and the back of Tidwell's neck.

Tidwell's arms locked themselves around Ratliff.

". . . all right now," said Ratliff.

Tidwell's cousin McGraw still stood off to one side, and now McGraw also was weeping. He kept digging at his eyes with the hand that was wrapped in the dirty rag.

Ratliff nodded in McGraw's direction and said to McGraw: "You an me an this here cousin of yours, we're goin to make her, an at's all air is to it, by God . . ."

McGraw couldn't speak, but he did manage to nod. His face was all squinty and knotted.

Ratliff and Tidwell and McGraw dug a grave for Goodfellow. They dug it with the stocks of their brandnew rifles. Goodfellow's demolished skull leaked blood when they dragged his body to the grave. They lowered him into the grave as gently as they could, but McGraw's strength gave out, and he let go of the body's shoulders, and so it more or less flopped and bounced into the grave. McGraw fell into the grave after the body, and he cursed and wept. Ratliff and Tidwell pulled him from the grave. Tidwell wheezed. Ratliff breathed with his mouth open. Boom spoke a few words having to do with the sure and certain hope of the Resurrection, and then they all shoved the dirt back into the grave, and they went away.

BOOM

Monday, April 10, 1865.

Including Boom himself, only eleven of them remained that day.

Pendarvis and Nelson had been executed.

Llewellyn had been driven away more or less by acclamation.

Sgt Patterson had been shot and killed by the Yankees, and Goodfellow had been shot and killed by Tidwell.

And so the survivors—the ones still taking part in this march or retreat or whatever it was—were Boom, Coy, Miller, McGraw, Ratliff, Tidwell, Appling, Vincent, Pope, Petrie and Barber. Lord God, talk about your sorry raggletaggle lot.

Now, this morning, this miserable bunch was shuffling along a narrow rutted country road, wandering from side to side of that road, and knees buckled from time to time and made one or another of the fellers stagger and weakly flail, and they didn't talk much, and Tidwell wouldn't have been able to move at all if it hadn't been for Ratliff holding him up and steering him along. Poor Miller the cripple also was in a dreadful condition, and he was humming wordless hymntunes while the onearmed man, Coy, guided him and kept telling him what the hell, each step they took was a step closer to home, and hurrah, hurrah.

Boom stared dully straight ahead. He kept reaching up and adjusting his top hat, and he felt as though he'd just been elected

188

to the legislature and was preparing to attend some sort of fancydress ball sponsored by the Governor, or maybe even that prince among men, President Jefferson Davis. Boom's lips worked. He supposed he was dead, which meant this war would obtain and persist until six weeks past Eternity. He hoped he was right. Enough was enough, and he needed to become ectoplasmic and mysterious and waft himself home to his Lenore, his beautiful Lenore, his Leonore whom he loved, and never mind her poor sad bloody dead babies. O, he wanted to go home. He wanted to go home. He wanted to go home. He wanted to climb into the sky and sail home aboard the clouds, to grapple with the winds, to scoop up his Lenore and grimace into the rain with her. He needed romantic nonsense. He needed to posture and declaim. He needed to write a great breathy book and call it *The Sorrows of the Young Boom*. O, o, o, he was full of shit, and probably his brains were leaking from his ears, and wasn't he ever the *one* though, ha ha!

Jack Boom. The great *General* Jack Boom he'd been, and he'd understood how to sit a horse, and Old Catawba had clipped and had cantered along all bravely lipped and nostriled, and no less a personage than J. E. B. Stuart had taken Jack Boom aside and had told him by God we'll do great an splendid things before this war is done, Jack old friend, an I'm certain you'll always member to maintain your old élan, now won't you? And there had been a slapping of backs, and Boom and Stuart and several other generals had sat around a campfire outside Fredericksburg, and they'd offered toasts to the Confederacy, to Valor, to Honor, to Grace and to Gentlemanly Behavior, and their laughter had been decent and maybe even gallant, and they had spoken warmly of their women, the precious darlings, and photographs had been passed around, and all those fine courageous generals had nodded, and their port and their whisky had slid down their throats with a sort of easy stylish smoothness, and each of the generals had listened to expressions of admiration for his wife's beauty from each of the other generals, and saucy lips and gentle wavy hair and the thrust of certain flirtatious and jaunty bosoms and bellies had brought gentle exclamations and the slow respectful shaking of respectful officerish heads and beards and jowls, and after a time there had been tears in the eyes of some of the generals, and here and there a

temple had twitched and had danced, and a mouth had given way
at its edges, and Brig Gen Edmund Aspinwall (Jack) Boom,
commanding officer of the 11th Cumberland Cavalry, Pickett's
Corps, Army of Northern Virginia, had put away a trace too
much of the port and the whisky, and so he'd openly wept in
front of J. E. B. Stuart and the rest of them, covering his eyes and
his mouth, though, so this . . . this *demonstration* of his wouldn't
be too obvious. And the others had looked away. And they'd said
nothing. He'd supposed they figured he was weeping over sentimental memories of his Lenore. Well, he probably was, but in a
larger sense he was weeping because of four dead babies. And
later, as the contemptible Yankee U.S. Grant's insistence on a war
of attrition began grinding the Army of Northern Virginia into
dust and sawdust and shattered glass, Brig Gen Edmund Aspinwall
(Jack) Boom did a sight more weeping—as he mourned J. E. B.
Stuart, as he mourned T. J. Jackson, as he mourned his two dead
brothers, poor Sam and poor Carter, as he mourned his mother's
foolish dreams and imaginings, as he mourned the entire courtly
glorious arrogant courteous whooping lazy fragrant legendary
horseshitted South, as he mourned his own vanity and stupidity
that had caused him to lead his troopers into mad doomed skirmishes
with various Yankee cavalry forces that had outnumbered them
two, three, eight to one. And he mourned all the dead young men
who'd fought under his command. And of course he mourned his
brave Old Catawba, even though Old Catawba had given him and
the others temporary life in the sense of flesh and meat and bone
and gristle, dying calmly and making no sound after Boom pressed
the trigger to the great sad beast's skull. And Boom and his men
ate everything there was of Old Catawba, everything except Old
Catawba's eyes and maybe Old Catawba's asshole. (Boom couldn't
remember what had happened to Old Catawba's eyes. As for Old
Catawba's asshole, well, maybe Boom had sampled it but hadn't
been told what it was.) That final fight, the engagement that had
seen Boom so fucking maladroitly command and maneuver his
vast forces into that culdesac at the James River, there to be routed
by perhaps five times as many Yankees . . . ah, such a wonderful
time it had been, and such a general he was, and all he'd really
done to rectify the situation was leap down from the saddle and

stand and numbly fire his pistol and brandish his goddamn sword and pray that some Yankee would kill him along with the others, so that at least he would be spared the indignity of surviving them. But he wasn't even scratched. The skirmish lasted twenty minutes at the most, and he fired away, and he brandished away, but the Yankees didn't bother with him, and finally he hunkered down and tried to make himself inconspicuous. Finally, by dear sweet timid palpitating Jesus, the brave General Edmund Aspinwall (Jack) Boom hunkered down and made himself so inconspicuous the wonder was he didn't simply melt away and vanish forever. Finally he was able to stand up, and Old Catawba came to him, and Old Catawba was trembling and staggering, and he knew the war was over for Old Catawba. So he shot Old Catawba, and blood flew, and bone flew, and that was that. A dozen men or so helped him eat the old horse. The Yankee attack had been unexpected, and Boom's men had been dismounted, and so the first thing the Yankees had done was go after those skinny old nags and whack their rumps and send them off on a hoarsely whinnying skedaddle. The rest had been easy, and Boom and the other survivors were silent as they ate Old Catawba. Dead men lay all around them, and the survivors took turns digging a huge hole for the dead men, who numbered twentysix. Some of the survivors actually sucked on bones from Old Catawba as they dug the huge hole. Later, when they carried the dead men to the huge hole, there was weeping and howling, and Boom stood with his hands on his hips, and he tugged down his top hat, and he belched from the juices of Old Catawba, and the corpses were lowered into the hole, and the hole was filled, and then Boom said a few words from the *Book of Common Prayer* and told the men they'd done their duty and then some, and they were free to go home. He told them he wished them luck with the provosts and any bitterenders who might be roaming the countryside. They nodded. They walked away. None of them shook hands with Boom. They simply walked away. He slept that night at the edge of the river, and the next day he walked into Richmond, and he'd thrown away all badges and symbols of rank. He didn't believe his war was quite yet over, and so he caught on with those men who were guarding the railroad yard, and one thing had led to another, and five men (including G. W. Mossman, the politician who'd killed himself on that lawn back in Richmond) were dead who hadn't been dead (and of course neither Boom nor anyone else had the slightest goddamn notion what had happened to the big belligerent Llewellyn), and Boom knew damn well he should have quit this war at the instant he'd given his own men that particular option back on the banks of the bloody James. Ah, but perhaps Heaven had more auspicious plans for him. Perhaps God and all the Seraphim and all the plumply adorable Cherubim had chosen him to be this conflict's final casualty. Perhaps his eyes would be blown out. Or his balls perhaps? Or perhaps he was destined to fall in a cistern or be pecked to death by birds or eat a poisoned pig or walk into the path of a locomotive. Perhaps he would be scalped by some Yankee's victorious sword. Perhaps he would be sucked to death by the wind. Ha. Oh. Ha.

And now Boom grimaced. He told himself there was no need to yield to foolishness. He got to thinking of the late Goodfellow. Dead because of a goat . . . poor Goodfellow. What had he been about to do with that goat? kidnap it? elope with it? seize it and eat it alive? ask it to dance with him? hand it his rifle and tell it to die for the Confederacy? propose it for membership in the Free-masons? Boom shook his head. No, that boy had loved *locomotives*, and he'd not said a word about loving *goats*. But why hadn't he simply *shot* the goddamn thing and been done with it? Why were men so often so absurdly compromised and made trivial at the moment of their death? Why did men have to die while they were sitting in the privy or picking their noses or masturbating or spitting greazzy hockers or pouring sugar into their coffee or trying to add sixtyseven and fortyone? Boom needed to grieve for all such men, but a sort of dry cruel laughter kept getting in the way, and all he could manage to do was grimace—and muse on the abundant mysteries of truant goats.

He sighed. He glanced back, and the men all were carrying their rifles at a trail and cutting shallow wandering tracks in the road's muddy surface. But the surface wasn't *too* muddy. There had been no rain for several days now. Boom wasn't sure whether this was good news. If the war were in fact over, then the men would be hurrying home so they could do their spring planting, and he didn't suppose they wanted a goddamn drought. He hoped the war was over. He wanted to go home. He was hungry, and his feet were all scabbed and filthy, and he wanted to go home. They stopped for the night in a woods, and they listened to owls, and he told them they were free not to pay attention to anything he said . . . right then or in the future or after he was dead and buried or whenever the hell. Then, laughing a little, he told them he had no more idea of what was happening than they did.

PITT

Tuesday, April 11, 1865.

Pitt and Brig Gen Snell stood on a low ridge with their hands on their hips and watched a gang of deserters come straggling out of a deep piney woods and weave and stumble toward them—like lazy shuffling niggers maybe—along a narrow road. These fellows carried rifles, though, and so maybe they weren't deserters, after all. Maybe they'd remained loyal to the Confederacy and simply were exhausted.

"What do you make of em?" said Brig Gen Snell. He tugged at his lower lip. His eyes were pink, and the knees of his britches just about were worn through.

"I don't believe I quite know, sir," said Pitt. "They appear to be irregulars of some sort, perhaps militia, perhaps home guards."

"They are not movin along at road in military order," said Brig Gen Snell, shaking his head. His flesh was gray. Too gray. Every so often he bent down and scratched his ankles. This was the man who liked to fancy himself as The Little Whirlwind, and now there were scabs on his neck and his cheeks, and his finger-nails were torn, and his knuckles and palms were layered with dirt and runny grime, and he was no more a Little Whirlwind than Pitt was the Archbishop of Canterbury. Now Brig Gen Snell shook his head and scratched one of the scabs on his neck. Then

194

he said to Pitt: "I expect we should take a walk down air an find out what air up to."

". . . right now, sir?"

Brig Gen Snell frowned at Pitt. "Of course right now. What do you suggest we do? Let em run round the countryside without the proper authorization? They need documents. An *we* need to know what air plans are. Perhaps we can be of assistance, don't you know . . ."

"Yessir. Sorry. I suppose I never thought of it at way."

"You still think it's all a comedy, don't you?"

". . . yessir."

"Well," said Brig Gen Snell, known to his legion of admirers as a man who'd more than earned his sobriquet as The Little Whirlwind, who was as tough and unyielding as corncobs and artillery and brick walls (which nobody could deny, don't you know), "I would argue the point with you, but I expect it doesn't matter, does it?"

"I suppose not."

"Didn't I say to you we must play it out?"

"Yessir," said Pitt.

"If you want to laugh, fine, but do your duty anyway, God damn it."

"Yessir," said Pitt.

Brig Gen Snell glanced back over a shoulder. The six men he and Pitt commanded . . . Burns, Lillis, Ford, Lavelle, Shankland and Sgt Crabtree . . . were lounging on the grass. Lillis and Lavelle were cleaning their new rifles. The others had shaded their eyes and appeared to be dozing. Brig Gen Snell inhaled. He shrugged. He grunted. Then, turning to Pitt again, he said: "We need to question those fellows down air an find out what air up to. If we show force, they'll be less inclined to argue with us."

"Force, sir?" said Pitt.

"At is correct," said Brig Gen Snell.

"Six men, sir?"

"Eight," said Brig Gen Snell, "countin ourselves."

Quickly Pitt nodded. He needed to laugh, but he didn't want to upset the poor old fellow. A man needed to be careful when he dealt with craziness. So he shouted back to the men to fall in, column of twos. The men stirred, rubbed their eyes, stretched, yawned. Sgt Crabtree was the first to stand up. He spoke quietly to the men, and they fell in behind him. They carried their rifles at right shoulder arms, and for some reason Pitt just about wanted to kiss them. They marched down the side of the ridge and met the stragglers in the road. Birds called, and there was an odor of remembered manure. Everyone stared at everyone else. Pitt didn't like the looks of the stragglers. Perhaps, for all he knew, they were outlaws. One thing was for certain—they didn't appear to be too terribly disciplined. (Here Pitt coughed and hawked and covered his mouth. He needed to laugh out loud, but he was wise enough to know this wasn't quite the time.) The stragglers . . . or whatever they were . . . slumped and stared. A onearmed man appeared to be trying to hold up another fellow who apparently had something the matter with his legs. Two other men were more or less embracing, and one of them appeared to be weeping. A stocky bearded man in a top hat walked up to Pitt and Brig Gen Snell. The stocky bearded man did not salute. He was smiling, though, and he said to Brig Gen Snell: "Well, good morning to you, General. You're General Snell, correct? The old Hartstone Zouaves, unless I miss my guess?"

Frowning, Brig Gen Snell said to the stocky bearded man: "Do I know you, sir?"

"I am Jack Boom, sir," said the stocky bearded man. Casually he saluted Brig Gen Snell. "At your service, sir."

Brig Gen Snell managed to return the salute, but his mouth was lax and his eyes were white and wetly bewildered. "Boom Jack hey who?" he said.

Several of the stocky bearded man's bunch sniggered a little, but he motioned to them to be quiet. They coughed. Most of them stared down at their bare feet.

Pitt looked around. Sgt Crabtree and his men were standing in their column of twos. They were expressionless.

Sunlight came down in a sort of humid golden blare. There was a sound of field birds. The stocky bearded man said to Brig Gen Snell: "My men and I were bivouacked near you for two nights near Sharpsburg back in September of '62. One of those nights you very generously invited me to take supper with you,

General. We had quite a spirited conversation, as I recall, concernin the relative merits of the infantry an the cavalry. I am a cavalryman, as you may recall, an our dialogue was . . . vigorous. You made a good case for the infantry, sir, an I member the evenin with great pleasure . . ."

". . . I'm sorry," said Brig Gen Snell, blinking.

"Sorry, sir?" said this Jack Boom fellow.

Brig Gen Snell glanced at Pitt and said: "Do you member him?"

Pitt shrugged. "I believe so, but that was what? two an a half years ago? I'm sorry, sir, but I just don't know for sure."

The Jack Boom fellow smiled. "Well, believe me," he said. "Much as I regret it, I am who I say I am."

"Boomy Jack, eh?" said Brig Gen Snell. "Boom. E. Jack. Jack an the Boomstalk. Climb, climb, climb, brave Jack . . . Jack, Jack . . . Jack the Smokestack. Jack the Flack."

Jack Boom glanced at Pitt, who raised his eyebrows.

"Why are you here?" said Brig Gen Snell to Jack Boom.

Blinking, Jack Boom said: "We're on our way home, sir. Now at the war is finished, we want to return to our families an sort of . . . reassemble ourselves."

"The war is not finished, sir," said Brig Gen Snell. "We have not surrendered, sir, an I regret to say neither has the enemy. The enemy will be the end of me, but until at time we shall remain resolute in our pursuit of our ultimate end of me enemy victory don't you know . . ."

Jack Boom shrugged. "Fine an dandy," he said. "Whatever you want to believe, you just go on an you believe it, sir. My friends here an I have disaffiliated ourselves, however an we— "

"Fuckin deserters," said Brig Gen Snell. He glanced at Pitt and said: "This is a bunch of fuckin cowards an cuckin fowards, don't you know . . ."

"Yessir," said Pitt.

"You're under arrest, God damn you," said Brig Gen Snell to Jack Boom. "You an the rest of you. It's arrest tarrest arrest the rest for you, an a firinsquad will be prepared." Then, to Pitt: "Arrest this bunch, Captain. See at a firinsquad is detailed. We shall execute em all, Captain. This is The Little Whirlwind speakin,

Captain, an see you obey him." Then Brig Gen Snell leaned from side to side and resumed speaking to Jack Boom: "You are dealin with righteous men here, sir, men who understand Duty an Bravery . . ."

Jack Boom was smiling. "We don't want to be impolite, General," he said, "but, wellsir, the truth is, you can take your firinsquad an your righteousness an shove em up your rosy red asshole. Oh, an tell me somethin—who's The Little Whirlwind?"

Brig Gen Snell got to shouting. "*I'm* The Little Whirlwind! *Everone* knows *at!*" He shook. He began beating his palms together. He jumped up and down.

"Oh, shit," said Jack Boom.

There was a general fuss and commotion. Jack Boom wheeled around. He shouted at his men to follow him, and he ran back up the road. His men followed him, all right. Even the one with the bum legs followed him, and so did the two men who were embracing one another. They had been carrying their rifles at a trail, but now they were holding their rifles across their bodies. Jack Boom led them into an open field, and he hollered at them to spread out. Brig Gen Snell yelled at Pitt and their six men to pursue the traitorous buggers. Pitt was laughing, but the sound of it was lost in the general brouhaha. He waved his sword, only in truth it wasn't his sword at all; it was the sword he'd confiscated from Brig Gen Snell. He also waved his pistol, only in truth it was the pistol he'd confiscated from Brig Gen Snell after he (Brig Gen Snell) had foully assassinated his (Brig Gen Snell's) holster. Brig Gen Snell stumbled back and forth across the road and ordered his men to form a skirmishline and advance on the treasonous buggers. Pitt just about wanted to sing. He advanced with the others toward the field, and he was able to see Jack Boom's top hat. He did not remember Jack Boom from a pile of sticks. Everyone spread out. Pitt wanted to tell Brig Gen Snell (who, after all, was unarmed) to stay back, but he said nothing. He figured it was up to Brig Gen Snell to decide what Brig Gen Snell should do. Now he and the others were on their knees and firing at the stragglers, and just about everyone was yelling. Just about everyone except Pitt, who wanted to sing. Sunlight rubbed his face, and his forehead was itchy with golden sweat. He was beyond yelling, just as he was beyond laughter. Now he only required a little music. As a publisher of hymnals and Bibles, surely he needed to sing of sheaves, lambs, angels, the Throne of God. There were puffs and pops. Brig Gen Snell and Pitt and the others stood up and ran forward.

BOOM

Tuesday, April 11, 1865.

The fight lasted no more than half an hour, and it was reasonably unspectacular, even though most of the men on both sides were killed. Boom lay on his belly and kissed the barrel of his rifle and began firing. O, God damn these stupid muzzleloaders; a man needed a full minute and maybe a minute and a half between shots. Boom had heard it said that the Yankees now had breechloaders requiring only a few seconds to be reloaded, and he surely would have had use for one that morning. He watched the little general, that deranged Snell fellow, stagger back and forth, and Snell hollered and howled, and his mouth appeared black. Maybe he was without teeth. His britches appeared torn. Someone shot him through the throat. He dropped to a sitting position, and he still appeared to be trying to holler and howl, but all that came from him was a quick blotty spray of blood. Finally he fell forward. His buttocks undulated and he made fists for a few minutes before he finally went ahead and died. Boom glanced back at his men, and they were popping away with their rifles. The sounds were like dull perfunctory slaps. There wasn't much smoke. He stood up and motioned to his men to pull back. This entire business was ridiculous, and he knew it was ridiculous, and all he wanted was to go home. He needed warm milk. He needed his Lenore to suck his bellybutton and gather his balls in her tiny

gentle hands. Now he had a boner, but then he'd often had a
boner when there was a fight. He ran back, but his men weren't
moving. Several bullets went whirring past his skull, and he
glared at his men, and then he removed his stupid top hat and
hugged it and again dropped to the earth. He told himself he
needed to stop thinking of these fellows as *his* men. He was
nothing more than an unofficial, ah, custodian, and he would do
well to remember that. He kept firing, and he winged one of the
other fellows, who stood up and whirled and hooted and threw
away his rifle and began running back up the road. A shot was
fired behind him. It came from the crippled Miller, who was
sitting in the meadow with his legs splayed in front of him. The
shot did away with the small of the back of the fellow Boom had
winged. The man flailed, and he kept lurching forward, forward,
the sonofabitch, and so Boom shot him a second time, blowing
away most of his right foot. Finally the fellow fell. He didn't
move, and surely he was as dead as he ever would be. Then the
other men came running in a charge, and they were at once
hollering and grunting. Boom was able to make out just six of
them, and one was the officer who'd been standing out there in
the road with the late Brig Gen Snell. According to the insignia
that had been sewn on the shoulders of his shirt, this man was a
captain, so why hadn't he tried to stop all this foolishness? What
was happening? Boom wanted to go home. Boom wanted to go
home. Everybody wanted to go home, but Boom most of all. He
should have clubbed the little general to death right out there on
the road. There wouldn't have been much to it. Why, it would
have been like clubbing a starving child to death. An orphan
maybe, who was fed thin soup and not much else. Boom and his
men stood up. The other men appeared to have new rifles, and he
supposed o shit an go to hell, the new rifles had been taken from
that same abandoned ordnance wagon back in Boxerville. None of
this should be happenin, said Boom to himself as he stood and
braced himself to take the charge of this lunatic enemy. A boy of
no more than nineteen, gray and skinny, with a cluster of warts
on his chin, came at Boom swinging his rifle like a club, but Boom
also swung *his* rifle, and it caught the boy smack on the cluster of
warts, and the boy's head snapped back, and his neck broke with

a sound that was like an abrupt shredding of sticks. He flew backward, and his rifle sailed from his hands, and he landed flat on his back, and his head lolled, and his mouth was bloody, and his eyes were bloody, and his nose was bloody. Coy, the onearmed fellow, gave a cheer. He'd been sitting with his crippled friend Miller, but now he came forward and grabbed the dead boy's rifle, grabbed it lefthanded, then lay down and pulled the rifle closer and aimed it and waited for someone to pass before him. Miller was a few yards away, and he loaded and fired, loaded and fired, and they both were weeping. No one was falling back, and Boom was just about ready to kill them all, and now he wasn't quite sure who was on whose side, and the sun wobbled and fumed all hot and blinding, and Boom kissed the stock of his rifle and even licked it. He supposed this was both ultimate and logical. Surely there was no retreat, and surely it was fitting and proper. Tidwell ran toward Coy and called him a piece of shit. The captain shot little Petrie with his revolver. McGraw, Tidwell's cousin, ran after Tidwell. The captain's bullet passed through Petrie's groin, and he screamed and fell, and the captain knelt next to him and shot him through the skull. Tidwell kicked the onearmed Coy, and McGraw tackled Tidwell, and the captain shot Ratliff in the face. The captain was shouting words that had to do with God and Redemption, and maybe he even was singing them. Ratliff lay dead, and he appeared to be hugging his face. Tidwell and McGraw rolled on the earth, and Boom went to Coy and stood over him and told him he was pathetic and knelt over him and strangled him. Two of the other attacking fellows began cursing one another. They pulled knives. One of them—the larger of the two—stabbed the other fellow in a temple, and the other fellow slowly sank to the earth. The victor appropriated the loser's knife. Wielding both knives, the victor looked around, and the captain speared him in the groin with a sword he was carrying. The man fell, and then the captain had the devil's own time pulling the sword from him. Boom's hands were warmed and perhaps even a bit chafed from his strangling of Coy. He stood up and rubbed his palms across his shirtfront. He still was wearing his top hat, and he wanted to go home. He wondered whether they all were dead yet. He supposed they weren't. He supposed they lacked the

manners to be dead yet, and he wanted to go home. Appling and
Vincent threw down their rifles and tried to run away, but the
captain and a man wearing sergeant's stripes intercepted them.
The captain nearly beheaded Appling with one swipe of his
sword, and the sergeant fell on Vincent and gouged out Vincent's
eyes and shoved them inside Vincent's mouth, but Vincent made
no sounds, and Vincent never would make sounds, seeing as how
this sergeant twisted Vincent's neck and broke it. Somehow Boom
was exercised by all this, and so he knelt and aimed and shot the
sergeant through one ear and out the other. Boom smiled. Boom
wanted to go home. He had to smile, though, at the accuracy of
his aim. He was quite the brave and skillful fellow, was this
Boom, and he only wished someone had thought to call *him* The
Little Whirlwind. McGraw killed his cousin Tidwell by picking
up a large pocked rock and smashing Tidwell's skull with it. Pope
and Barber stood up and began to run. Boom shot Pope, and the
captain shot Barber. Boom did not know Pope's first name, nor
did he know Barber's. There was another man—Vincent—to
whom he'd never even spoken. Pope and Barber both still were
alive. They'd both been shot in the legs, and they lay weeping
and twitching. Boom reloaded his rifle. He touched his top hat,
and he supposed it was bloody. He wanted to go home. He killed
Pope with a shot to the head, and the captain fired his pistol two
times in the base of Barber's skull. Then was a silence, and no
more shots were fired . . . at least not for a moment or two. Boom
looked around, and he believed all his people were dead. An
image of the enormous Llewellyn went grunting across Boom's
mind for a moment or two, and Boom supposed Llewellyn surely
was the lucky one, wasn't that so? Boom and the captain did not
speak. They breathed loudly, though, and Boom wanted to go
home. He reloaded his rifle. He kept looking around. McGraw
came toward him, and McGraw's shirtfront was sopping with
blood and vomit, and he fired at Boom, but his rifle simply
bucked straight up, and so Boom grabbed him around the knees,
and Boom and McGraw rolled on the earth, and then McGraw's
chest erupted with blood and stringy tissue, and he was dead.
Apparently a stray bullet had hit him. At any rate, Boom had no
recollection of firing at the fellow. He wandered. He stepped over

bodies. The captain also wandered. The bodies were crooked and crimson and absurd. Most of them were staring at Boom . . . or at least that was what he believed. He wanted to go home. He supposed he was crazy, but he was afraid he was not. Then he saw the crippled Miller sitting there on the earth, and Miller was speaking to an invisible woman named Ruthie, and he was telling this Ruthie he just knew she would be ashamed of him, and finally Boom killed Miller with a shot to the skull from about ten feet. Miller erupted, and fair enough . . . who gave a damn? Boom stood gasping and watching the captain pursue two men across the road. The men were flapping and screaming, and the captain killed them sweetly with single shots that caught them in their spines and sent them flying in a sort of hapless spiral as though they were sick geese. Now surely no one was left alive except Boom and this captain. Boom waved at the captain, and Boom was smiling. The captain waved at Boom, and the captain was smiling. Boom wondered when the last time was this captain had fucked his mother. But all Boom did was wave at the captain, and Boom smiled and smiled. Carefully the captain aimed his pistol at Boom, and Boom continued to smile, and the captain was singing, and there was that word again: Redemption. Boom did not move. He waited for whatever. Now the captain laughed as he sang. Boom nodded. "Right," he said.

BOOM

Tuesday, April 11, 1865.

The captain squeezed off two rounds, but nothing resulted except a couple of cottony clicking sounds. All the bullets had been fired from his pistol, and so his singing trailed away and he gazed muzzily down at the damn pistol and shook his head. Then he looked up at Boom, who still hadn't bothered to move. He spoke loudly enough so that Boom could hear him, but in no way did he shout. The time for shouting probably was gone. He briefly coughed, and then he said to Boom: "Wouldn't you goddamn know it? Just when this thing needs bullets, air are no bullets."

Boom nodded. "Happens to all of us," he said.

"Oh, I believe I do have bullets, understand," said the captain, and he patted his pockets. "But I'm damned if I'll stand here in front of you an *reload*. At would be needlessly cruel, wouldn't it?"

"Oh, of course," said Boom.

"I don't want to be cruel, needlessly or otherwise," said the captain.

"Thank you kindly," said Boom.

"I'm only tryin to be logical," said the captain.

Boom was silent for a time. He wanted to go home. He threw down his rifle and embraced himself. "I wonder," he finally said, "how we'll answer for all this."

"At's why I'm tryin to be logical," said the captain.

205

Boom shuddered. "Perhaps no logic is called for."

"One thing is for sure, though."

"What might at be?" said Boom, relaxing a little, lowering his arms to his sides and flexing his fingers.

"It's not even noon yet, but we've already put in what in my judgment is a full day."

"Yes," said Boom. "Come to think of it, I expect you're right."

The captain came toward Boom. He made no effort to reload his pistol.

Still, Boom's legs tightened. He glanced down at his rifle, but what the hell, what the hell, he did not try to pick it up. He wanted to go home. But then he got to blinking, and he said to himself: No. At is incorrect. I no longer want to go home. Air is no way I can go home. Not now.

The captain was smiling a little.

Boom held out his right hand.

The captain nodded.

Boom and the captain shook hands. Boom just about wanted to embrace the man. Maybe there was something to this logic business.

The captain stuffed his pistol inside his belt. He grunted. "The logic," he said.

"All right," said Boom.

"We have gone beyond laughter into final blood," said the captain.

"I'm not so sure . . ."

"But what more could air be?"

"Ask me tomorrow," said Boom.

"This is called a civil war," said the captain. "Myself, I call it an uncivil war. After all, how can a war be civil?"

"I expect I don't know," said Boom.

The captain was breathing with his mouth open. "At's quite a jaunty hat you're wearin," he said. He touched one of Boom's shoulders. "You've demonstrated spirit, haven't you?"

Boom shrugged. His chest and belly were clogged with he didn't know what. His eyes were hot, and now it wasn't necessary that he go home. It wasn't necessary at all. Now all that was necessary was that he blow up.

"The Throne of God sat at the edge of a foul stinkin river of goddamn blood," said the captain.

". . . yes," said Boom.

"Are you as amused as I am?" said the captain.

". . . maybe so," said Boom.

"But I no longer really am amused, sir," said the captain.

". . . oh," said Boom.

"I am taken only by blood, sir," said the captain.

"All right," said Boom.

The captain squeezed Boom's shoulder, then released it. "I have been despondent," he said, "an *en* I have been quite profoundly amused, if I do say so. An today I sang. But now . . . well, *now* nothin remains other an the blood. I am quiet again, sir. A little while ago I was loud an jubilant, but now I have returned to my natural state. Do you understand?"

"I don't know," said Boom, "but does it matter?"

"I do propose to kill you, sir," said the captain.

"Yes," said Boom.

"Logic dictates such a thing."

"If you say so," said Boom.

"Are you afraid?"

"Of course not," said Boom.

The captain smiled.

Boom adjusted his top hat. He tapped it. He grimaced.

"Logic is all we have remainin to us," said the captain.

"Ha," said Boom, clearing his throat.

"It was logical at I remained with General Snell. Logical because I no longer could see any logic in anythin, because I'd lost sight of all the *issues* an all the *passions* at had brought is to where we were, an so I told myself I needed to follow it all through to whatever its ugly and perverted conclusion. So we apprehended two looters an one deserter, an we—"

"Please tell me what air names were."

"I'm sorry," said the captain, "but I'm afraid I don't know. We never asked for air names. We shot em, an at was at."

"Was one of them a great big fellow with a beard?"

"Yes."

"And were the other two nothin more an boys? An did you

shoot those two boys near a little country store at had been emptied?"

"Yes."

Boom thought for a moment, and then he nodded. "You're right bout the logic," he said.

"Oh?"

"Those boys were mine . . . in a manner of speakin. An I was sort of hopin the big one got away."

"Well," said the captain, "they were caught up with by logic, all right, logic at called itself The Little Whirlwind. Or they were caught up with by vengeance. Or they were caught up with by duty. Or they were caught up with by obligation. He was mad as a bedbug. Did you hear the way he was talkin today?"

"I did," said Boom. "He was mad, all right, but I expect he had a right to be mad, didn't he?"

"Of course he did," said the captain.

"I know what you mean when you say logic. Don't think I don't."

"It was why I stayed with him," said the captain.

"Out of curiosity, you mean."

"Absolutely," said the captain.

"Logic dictated we had to kill one another," said Boom.

"Indeed," said the captain.

" . . . as a sort of distillation of the madness," said Boom.

"Yes," said the captain.

"Blood is blood, and it is just as tasty no matter whose it is."

"Correct," said the captain.

Boom nodded. He smiled at the captain. They linked arms. They crossed the road to where all the dead men lay. Arm in arm, they walked from dead man to dead man, and flies already had gathered. The two men did not speak. Neither did they weep. Neither did they beat themselves across their chests. They stood over the body of the onearmed Coy. Boom's wrists still ached from the strangling of Coy, whose tongue protruded. Boom seemed to recall he'd had a boner while all this killing had taken place. He shuddered. He made sure he did not look directly at the captain. He kept tapping his top hat. He did not care whether he went home. He stared down at the boy who had the cluster of warts.

He stared down at Petrie and Ratliff. The captain had killed both of them, and Ratliff had no face. Boom poked at each of the corpses with a toe. He and the captain did not let go of one another. A crow hopped back and forth across the corpse of the man who'd had two knives. The crow made hoarsely jubilant sounds. Boom wanted to kill the crow, but what the hell, what the hell. Boom stared down at the eyeless dead Vincent, the one whose eyes had been stuffed into his mouth. Boom's boner was returned, and he had to swallow a number of groans. The captain glanced at him for a moment but said nothing. They came to the corpse of Brig Gen Snell. The captain disengaged himself from Boom and rolled the corpse of Brig Gen Snell onto its back. Brig Gen Snell appeared to be smiling. The captain touched Brig Gen Snell's bloody ruined neck and then rubbed several blots of Brig Gen Snell's blood across his own forehead and cheeks. He smiled at Boom, and Boom nodded, but nothing was said. Only the crow and a few uneasy fieldbirds made sounds. One or two of the fieldbirds whistled and trilled, but the rest of them were silent. Boom breathed blood and gunpowder, and he breathed more blood than he breathed gunpowder. The sun slammed and danced, and Boom's eyes watered. Idly he wished the captain would hurry up and kill him and get it over with. He thought of logic. He thought of logic. He thought of logic. He did not want to go home, and there was no way he could go home. No logical way. This . . . what he was seeing, what he was breathing and smelling and rolling across his tongue . . . was the only logic that mattered a damn. In the midst of war, he said to himself, we are in war. If we exhaust and demolish one enemy, we always can engage ourselves, which of course we have been engagin all along, correct? Our enemies are numerous, but surely we are the best an the most deservin of the lot. O, such a lucky fellow I am. I am so grateful for his knowledge, so grateful to be understandin the logic. All we need now to do is lick the blood an chew the bones, an maybe after a time we can irrigate all this with our puke. In the meantime, air surely are no prayers, an so if we laugh an sing, what the hell, what the hell.

PITT

Tuesday, April 11, 1865.

It was late in the afternoon, and Pitt and this Jack Boom fellow walked north toward a place called Appomattox Court House. According to Jack Boom, a cavalry officer had told him Lee had surrendered and so the war was over. Pitt didn't know what to believe, but what difference did any of it make? Now the time was gone when that sort of thing really mattered. The killing of all those men this morning had meant no surrender was necessary. After all, who really was left to do the surrendering? The dead men back there in that pasture of course had gone unburied, but that didn't matter, either. Someone would come along and bury them. People always seemed to be available for that sort of thing. Maybe, come to think of it, half the world fought the wars and the other half served as pallbearers. Pitt's jaws were tight. He tried to think of hymns and supplications, but the words would not form themselves. He and Boom were silent. He needed to kill Boom, and Boom surely didn't appear to give a damn about it one way or the other. Pitt smiled. He was thinking of all the logic, and so he figured he had a right to smile. Trees curved over the road, and some of them were budding. Pitt always had loved the spring. It had performed sweet miracles as far as his flesh and his juices had been concerned. He breathed with his mouth open, and his tongue captured a flavor of earth and new leaves. He and

210

Boom walked steadily. He still carried his pistol, but Boom hadn't bothered to retrieve the rifle he'd thrown down. Boom's arms swung easily at his sides, and every so often he reached up and tapped his top hat. Neither he nor Pitt had wept, and Pitt had reason to believe they never would. Tears were altogether too trivial. So were grief and guilt. Laughter was more important. Music was more important. (Madness fell somewhere in this catalogue, but Pitt wasn't quite sure where.) He tried to summon a vision of flags and politicians and philosophers and whores and preachers. He knew he needed to confront the finite and the banal and the trite. They had to do, people said, with what was defined as the real world, and they were the elements that in truth governed the politicians and the whores and all the rest of them, wasn't that so? Ah, the real world. A fellowship of villains and cannibals, orators and liars, traitors and deviants. Owls and bats flourished in this real world, as did the shedding of blood. Pitt sucked spit. He rolled it on his tongue, and it was sour, but he swallowed it. He didn't want to spit in Boom's presence. He didn't want to appear all that indelicate. He cleared his throat, and then he said to Boom: "Is air anythin else we can do?"

"No," said Boom. "Air is nothin else we can do—or at any rate air is nothin else *I* can do. I can't exactly go home an hug my wife an tell her hallelujah, the war is over an I did my duty, now can I? I'd choke after bout two syllables, wouldn't I?"

"I suppose you would," said Pitt.

"I'm thinkin now bout dreams," said Boom.

"How so?" said Pitt.

"All the dead ones, they must have had dreams an plans," said Boom. "An memories, of course. An now everthin's been . . . interrupted. An interrupted forever, a person might say. Frozen. Buried. Hidden away forever."

"So you know why we must die?" said Pitt. "You know why air's no doubt we must die?"

". . . yes."

"It's logical, I'd say," said Pitt.

". . . yes," said Boom.

"An I'm not talkin bout punishment. I'm only talkin bout logic."

Boom cleared his throat and nodded.

"I'll be followin right along, you know," said Pitt.

"Fine," said Boom.

Pitt's mouth was dry, and so he summoned up more mois-ture, and this time he did spit it out. Noisily, and it was rubbery, and some it it even emerged from his nose. He swiped at his nostrils with a sleeve. "I beg your pardon," he said.

"Thank you," said Boom.

"Pardon?" said Pitt.

"For bein so polite," said Boom.

Pitt smiled. "Well," he said, "I only wish I could say I come from good stock. But I'm afraid I don't, you see. My mama used to tell me our family was FFV. She forever was tellin me I should be proud. But air wasn't quite the whole ring of truth to her words. So later I made some inquiries, an it turned out *her* mama had run a boardinhouse for sailors in Norfolk, an the place had had a *reputation*, if you know what I mean. An it turned out at my *father's* mama had been the mistress of some banker in Baltimore for somethin like twenty years. So air you are. No FFV lineage for me, I'm afraid. And if I'm as you say polite, it comes from watchin the behavior of others; it certainly isn't somethin I learned naturally. So don't think it's good stock. All my life I've had to overcome certain . . . blemishes . . . in my history. An don't ask me how I came to be a publisher of hymnals an Holy Scripture. I was left a bit of money, an I had a certain small talent for commas an typefaces an the courtin of certain of the lesser Protestant denominations when it came to obtainin printin contracts, and back home in Hartstone, Virginia, I have—believe it or not, whatever you like—I have a certain reputation for . . . probity. An I always beg a person's pardon when I spit out a particularly repellent gob of whatever corruption might be lurkin in my lungs. Oh, I possess a goodness at is enough to bend the heavens, don't you know . . ."

"Bend the heavens?" said Boom.

"Hyperbole," said Pitt.

Boom nodded. He kept stepping right along, and his elbows churned. He was silent, though, for a minute or so, and then (his voice a trifle rusty) he said: "How do you propose to do it?"

212

"I have found two bullets in the pockets of my britches," said Pitt, "an two should be sufficient, shouldn't they?"

"I expect so," said Boom.

"You don't want to change your mind, do you?" said Pitt.

"Of course not," said Boom. "I can't go home now. I have abdicated this life. At's at, an so it will be good when I die. I am a general who lost all the important battles an lost all his men an ended his career by killin anyone who entered his line of vision. Anyone. Friend or foe. I neither *deserve* to live nor *want* to live. I seek only to be erased. You should have killed me back air."

"I would have, but I didn't realize I was carryin those bullets. I mean, I wasn't all at sure, an at the time I was sort of . . . worked up."

"Stand close to me when you do it," said Boom. "I don't want you to need to aim."

"All right," said Pitt.

". . . an the last bullet will be for yourself?"

"You have my word," said Pitt.

"All right," said Boom. He shrugged. He tapped his top hat.

"May I wear your splendid hat when I die?" said Pitt.

"Of course," said Boom. "I won't object."

Pitt cleared his throat. *"Lord,"* he said, *"let me know mine end, an the number of my days . . ."*

Said Boom: *". . . at I may be certified how long I have to live."*

Said Pitt: *"Behold, thou hast made my days as it were a span long, an mine age is even as nothin in respect of thee . . ."*

Said Boom: *". . . an verily every man livin is altogther vanity."*

Said Pitt: *"For man walketh in a vain shadow, an disquieteth himself in vain . . ."*

Said Boom: *". . . he heapeth up riches, an cannot tell who shall gather em."*

Said Pitt: *"An now, Lord, what is my hope?"*

Said Boom: *". . . truly my hope is even in thee."*

Said Pitt: *"Deliver me from all mine offenses . . ."*

Said Boom: *". . . an make me not a rebuke unto the foolish."*

Said Pitt: *"When those with rebukes dost chasten man with sin, thou makest his beauty to consume away, like as it were a moth frettin a garment . . ."*

Said Boom: "... *every man therefore is but vanity.*"

Said Pitt: "*Hear my prayer, O Lord, an with thine ears consider my callin* ..."

Said Boom: (and now his voice was blurry with tears): "... *hold not thy peace at my tears* ..."

Said Pitt: "*For I am a stranger with thee, an a sojourner* ..."

Said Boom (gulping and shuddering): "... *as all my fathers were* ..."

Said Pitt: "*O spare me a little, at I may recover my strength* ..."

Said Boom "... *before I go hence, an be no more seen.*"

Pitt nodded. Boom lurched against him, and Boom's knees were beginning to give way. Boom kissed Pitt on the mouth, and again Pitt nodded. Pitt pushed Boom against a treetrunk and shot him through the heart. He snatched Boom's top hat as Boom fell. Brig Gen Snell's stupid blood had dried on Pitt's face, and now it itched. Pitt grimaced. He dug at the dried blood with his fingernails. He fired his final bullet straight in the air. He was human, by God, and he sat down in the road and he waved Boom's top hat back and forth and he screamed and he screamed.